"Val H. Stieglitz has wı
memoir of adolescent av
this lawyer-turned-write
with an intriguing twist.

counting of a young man's pursuit of mastery in sport -
in this case, mastery of the vexing game of golf - and the
ways in which his pursuit awakens his very consciousness.
Stieglitz's prose is highly refined, lyrical, and engaging -
with not infrequent moments of breathtaking beauty. *Gale*
is a love-letter to a time and a place and a wonderful cast
of characters. It is marked throughout with an elegiac tone
that is deeply affecting, but never sentimental. I could not
put this memoir down, and it lingers."

*Stephen Cope, best-selling author of*
*'The Great Work of Your Life,' and many others.*

"In his elegantly written debut book, *A Gale Stronger Than
Longing*, Val Stieglitz gives us an intriguing coming-of-
age work wherein he wrestles with learning the intricacies
of golf while navigating moving into adulthood, amid the
challenges of moving from his childhood home to Milford
Haven, Wales, then returning to America. If you love the
game of golf, competitive golf drama, and encountering
a lively array of characters - such as the rotund Irish golf
pro, Dick Flynn - then you will find *A Gale Stronger Than
Longing* as refreshing as a stroll through the Welsh countryside while listening to a reading of Dylan Thomas.

*Thomas Cofield, author of 'Scuffletown.'*

A GALE STRONGER THAN LONGING

Charleston, SC
www.PalmettoPublishing.com

*A Gale Stronger Than Longing*
Copyright © 2023 by Val H. Stieglitz

First Edition

Hardcover ISBN: 979-8-8229-1766-8
Paperback ISBN: 979-8-8229-1767-5
eBook ISBN: 979-8-8229-1768-2

# A Gale Stronger Than Longing

OR

*How To Play Golf
In The Land Of Memory*

VAL H. STIEGLITZ

# FORWARD *and* ACKNOWLEDGEMENTS

The title of this work – *A Gale Stronger Than Longing* – comes from a phrase in the poem *Sea Virus,* by Gwyneth Lewis. Ms. Lewis was named the first National Poet of Wales in 2005, and has been widely recognized for her poetry. I believed the phrase captures the spirit and mood of this book.

There is an observation in the introduction to Tobias Wolff's memoir, *This Boy's Life,* which expresses how I think about this book. The observation reads, "… this is a book of memory, and memory has its own story to tell."

In the same way, this work is a story told by memory. It sits somewhere between fiction and memoir, and is not meant to be literally factual or historically precise in all respects. It is meant to reflect and convey the way in which my experiences in a small town in southwest Wales settled within me over time, and affected my larger life and larger perspective. It is the version my memory wishes to tell, not a recitation or checklist of facts. Thus, no person should see themselves, or anyone else, in any character, or any specific description of events. I did live in Pembrokeshire as a youth, and did learn to play golf there, on the 9-hole course described herein, which is now a full 18. And I did return some 35 years later. The people, places, and events described in these pages are inspired and informed by my time there, but represent a mixture of the true, the imagined, the embellished, and the remembered. My feelings for the place, the people, and this period of my life are, however, entirely real.

I should acknowledge several people who were crucial to the commencement and completion of this book. First, my wife, Sandra, who is always my biggest supporter, in matters small and large. Then, my mother and father, who undertook the logistically daunting family relocations described in the story, with four children in tow, and not only made it work, but work like a charm. I think then of the many friends who shared my time in Milford Haven, Wales, but especially Gillian Knowles, who tracked me down to return to the school reunion that sparked my commitment to writing this book, and who read and commented upon a very early draft. I also thank Joanne (Arkell) McCay, whose family resided in Milford the same time as mine, as our fathers worked together on the construction project I describe, who read and commented upon a much later draft. Thanks also go to my brother-in-law, Stephen Cope, himself a noted author, for his encouragement and advice. Finally, I appreciate the professional editorial counsel of Alexia Paul, who opened my eyes not only to the many ways I could improve this book, but to becoming a better writer as well; and Ellen Fishburne Triplett, for applying her artistic imagination and skill to the cover artwork and design.

As for a formal dedication – well, that is easy: to my children, Henry and Catherine.

October, 2023
Columbia, South Carolina

# THE DYING DAY

The town of Milford Haven, in Pembrokeshire, sits along the northern edge of a great cleft sliced into the southwest flank of Wales during the last Ice Age. This cleft is vast and wide and deep, fed by cold waters from the turbulent North Atlantic but calmed to a smooth sheen by the myriad bays, inlets, marshes, and mudflats that line and protect the sinuous, winding estuary. In winter, the weather can turn wild and unpredictable. In the brief and poignant months of summer, however, the northernmost influence of the Gulf Stream warms the seas, the days assume a kind of sleepy languor, and all feels at peace along the tranquil Milford waterway.

Sun and light command these mild, mid-year months. Tankers, sailboats, watercraft of all kind, glide serene and untroubled upon the glistening Haven. The sky is rich and blue. Seabirds swoop in lazy circles. The breeze comes warm and gentle, fragrant of salt and blooms and wild grasses from the hills, tilting the mind toward gentle thoughts and optimism.

It is only a passing thing, however, this fair and placid season. Soon enough, the skies will fill again with rain and cloud. Winds will whip the waters. The land will brown with autumn. The season will have changed. As if knowing their time is short, therefore, the splendid days of summer glory in their brief and transient reign and refuse to yield the skies. And thus, as each sun-sprinkled summer day nears its close, a quiet struggle grips the quiet, drowsy Haven.

It begins with what the senses perceive as an alteration in the composition of the air, as if something is withdrawing, draining away. Nothing is definite or measurable – the day simply loses its solidity, ceases being what it was, and changes. The warm air cools. The waters lap. Bird cries soften. The colors of the sky, the landscape, the sea, all darken a shade ⊤ or appear to, at least, the eye less reliable with the advancing hours. A hint of mist, at first a mere wisp, collects atop the soft, green hills. The sensation of lassitude deepens, accompanied by an impression that the light itself, that thin, frail, northern summer light, is disintegrating.

As this subtle contest hastens, thin ribbons of pink and orange materialize above the western horizon, flooding the skies with blazing streaks - then fade and disappear, all spent. Passersby on the streets, gardeners tending their roses, shopkeepers closing their shops, children at play, all feel the approaching chill, gaze skyward, and tighten their jackets. As the fiery color-bursts recede, a pale, translucent outline forms, and the ascending moon emerges as a faint sketch, barely visible against the graying background. The earlier mood of weary indolence, so benign, gives way now to a hollow foreshadowing of the impermanence of things, and this empty feeling threads steadily through the atmosphere.

It feels unnatural, this silence, this emptiness, and cannot last. Into the solemn stillness, therefore, arises an anticipation, a suggestion of vibration, pitched just beyond hearing, humming from sea to sky to land - then suddenly it is done, the day has died, and dusk drops full and quick like a violet cloak across it all – the hills, the towns, the country lanes and fields, the houses and the waters – and another summer day along the sheltered Haven has met its end.

On one such evening, a balmy July Monday, in the year 1968, we find this familiar little drama repeating itself. The day has been long and warm and filled with light; but moves now toward its familiar conclusion. A chill rises from the water. Mist gathers in the hills. Flames of gold blaze resolutely on the western horizon, only to expire. Evenfall steals over Milford Haven and descends upon the weathered Milford Railway Station, there to circle and swirl about a train that crouches taut in readiness, blue and silver on the iron track.

This waiting train is the Great Western's overnight express to London, which departs at 8:45 p.m. every Monday in the summer – and its departure this evening is imminent. Slanting rails of willowy sunlight are fading against the coming darkness. Night, with its sudden sea-borne draught and strange, lonely quiet, is draping steadily across the waterway, and the thick, leafy trees surrounding the station sway loosely in the freshening breeze. Little collections of passengers – mothers and fathers shepherding wide-eyed children, white-haired ladies carting worn-out bags, frowning men bearing briefcases - scurry aboard the express as the conductor whistles shrilly to sound its departure and the steam begins to blow. Moments later, there emanates from the train a low, menacing rumble, then another, followed by an eerie interlude; and then abruptly, almost without warning, like a dark creature rousing fitfully from slumber, the big train shudders and coughs and lurches and begins to labor away from the station, its enormous wheels straining painfully against the rails, its cars and couplings clanking in a high, metallic cry that cuts against and through the silver faint-light's calm repose. The rending cry sharpens as metal grinds against metal, as thousands of tons bearing hundreds of people to a hundred different destinations stir agonizingly to life. 8:45 p.m. has arrived and the train, indentured to its timetable, is on the move.

Although the express departs every Monday with monotonous sameness, and nothing of interest ever occurs, as the engine now heaves forward the form of a young man of sixteen can suddenly be seen, craning out the window of one of its compartments, waving his arms round and round at a circle of youths gathered together back on the platform. And these clustered figures, alone on the now-deserted siding, eight or ten of them, bright-eyed, fresh-faced, red-cheeked - they cry out to the one on the train who is leaving. He can tell they are calling to him, for their mouths are wide and straining, and their expressions urgent, but he hears nothing above the tumult of the departing train. Inaudible against the furious roar, they may as well be a ring of mutes. Leaning from the compartment window, however, he knows otherwise; knows without hearing that they are shouting, imploring him to come back, to stay, and never to forget them. But the train presses forward, on and on, louder and louder, leaving them behind.

The young man's face falls stricken. Squinting his eyes against welling tears, he watches the small knot of his friends and companions draw together on the platform, recede, recede, and grow ever smaller against a backdrop of dirty yellow clouds drifting in from the sea, smudging the darkening sky. From among the little corps, arms reach into the dusk – two, three, four arms reaching out as if to grab and pull him back; and out he stretches too, in helpless reply.

Now, however, to the strengthening beat of the train, it all begins to blur, and he grimaces with one final effort to catch and keep just one brief word or call; to no avail, however. For night has fallen over the little station, and over the trees and the hills and the rippling waters, and the whipping wind cuts cold against his face and smells suddenly of rain, and the boy's eyes sting in the gathering rush as he stares back blank and still. The train picks up speed and power and wraps him within its hurtling mass; and then his tiny group of friends draw together on the platform as if one, then vanish, leaving his eyes to scour the darkness. There is nothing to see, however; nothing save the pale half-moon lifting timorously against the purpling sky as the speeding train leaves Milford Station far behind and thunders on through the night, far away.

# THE MAGIC WAND

The Milford Haven Golf Club's opening hole is a modestly short par-5, bordered to the right by an immense, thick hedgerow thrusting up luridly from a muddy bog. This dense and untamed growth - never trimmed - presents a sinister jungle of vines, brush and nettles, disarmingly so in springtime, when adorned with thousands of pastel-hued coastal wildflowers. Beyond the hedgerow's greedy grasp, however, and farther to the right – off the property completely - the terrain elevates, dries, and unfolds undisturbed into a broad pasture littered with stubble, rocks, and rabbit-holes.

Playing the course as a youth, just learning the game, my concentrated objective had been to hit the ball hard, not straight; and thus, I catapulted countless golf balls deep into the hedgerow's spiny maw, or high and wild into the rough pasture, leaving them lost forever, to be nibbled lazily, perhaps, by a wayward goat on a windy stroll, or rolled upon lasciviously by a farm dog marking a new and treasured possession.

I was slight of build, and Gary Player was my idol. How could it have been otherwise? His eyes glimmered like hard steel in the late afternoon sunlight. His garb was all black; black trousers whipping in the breeze, black turtleneck clinging to his lithe and wiry frame, black cap pulled tightly down upon his black-haired head. Surveying his shots, he narrowed his gaze like a sharpshooter. Stalking the fairways, he leaned into the gales, calling to mind some fearless hero striding to meet some unknown danger, or a hunter tracking prey. His every aspect claimed attention and respect.

Along with my family, I had migrated from hot and sunny Miami, early in 1966, briefly to London, and then to Milford, unknowingly primed for adventure and new things. Looking back, I came to Milford as a boy. When I left, however, it was as something else – not yet an adult, but something more than a boy. A fledgling explorer, perhaps, in a small kind of way. For in retrospect, my time in Milford had been a first discovery of that wide, deep expanse of experience, both within and without, which lay waiting ahead in life. And for me, golf in Milford became not only a part of this exploration, but an exceptional realm of discovery all its own, mysterious and rich, in which some part of me has remained ever since.

Not long after arriving in Milford, my father bought my first set of clubs, which he presented to me one windy Saturday afternoon, with a conspiratorial gleam in his eye. I remain confident even today that my reaction did not disappoint, for never before had I beheld objects of equal purity and grace, much less been entrusted with such voluptuous instruments. Touching them, feeling my fingers close around their tacky rubber grips, my father beaming, I felt a solemn kind of awe; a peculiar form of responsibility, almost. I possess them still, these first golf clubs – old and dusty in the basement, where every now and then I pick one up and turn it slowly in my hands, feeling again the weight, fashioning a half-swing, re-membering the excitement – both mine and my father's - with which they first became my own.

Shortly after my clubs, I next acquired – from where, exactly, I cannot recall - a paperback instructional book by the great Mr. Player, perhaps thirty pages of pen and ink drawings, accompanied by dozens of pithy admonitions and tips, and several grainy photographs. He illustrated the proper grip. He demonstrated the backswing and the subtle shifting of the weight onto the right side. He depicted the position of the club at the top of the back swing, slightly past parallel, poised and almost quivering in anticipation of its downswing, then the controlled explosion at impact and the long, full, sweeping follow-through.

The book's cover displayed a black-and-white photo-graph of his flinty visage glaring at the ball as it sped away down the fairway, as if in a great rush to escape his piti-less stare. I studied this picture, and played at reconstruct-ing the circumstances in which it might have been taken. Perhaps he needed a birdie in order to claim an important tournament, and was going for the green with a one-iron, into a driving tempest, over a perilous brook, on the final and deciding hole. Something dramatic was clearly afoot. Unquestionably, some great prize lay in the balance, so stern was his countenance, so implacable and hard.

On the back cover appeared a different photograph, however, suggesting a different mood; the smiling, debonair sportsman now cradling a large trophy from some exalted championship, not a single jet-black hair out of place, at ease and affable but not fawning, never fawning, the pinnacle of style and grace and strength. He represented all I held to be fine in a golfer – indeed, in a man, as I imagined at that time of my young life a golfer to be the finest sort of man. And the sum of his counsel, in my mind, seemed to congeal into one simple rule, which I adopted as my supreme command: *Hit the ball hard.* Thus it settled into my consciousness as the undiluted essence, the distilled quintessence, of the sage's philosophy. As I was nothing if not the most devout of pupils, therefore, this is precisely what I strove to do, with unwavering zeal. *Hit the ball hard.*

Right from the beginning, I took to the game. There was no period of uncertainty, no dipping a toe into the water, pulling it out, then coyly dipping in again. No passing flirtation. It was enchantment from the start, and full immersion. Immediately after procuring my clubs – McGregors, if you are curious, regal in their place of honor in the basement - my father placed me under the tutelage of the Milford club professional - an Irishman named Dick Flynn, who came to feature prominently in my golfing career.

It must be emphasized at the outset that, upon first sight, Mr. Flynn seemed designed for virtually any occupation other than that of a golf pro; or, to state the obverse, he appeared to be utterly unsuited to, and perhaps most likely masquerading as, a golf pro. He must have weighed three-hundred pounds, and truthfully it could have been more. Most outstanding was an enormous stomach, that completely overpowered and engulfed his capacious trousers – which themselves seemed at any moment about to relinquish their struggle against his frightening paunch and fall ingloriously to his ankles. His forearms and haunches were massive, on a scale suggestive of a Belgian draft horse, and he trod the course with the dogged, stolid step of just such a creature, on his face the concentrated stare of a man trying hard to remember something just beyond his memory's reach. He was forever hiking up his pants, or tucking in his fluttering shirt, or adjusting his drooping belt, or reaching into his pockets, or fidgeting with his collar, or scratching his stubbly chin, or clamping his cap down upon his head - but somehow Mr. Flynn, my first instructor, could strike a golf ball with shocking grace and power, and soon enough stood, after the black-clad South African, second in my pantheon.

My relationship with Mr. Flynn and the pursuit of golf commenced late one September afternoon, when my father picked me up after school and made directly for the Milford Haven Golf Club. In the morning, the rain had blustered, but it passed and the sky had brightened. Now it was a cool, mild afternoon, the sun hovering low and round and pinkish above the trees, like something big and ripe. In retrospect, I realize my father must have left work early, which he rarely did – and perhaps the rarity of that event explains the sharpness with which the memory has endured, for so readily do I today still feel the crisp air playing about my neck and arms, and savor the scent of newly-mown grass, rich and thick and heady.

My father's gray Austin pulled into the gravel parking lot. Out I hopped. He walked on ahead as I wrestled my bag from the boot, the clubs clanking noisily, their weight tilting me first one way then the next. When I finally got the contraption under control, I circled around the back of the clubhouse to a broad, fresh-cut field, scattered with a dusting of early-fallen leaves.

And that, for me, was the moment golf began.

On the nearest edge of this field, in a patch of late afternoon sunlight, a large, disheveled man – frankly, I thought, a ridiculously obese and scruffy man, who bore no resemblance to Mr. Player - stood lazily swinging a golf club and hitting balls toward a red flag stuck in the ground at the far end of the field. Despite the evidence before my eyes – he cut a shapeless and unruly figure - I knew this had to be the local pro, he to whom the secrets of this game were known; he who would impart to me these secrets. I contemplated him with an uneasy shudder – his easy motion a blunt and disorienting contrast to his great bulk, even to a completely ignorant observer like myself. And then the untidy man finished hitting balls, looked our way, and commenced shambling in our direction, increasing in size in some disturbing geometrical progression as he approached.

He halted before us, this giant, and seemed to tower into the sky. I stared blankly. After a moment, my father spoke

up to introduce me. Mr. Flynn extended an enormous, calloused hand and expelled something incomprehensible in
a thick brogue, accompanied by the stench of cigarettes. I
smiled tentatively, placed my hand in his and, for lack of
anything more appropriate to the moment, nodded and said
"Yes, Sir." This vague rejoinder evidently sufficed, however,
for Mr. Flynn thereupon released my hand and pawed me
on the shoulder, which caused me briefly to lose my balance.
He exchanged a few more words with my father – again in
some dense, heavy accent – then my father too clapped me
on the shoulder and disappeared back around the clubhouse,
leaving me alone with this unnerving behemoth speaking
an indecipherable tongue.

I heard the Austin pulling away, crunching on the gravel,
and thought it was getting a bit chilly. I wondered, actually,
whether it might not be a tad too brisk to be undertaking
this new and daunting venture, which naturally lead to some
brief consideration of whether I was really all that interested
in golf at all – the entirety of these musings, however, occupying only a second or two, before I turned again to face my
new tutor. Like a mountain, he loomed before me, hands on
hips. I looked up impassively. Mr. Flynn gave me a brief ap-
praisal, then flashed a mysterious smile that revealed a mini-
mal number of teeth – I glimpsed a couple of brownish nubs
amid dark pink gums - but which also seemed to flick on tiny,
playful lights in his eyes – blue lights, like small flashing blue
sparks, and I felt myself smiling back – and then we began.

It was, I reflected later, just the strangest thing. The time
passed wholly unnoticed, surreptitiously, as it does when we

become engrossed in something unexpectedly captivating. Mr. Flynn told me what to do and I obeyed. He demonstrated and I watched and copied. He spoke and I listened. I examined how he gripped the club, and watched him swing. He bade me repeat and I repeated. He moved my hands, my shoulders, my feet, my head. It was only the two of us, alone. I forgot the chill. It grew quiet. The late afternoon light waned and softened, and before long my exhalations were accompanied by thin, smoky contrails that wafted up and away into the dissolving day.

And then, miraculously, by the time my father returned some ninety minutes later to gather me up, I was lofting 7-irons toward the red flag stuck at the far end of the scrubby field and had fallen completely into something like a trance. In my hands I held a rod of steel; I drew it slowly back and up, then allowed it to fall, but also guided and propelled it through the back of a dimpled white ball waiting bright and snug atop the grass. There was a click, and a movement traveled up the rod of steel into my hands and arms, as the ball rose seemingly of its own volition into the air, my arms following its flight, my weight shifting from one side to the other, and my left foot beginning ever so slightly to turn over.

And the club? Well, that prosaic shaft of metal was now somehow a wand, a baton, a magic wand, through which I had become the author of a delightful little trick. The ball arced prettily against the blue-gray sky, then dropped back to earth with a soft plop, by which time the rod of steel that was my club had traveled over my left shoulder, and the echo of the little click had vanished, and I posed admiringly as the wind tussled my hair and ran noisily though the bushes surrounding the clubhouse. And then I wanted to perform the trick again. And again and again, over and over. And when the trick didn't work as I wished, I determined to do it again and make it work. And then when it did work, as my confidence grew from one lesson to the next and the next, I felt the urge to perform finer sleights of hand, the kinds I quickly realized Mr. Flynn could perform, making the ball veer left and right, drill low, or soar high. And if such feats resided within Mr. Flynn's repertory, I reflected, executed in a lumpy field behind a nondescript brick clubhouse, in a remote little town in southwest Wales, imagine what wizardry the great Gary Player must be able to work with a club and a ball, what legerdemain that severe and dark-eyed master must have at his command, the secrets hidden within his cultivated game.

And so, spellbound from the beginning, I took lessons from Mr. Flynn twice a week, played on the weekends, swung a club in our backyard every day after school, pored at night like a cultist over my instructional book, and consumed large swathes of classroom time mentally weighing the merits and demerits of an open stance versus a closed stance, a strong grip, a weak grip, foot placement, ball position, and generally turning over and over in my mind everything I had thus far seen or read or heard or imagined or experienced about hitting a golf ball, hungry for every nugget that might possibly be turned to my advantage. I tumbled happily into complete devotion, therefore, swallowed up like Jonah by the thrill of mastering the art and craft and avocation of golf.

*Swept away* ... that is the phrase my memory offers up. *Swept away.*

And then, incredibly, before long, in what I took as firm evidence that indeed we inhabit a just world, my devotion produced its first concrete reward.

Golf enjoyed widespread popularity throughout western Wales. Sprinkled across the coastal counties were courses and clubs of all sizes and sorts, each with its own special history, its own loyal membership, and each with its own resident professional. The pros from these various clubs competed regularly in tournaments staged across the region. Each pro was attended by his own personal caddy, and the competitions were quite serious business.

Possibly, it was my conspicuous zeal – he couldn't have missed it. Or perhaps it was entirely random. Or maybe I was simply his last remaining option. I never knew the reason, but the fact is that at the conclusion of a particularly good lesson one day in late October, during which Mr. Flynn had smiled his approving, stub-toothed smile more than once, he inquired brusquely if I would be interested in serving as his caddy in the next upcoming tournament. I hesitated for an instant or two – never entirely sure I had understood precisely the words emerging from his mouth - then blurted *Yes, Yes Indeed*, before he had a chance to rethink the proposition.

"Eight sharp on Saturday," the terse Mr. Flynn growled. "And wear a jacket."

Well ... dizzy and swimming, I was. So joyously astonished by the invitation that had he further commanded me to remain at attention in the parking lot until the appointed hour arrived, gladly would I have done so, and counted myself lucky to boot.

Once the burst of giddiness slackened, however, it dawned upon me that I now occupied a position of no small importance, and had responsibilities. The time for puppy-like eagerness was over. Now it was time to buckle down. My duties were simple and clear, with no room for error. Mr. Flynn was not a dour man – indeed, his eyes could light and skip and play at times - but neither was he talkative, and he sought neither companionship nor conversation from his caddy. What he sought, I understood without the need to ask, was only competence; efficient and unfailing competence.

My task was to haul his bag without staggering or stumbling, promptly hand him whichever club he requested, clean it after he hit, and watch where his ball went. If it flew into the rough, I was to locate it. If it landed in some disagreeable spot, where he did not wish to venture, such as in the middle of a nest of briars or out of bounds in a mucky quagmire, I was to retrieve it, clean it, and bring it to him. On the green, my function was to tend the pin and lift his ball from the cup. If it began to rain, I pulled his jacket from his bag and handed it to him. When it stopped raining, I shook his jacket out, folded it, and returned it to the bag. I kept spare tees and a ball marker in my pocket. It was also understood – at least by me – that I was to pray fervently for the complete disintegration of his opponent.

Mr. Flynn never asked me to indulge in such unsporting supplications, but I believed he knew this was my intention and my practice, so that whenever I concentrated with special intensity on willing disaster upon our foe, I felt him to be both aware and approving. Many was the time we exchanged a swift, unreadable glance in the wake of an adversary's particularly poor shot. I understood, of course, that there was to be no outward sign of gloating, and none was ever shown.

In return for service as Mr. Flynn's caddy, I was allowed to play his course as much as I wished. Occasionally he even gave me an old ball or two or three – most welcome booty, badly needed to replenish my stock, as I continued with disheartening regularity to smash my drives into the miserable pasture beyond the insatiable hedge-bank alongside the first hole. I played in rain, gentle mists, and pelting storms. I played in bitter cold, when the ball was like an oval stone and its clanging impact against my irons sent stabs and shivers shooting up into my hands. I played under cloudless skies in the late days of spring, when the smell of new grass and clover was strong, and in the summer twilight, when the stubborn day held on and struggled and objects grew formless in the distance. Caddying for my pro, and playing what I thought of as his course - and ultimately mine as well - I dreamed of being a pro as well, and playing golf forever.

In addition to learning the rudiments of the game, embracing and adopting its practice and ritual, I somehow also absorbed a certain approach or attitude toward the pursuit of solitary, difficult goals, which eventually grew into a way of approaching the wider world that lay waiting in the years ahead. I did not know this at the time, and could have put none of it into words as a stripling of fourteen or fifteen. As I grew older, however, and began to reflect on where and how I had become the person I became, and why I looked at life as I did, so many paths lead back to Milford Haven, what I did there, how I lived there, and the people who shared and filled my life in that small town on the southwest corner of Wales; where, despite being a foreigner, an outsider, I inexplicably fit more true than any other place in the world. Some of these paths lead to particular people I had known, and particular things I had done or seen. And one path lead back to the Milford Haven Golf Club, and golf as I learned it on that plot of land, in rain and sun, under the stern, unsmiling, but light-hearted care of Mr. Flynn, when I was young.

# THE GENTLEST OF SKIES

It is a cruel paradox that time does not stand still, that nothing remains as it is, and everything changes – the consequence being that, despite our deepest yearnings to anchor fast forever the people, places, and things that make us happy, the tides move us on, and longing for good things past, good things lost, lurks at the core of each and every joy and pleasure, for none of it will endure. However, this same ruthless, relentless current of time, which destroys so thoroughly that which we wish most desperately never to be marred, is also our greatest good fortune and our greatest balm. Just as we cannot help but know the scorching sting and bone-deep ache of separation and absence, so we also build our own healing walls and towers as the present continually unfolds into our individual futures, and each person stows away their past and everything associated with it – every wince and triumph and regret - somewhere inside those walls and towers, stockpiled like heirlooms boxed in a warehouse. And this is how our days progress. Some boxes remain closed forever, their contents moldering into dust; to others you return, however, and open now and again, as you choose. It is a mystery, this dual aspect of time; at once the thresher of our deepest attachments, yet also the mender of their shattered, sharp-edged remnants.

Well, so may it be. So I believe it to be, in fact. Time gives and time takes. And we can never comprehend, really, how it works; and will certainly never control it workings. But today, however ... well, this day was no day for threshers and boxes and healing walls, for a brilliant confluence of events had returned me to Milford more than thirty years after departing, where now I stood upon the first tee with Hugh Evans, my oldest golfing companion in the entire world, surveying the familiar rolling landscape of the Milford course. Half a lifetime ago, a hulking train had carried me away, with no real means of keeping alive the bonds which had taken root here. Only a daydreamer would have harbored any expectation of return – which is precisely why those years in Milford had gone into a sturdy box and into the warehouse. Out of the blue, however, ties long submerged had resurfaced, a reunion of old schoolmates had pulled me back, and here I stood, in a place I had consigned to the quicksand of the past. A place which, though never far from mind, I had resigned myself to never seeing again.

The sheer unlikeliness of it had me in a bit of a daze.

"You go ahead," I told Hugh. "It's your course."

"No, no," he demurred. "It's as much your course as mine, you know that. Your honors."

I paused, for it was a moment to enjoy. The wind nudged slightly from behind and a little to the right, wafting soundlessly and effortlessly through my memories; a mild and generous breeze, a mild late-May breath full of the rich fragrance of wildflowers and the warming earth, streaming across the tee and filling my head with reverie. I glanced up toward the sky and smiled, then tugged my cap down upon my head and fixed my gaze down the fairway that I knew so well, ready and excited, thinking no more about boxes or warehouses or healing walls. Thinking, instead, about golf, and the years gone by.

Effective golf requires critical thinking. Accordingly, I put aside my fluffy, sentimental ruminations, and turned an analytic eye upon the course. Before me unfolded the entire scene, precisely as recalled, the hole draped lazily over and upon the rolling green terrain the way a towel flung carelessly upon a bed settles in little rises and rills and folds. Still beckoning ominously along the fairway's rightward boundary, the grasping hedgerow called to mind an unkempt but ageless siren, doom to the gullible competitor. At about the spot where a well-struck drive would land, there jutted up a small earthen dike, perhaps three feet high, running nearly halfway across the fairway from the right to left, but affording a gap on the left. This unobtrusive mound appeared to be much nearer than it actually was, and the cocky golfer unfamiliar with the course invariably threw his gaze beyond it, ignoring it, giving it no consideration at all. I had seen it happen many times, always with the same result. Peering far down the fairway, and brimming with bravado, some brash sport, ignorant of the course's peculiarities, thrashes his drive with abandon, pushes it slightly right of center, ends up plugged against the innocuous grassy wall, stalks puzzled off the tee, has no alternative but to chip out sideways, and, before even halfway to the first green, descends helplessly into a foul temper, his confidence punctured for the remainder of the round.

If these twin evils can be avoided, however – the cooing temptress verge and the sly earthen hummock – a pleasant stroll up a gentle rise to the green awaits, and I thought par was not at all out of the question as I stepped upon the tee. And it was in this drifty, tranquil frame of mind that I drew my driver back slow and smooth, turned, swept forward and through, and sent my ball speeding low and straight down the fairway..

"Lovely shot," commented Hugh nonchalantly, as my ball drew, sailed through the gap on the left, and skipped easily past the earthen rise to safety. "Well struck, well done."

I smiled to myself, for I was well-acquainted with the speaker of these words. Which, I believed, afforded me a certain insight into the workings of his mind, at least as far as golf was concerned. Stepping off the tee box, I gave a genial nod, confident his keenest hope had been for me to fire off a horrible slice, sending my ball into the deepest heart of the hedgerow's maze of thorns, or wildly over and into the pastoral wasteland beyond.

"Thank you very much," I replied jauntily. "As you expected, I'm sure?"

He replied with a small, wily grin. My first goal of the day – to thwart my old friend and golfing companion's cruel wishes, and demonstrate a solid, mature grasp upon my game – had been accomplished.

Hugh teed his ball and struck a respectable drive, a bit right but clear of the muck and short of the grassy hump, and we set off down the fairway into the softest of breezes, under the gentlest of pale blue Pembrokeshire skies.

# THE AGE OF OIL

They were building oil refineries in Milford Haven in the sixties – the years they would later come to call the 'Age of Oil.' It was a time when oil towered astride the center of the world's economy. Everyone everywhere cried for oil, demanded oil, begged, borrowed, paid, and prayed for oil. Governments and fortunes and careers rose and fell on oil. Machines sparked to life, hummed and thrummed and churned and sputtered on oil. Stupendous sums of money circulated in, throughout, and around the slippery stuff – and the health, vitality, and very existence of everything from dusty villages in arid wastelands, to tiny shacks on the spare Texas plains, to skyscrapers, palaces, and the planet's great metropolises, depended upon the endless flow of oil.

The world's thirst was, simply, insatiable.

New technology was finding new oil, hitherto unknown or inaccessible reservoirs of oil, drilling deeper, faster. Across the world, by every means and mechanism possible, oil was moving; by truck, by train, by ship. And the tankers that conveyed the precious substance across the oceans were growing ever-larger by the day, transporting ever-greater quantities, between ever more far-flung locales. The increase in scale was eye-popping. Veritable rivers of crude were being sucked out of the ground, spirited across some vast sea for processing and refining, then across a different vast sea to feed some new starving market. Oil was circulating from one corner of the map to the other, sloshing in the giant bellies of the giant tankers, amid an extravaganza of exploration, testing, financing, drilling, piping, pumping, loading, shipping, off-loading, refining, processing, more piping and more shipping, trucking, storage, and more delivery. At every crossroads, there stood oil, like a mighty colossus, and little Milford – due to a simple fortuity of geography and nothing more - had suddenly become a critical connecting point in oil's labyrinthine journey from deep in the ground beneath landscapes barren and remote, to every nook and cranny of the globe.

And what exactly was this fortuity of geography? How and why had Milford become an indispensable cog in this conveyer-belt of commerce? It was simple, really. Milford Haven was situated along one of the deepest natural estuaries in the world – the Haven, the Milford Waterway, an underwater ravine gouged deep into the southwest extrusion of Pembrokeshire County by ancient geologic forces. And thus, as a natural result of its great depth, combined with its tranquil, protected currents and ease of access, it was as if the Haven had been expressly designed with shiny, state-of-the-art oil refineries in mind, as companies like Esso, BP, Texaco, and Gulf began shopping the world for new sites in the 50's. When the Milford Haven Conservancy Board was established in 1958, therefore, explicitly charged with commercializing the waterway's unique topological attributes, and given civil jurisdiction in the Haven up to the high water mark – well, the stage was set (the pump primed, so to speak) for a new Age of Oil in Pembrokeshire.

Esso played the pioneer, breaking ground on the Haven's first refinery in 1957. Officially opened by the Duke of Edinburgh in a stately ceremony on July 8, 1960, the Esso facility was only the second of its kind to be built in the UK since the war, and boasted an impressive processing capacity of 6,000,000 tons of crude oil every year. Fortunately, the fact that a fire broke out the following day on the inaugural tanker to berth at the site, the *Esso Portsmouth*, did nothing to dim prospects for the future.

Next in line came BP's terminal and storage depot, completed at Angle Bay in 1961, featuring two marine berths for offloading, and pumping 8,000,000 tons of crude each year through a 62-mile long pipeline to the BP refinery in Llandarcy. Nothing caught fire following the opening ceremony.

Milford was now drawing more attention as a site of choice. In 1963, work commenced on what became the Texaco refinery and marine terminal, occupying 450 acres along the Haven's southern shore, providing five ship berths, and refining 5,000,000 tons of crude per year. Remarks made by the local MP at the opening festivities captured the poignant flutter of hope surrounding this burgeoning new industry: *This is the rebirth of Pembrokeshire. I only wish the men who were discharged from Pembroke Dockyard during the dark, depressing days, were here today to see it taking place.*

And it wasn't over yet – there was more to come, and ample opportunities for local political exposition lay ahead. For in 1966, a site along the Haven's northern shore was commissioned for construction of one more refinery – this one to be owned and operated by Gulf Oil, the next-to-last along the entire Haven - and this is where we came into the picture.

Each of these mammoth installations had to be designed and built from the ground up, which required engineers with backgrounds in the oil business. My father, armed with a degree in Petroleum Engineering and 16 years of experience, had recently landed a position as a field engineer for the Bechtel Company, and Bechtel had the contract to build the Gulf refinery – three tanker berths, road and rail tanker facilities, adding 3,000,000 more tons of annual capacity to the Haven's already-swollen refining proportions. In 1966, therefore, from the U.S. via an intermediary stint in London, with a handful of other Americans and a peppering of Canadians and Australians, my family and I arrived to live in this sleepy fishing village by the sea, tucked inconspicuously against the rocky southwest coast of Wales.

# THE VANGUARD

L eading the way, in the vanguard, one might say, were my father and I. Leaving my mother, two brothers, and sister behind in London, the plan of action called for us to embark first for Milford, scout out the terrain, and attend to settling all the logistics, preparatory to the remainder of the family joining us a month later. Circling around it was a definite air of adventure, blazing a trail, off into the unknown; and my mind, at that time just beginning to flex a new-found yen for new experiences, embraced the prospect without hesitation.

According to schedule, therefore, on a dreary Sunday afternoon in August, my father and I set forth from Paddington Station in West London, majestic terminus of the Great Western line to west Wales since the mid-1800's, booked on the overnight express to Milford – the end of the line.

Certain structures exude a gravitas, somehow harness and concentrate within their confines a singular aura of force and power; and this is the feeling that came strong upon me at Paddington. One of the venerable old London train stations produced by the energy and largesse of empire and the Industrial Revolution, Paddington, with its stolid Victorian architecture, its age and command of place, its huge train shed, wrought-iron arches, and triple transept, created in my mind both a cavernous, imposing effect, and a smothering sense of confinement, an uncomfortable feeling of enclosure within some alien hive of metal and machinery.

And this enclosure, this hive – well, it was like nothing I had ever seen or known! A weird, self-contained city, over-run with huge, menacing, mechanical creatures, all buzzing, clanging, swarming, with an unseen, insect-like intelligence; creatures made not of steel and bolts and cable, but of some hard, glinting, metallic flesh; strangely sensate, heaving and straining on their tracks like muscled Dobermanns tautly leashed, and then, with enormous gaseous bellows, leaping alarmingly to life and bursting forth to hurtle fiercely off into the world. Such were the startling impressions the great station set to bubbling in my mind on the wet and dismal Sunday of our departure for Milford; bizarre and unnerving impressions, rising upward from the tangle of sound, motion, and activity in the overawing and vaguely macabre heart of Paddington.

Wide eyes swiveling left and right, I followed my father along wet, dirty platforms, solemnly absorbing the scene's iron immensity, feeling my own paltry insignificance amidst the flurry. Above, below, to every side - people hastening, announcements blaring, cold metal wheels wailing hideously, lights flashing. A jarring cacophony of voices, anxious, angry, joyful; faces drawn in introspection, faces wide and aglow with anticipation, blank with fatigue, with boredom, pinched by some inner turmoil; clothes shabby and rich, plain and colorful – and every soul moving, every soul in transit, heading somewhere on some private mission, as behind it all some unseen force pulled levers and manipulated switches so that indeed the myriad of living, beating locomotives came and went with dull predictability and delivered, in the end, astonishingly, every person to their precise desired destination, to waiting friends, warm hearths, and loved ones, or perhaps to loneliness and regret, all at their scheduled times.

To the blank, receptive slate of my mind, doused in Paddington's frantic torrent, it seemed an impossibility of logistics, as if only chance or luck could possibly hold it all together. The massive board meant to inform travelers of departures, arrivals, platforms – was to me incomprehensible and unfathomable, as if carved in scratches; its code undecipherable to my overstuffed brain. Even worse, it was impossible to make any sense of the language crackling from the loudspeakers into the hyper-agitated air – the garbled skein of sounds assaulting my ears with jagged waves of furious electronic noise. Odors of oil, dirt, sweat, and steam swirled and mingled into a vaguely sickening miasma, the stench of which roiled and rolled in wet draughts, causing my eyes to swim and my thoughts to stumble. Babble of ten thousand voices, kaleidoscope of countless skittering bodies, rough scuff of shoes against grimy, well-worn cement.

I sidestepped burly men and frail old ladies and bawling children. I bumped my knees on mounds of luggage stacked on the sticky platforms. It was too much, this sensual maelstrom, too stimulating, too disorienting – and yet, overriding the frenetic vibrato oscillating throughout the smelly air, overriding the madhouse tenor of it all – well, at the same time, my heart raced in a kind of thrall, and my eyes bugged big and bright so as not to miss a single thing; not one exhilarating, mesmerizing thing.

We maneuvered through a slick metal turnstile, wedged through another crowd, clambered up some stairs, then down onto a dirty, busy landing; shoved our way onto one of the waiting trains, then down a narrow aisle, then finally into our compartment. The door slid shut. Immediately, the clamor fell away. Throwing our luggage onto the overhead rack, we dropped heavily into our seats, where I sat dazed, breathing heavily, numbed by the sudden silence, isolated now from the press and uproar outside.

As I settled down, though, and began thinking clearly again, I noticed my father gazing with his own wide eyes beyond the window; and then, before I could inquire what it was, what was so fixing his attention, he turned to me with a grin and announced *"Hold on, here we go!"* For our own train had shuddered briskly to life, was easing forward, bumping and grinding over the maze of switch-tracks, laboring into motion – and then Away We Charged! Bursting out of the alien hive, out of the city, blasting down the track between rows of trees, past yellow-green fields, as the sun sank into the blue-to-grey western horizon and shadows settled gently upon the entire landscape. And then, before long, it was night, black as oblivion outside our cozy berth, and I dropped off to sleep sitting up, leaning my head against the cool glass of the darkened window, my mind empty and still.

I may have slept for a minute; or it could have been an hour. My father roused me with a hand to my shoulder. We tucked away a hearty meal in the dining car, returned to our nook – I went bouncing off the sides of the narrow passageway as the train swerved and swayed – and climbed into our bunks, where I fell immediately into the deepest of dreamless sleeps.

Behind us lay Paddington. Ahead lay Milfiord.

It would have been completely natural, had I been wracked with unease over relocating to this new locale, of which I knew nothing. In fact, however, I harbored not one whit of anxiety or foreboding. I realize now this phlegmatic attitude was unusual. In retrospect, however, its explanation is clear.

This move from London to Milford was really the lesser of our recent upheavals. A few scant months earlier, our family had undertaken a much greater and more daunting transit, picking up from my childhood home in south Florida and flying across the ocean to London; the site of Bechtel's European headquarters, where the planning and design phases of the Gulf project were to occur. This phase, it was expected, would occupy several months. Then, upon its completion, we would relocate to Milford for the actual construction of the refinery. Accordingly, London was our initial landing-place, as a way-station leading to a longer residence in Milford. And this first migration from Miami to London was unquestionably the more momentous adjustment. That move was a true rupture – yet also became, in an unexpected way, a revelation, a pivot point in my young life; one consequence of which was that I regarded our latest resettlement, this one merely from London to Milford via the Great Western's overnight express, with anticipation instead of unease.

My childhood had unfolded serenely, cocooned in a small and familiar world of parents, siblings, grandparents, uncles, aunts, and cousins, the close and comforting routines of school, church, Little League baseball, dinner get-togethers, Saturday evening TV, holiday gatherings, laughter, jollity, and a vigorous collection of small, eccentric, family traditions. Our extended familial life in south Florida had been wide and deep and rich. And, as the date of our departure for London approached, there formed an awareness – keener with each passing day - that I was leaving the only place and only life I had ever known, for something very far away and sure to be very different, and from which I already intuited a return to be unlikely. We were stepping off a safe and solid platform into the air, I sensed, and nothing that followed that fateful step would resemble what had existed before.

To my young mind, of course, this was a deeply disquieting prospect – exacerbated by my complete inability to influence the matter in any way. Yes, as we played catch one evening in the backyard, my father told me it was going to be a great job, the kind he had always wanted to have. And yes, I heard my mother tell her parents, on the phone one night, that she couldn't wait to see everything there was to see, that it would be a wonderful adventure. Behind it all, however, I perceived only a vast dislocation. Naturally, therefore, the immense unknowns surrounding this first transition had spawned a swirling cloud of trepidation; my first encounter with what I dimly grasped to be separation, finality, and loss.

I need not have feared, however. Little did I know the reshaping wrought within me by our journey from Miami to London would prefigure everything that followed, both during our tenure in the UK and afterwards – I can trace it, in fact, as easily as tracing a figure on a sheet of paper, so clearly does its imprint remain.

We departed Miami on a humid, sultry, overcast afternoon. The air had a texture damp and sullen, thick with intimations not normally present – tension, anxiety. I made a final, somber study of my boyhood bedroom. I glanced, on my way to the front door, at the tree-house my brother and I had cobbled together the previous summer in one of the backyard trees. I stared thoughtfully at the spot in the living room where our Christmas tree had always stood. As we loaded into the car I turned and paused to commit to memory – for I knew something irrevocable was occurring - the shape and appearance of our plain and ordinary house, its front steps, its color, the porchlight, the bushes, the shutters, the knocker on the door. And then, the farewells at the airport had been sad and tearful, grandparents, uncles, aunts, cousins, all gathered dolefully to see us off. All of it was real, and as morose as I had anticipated.

Then, however ... then came the unexpected thing, the big leap, the big change – when it all fell away. When all the fears, all the apprehension with which I had boarded the airplane and swooped across the Atlantic, fell away within hours after landing at Heathrow; the entire, heavy-hearted, shroud of hesitation and doubt crumbling to nothing on our very first day in London, replaced by some influence that pulled me irresistibly, willingly, into its grasp; some stimulus electric, magnetic, and transforming.

The unknowing author of this experience ... but is "experience" even the right word? It wasn't simply an isolated, definable experience. It was more like a general remolding, an overall reshaping, emptying a container of its old contents and filling it anew with something different, something more substantial ... the author of which was my father.

# TURNING THE SWITCH

The day of our arrival in London stands forth with intense and vivid clarity. The plane's descent, ears popping, gathering our belongings, bustling through the airport and customs, sleepy and dozing in the cab, the phalanx of liveried doormen at the Mount Royal Hotel, luggage delivered to our adjoining rooms. Then, in the barest of moments, after the last bellman takes his leave and our door snicks quietly shut, my father corralling me and my brother together for a walk – *Just to get a look around*, he assures us eagerly, hustling us down the elevator and through the plush, red-carpeted lobby, out onto the street. No opportunity to plead fatigue, make faces, or slump shoulders in disinterest – up, my father sweeps us, up, up, out the door and onto the street.

We loiter listlessly on the sidewalk before the Mount Royal, my brother and I, dopey from the long flight. My father is engaged in some energetic discussion with one of the doormen, concerning something or another - whatever it is, they seem to be pointing in various directions, alternately nodding and wagging their heads. It is cold and gray and dank, vaguely redolent of soot, the air moist and heavy as if you could wipe it off your brow or smear it on your hands. My brother pulls a small notepad from his pocket and says he plans to keep a list of all the Rolls Royces and Bentleys he sees in London. He has an organized mind, my brother, keeps lists of many things, and has his pencil at the ready.

As for myself, I begin examining the surroundings. Horns blare, people mill and scurry, cars belch brown fumes, umbrellas tap the pavement. Weird smells and accents circle as we wait upon our father. Not a single thing looks familiar in any way, not a single person sounds familiar in any way, and I have the odd feeling some arcane force is creeping stealthily into my consciousness, infiltrating my senses, sneaking into my mind and body. Suddenly, out of nowhere, I feel my cheeks broadening into a smile, then see my brother smiling too - as if some internal switch, which had reposed hidden and untouched the entire length of our childhood, had suddenly been turned on – illuminating everything in an astonishing new sort of light, and turning our perspectives to some heretofore unknown angle. I glance again at my brother; he feels it too, I can tell, and together we stand speechless on Bryanston Street, in a kind of vacant, expectant trance.

Finally, his lengthy conference concluded, and a comical, ever-so goofy grin plastered across his own face, my father comes bounding down the steps to join us. Briskly, he buttons his jacket, swivels his eyes up and down the street, cranes his neck toward the leaden sky. *Ready?* he cries, batting our shoulders. Simultaneously, my brother and I nod – then *Off We Go!* he exclaims enthusiastically, as if calling the start of the Indy 500. Off we go! And thus, indeed, Off We Went! Off into this new and unknown city! Off into London – that great city of which, I came to read in a book many years later, a man grows tired only when he grows tired of life itself! That city after which, for me, nothing was ever the same.

And our *"look around?"* Well, somehow it turned into an extended reconnoitering mission, the details of which could consume pages. Suffice it to say that, over the next several hours, we traversed sidewalk after sidewalk, rambled up and down alleyways and mews, squares and gardens, investigated tiny shops selling exotic items, and gawked at monumental structures cloaked in an aura of history perceptible even to my limited sensibilities. We perused plaques and markers, stared at impressive storefronts, navigated treacherous traffic circles. We dodged showers, skipped puddles, peeked inside churches, passed pubs with peculiar names, ambled down Oxford Street, Piccadilly, the Mall, our feet weightless, our breath smoking in the air, our hands and ears and the tips of our noses cold and red. What a panorama! My extremities may have been numb with chill but my brain, my imagination, was hot as a roaring engine! And our little "look around" had become, I later came to appreciate, an absolute conflagration – a veritable bonfire, in which so many prior conceptions, small, childish conceptions, were burned to the ground, incinerated in a great cauldron of … of transformation. Conceptions of history, the world, of life – of everything. Turned to ash so the rebuilding could begin. All that first morning in London.

It had to do, I believe, with the stretching of basic ideas. Stretching them wider and deeper. Every child learns that there exist places and people different from the places and people with which they live their daily lives. We read in books about faraway lands full of men and women who speak strange languages, dress in unfamiliar ways, and practice customs unlike our own. We watch TV shows and movies set in the world's grand metropolises, the exotic tropics, in deserts, palaces, and on the high seas. We receive postcards from aunts or uncles visiting unusual locales. As an abstract matter, we know full-well the world is bigger than whatever we see around us morning, noon, and night.

As an abstract matter, that is.

But we cannot truly know all this to be the case – much less grasp its import - till it hits us squarely in the face. And I don't mean a summer trip to New York or the Bahamas – I mean hit in the face as in, *this is where I live now, in this completely unfamiliar place and among these unfamiliar people, and I do not understand much of it, so better figure it out quickly.* I mean the blunt, hard reality of being thrown into the unknown and knowing there is no way out. I am reminded of the story that Cortes, upon landing in Mexico, burned all his ships, lest his soldiers imagine they could scurry back home if the going got rough. In a similar sort of way, this was the lesson I took from our first-morning expedition throughout

London – *see how big the world really is? It is as huge as they said. That wasn't just a story. See how much more there is to experience, learn, encounter, than you ever, ever imagined? See how very different it all is? This is where you are now – and you can't go back, so how are you going to fit it into it?*

My preconceived picture of how wide the world was – well, it got stretched, mightily, and in this one fell swoop.

And the 'deeper' part?

The longer we walked the streets, the more it dawned upon me that history, that time, ran far, far deeper than I had thought possible. It began with imagining I was able, if I concentrated hard enough, to discern the footprints of men, women, children, Princes and paupers, who had walked these same London streets hundreds of years ago. It was an astounding epiphany. In the previous incarnation of my young life, I had never trod a street that had been trod upon a hundred years earlier. Many of the roads and lanes of my childhood had not even existed fifty years ago, much less a few hundred. It was the same with buildings and structures. An historical plaque in Miami might proudly note the location of the city's first hotel, in 1883, in Coconut Grove. Or the oldest home still in its original location, built in 1891 – the "Barnacle." Or the Dade County Courthouse, one of the architectural prides of the city, when completed in 1928. You could keep your eyes peeled in Miami for days and see nothing to suggest that history extended beyond your grandparents' lives. How, therefore, could I not have formed the impression that history was something that extended back a few decades at most – prior to which it was all just a great bowl of undifferentiated mush? That time was, in truth, shallow as a puddle, and hadn't really lasted all that long.

In London, though? Well, that was all different, immediately – or, it struck me immediately, at least. I couldn't turn my eyes left or right without bumping into how elongated a thing time could be. All around were reminders that here, history was counted in centuries, not decades. And even more astonishing to a juvenile mind conditioned by south Florida's unique culture of modernity, and eternal transience in all things – was the palpable sense all this history was still alive, active, woven into all the little corners of the lives of the place and its people. The past wasn't gone – to the contrary, its reverberations, strong and unmuted, seemed to be zinging through the very air I was breathing.

The city, therefore, grabbed my paltry, stunted sense of what history actually was, how deep time actually was, shook it hard, and lengthened it out. Instead of being shallow as a rain puddle, history was deep as the deepest trench in the deepest ocean. It was a pool, a vast reservoir, into which you could dive and swim and encounter things you had neither encountered before, nor even imagined – without ever actually reaching the bottom.

These ideas ... well, they flooded my mind and made everything look different.

By the time we finally dragged back into the Mount Royal's lobby, therefore, late in the afternoon, our cheeks flushed and rosy, our feet worn out, hungry, chilled, wound up and down at the same time, my former life in the warm cradle of extended family in Miami had been lovingly but irrevocably consigned to the past. All this stretching and widening and deepening had done its work. Any sorrowful pining for what had been left behind was gone. Taking its place was a hunger to experience more of this fantastical place, ingest its new customs, adopt new habits and learn new ways, hear new people say new things in new accents, burrow headlong into it all and come to know it. Our post-arrival jaunt through London did something permanent to me. Something in the city's sprawling amalgamation of old and new, dirty and grand, imperious and eccentric – all jumbled together with fog and soot and the odor of car exhaust and drizzle, the footprints of generations strangely visible upon the pavement, and all against the roll and thump and flex of more lives being conducted in one place than I had ever conceived – well, it wiped clean the slate of my imagination, as it were, leaving it bare and pristine as a blank tablet, and lit in my mind the beginning of a fascination with new places that never went away.

I suggested a moment ago that the unknowing author of this experience was my father – upon reconsideration, however, I believe it more accurate to say it was London itself that worked the change.

Months later, therefore, I felt not a dollop of anxiety over our impending move to Milford Haven, another unknown place. My father had shown us its location on a map, and phrases in travel magazines like "coastal beauty" and "windswept cliffs" had aroused curiosity and anticipation, foretelling the possibility of another jolt of exhilarated discovery like the one I had experienced that first day in London, and was keen to recreate.

And thus, I slept deeply and free of care in our compartment as the train swayed rhythmically on the track and bore us through the night west from London toward the coast of Wales; then stepped out from our carriage onto the platform at Milford Station early the next morning, a brilliant blue morning late in August, 1966.

# MARSHAL HOUSE

So soundly had I slept, utterly sedated by the roll and rumble of the overnight express, that the groggy aftermath of slumber drooped heavy as a soggy blanket over my perceptive faculties. I stood upon the platform, blinking dully in the bracing morning chill, as if still asleep. It was extremely quiet; in fact, everything seemed exceptionally, unnaturally silent, save for an occasional gust of steam from the winded locomotive, expelled with a throaty rasp like a weary parting sigh. Bright pinpoints of dew glistened on tufts of grass poking up between the rails, and the weathered crossties were damp and discolored. Shallow puddles shimmered on the platform. A red-rimmed sun peeked above the roof of the station and threw glancing rays against the toil-worn train. I heard a noise in the sky and suddenly a flock of grey-white birds raced in overhead to settle, with a great flutter and noise, into a thicket of trees opposite the platform, across the tracks, where I gazed at them drowsy and torpid.

Nothing seemed to be happening. All was still, as if time had taken a short respite from its labors. I struggled to gather my wits and order my thoughts. A sparkling, luminescent wetness danced in the air, the way it might look if thousands of tiny sparklers were twinkling behind a gossamer curtain. And then, welling up into this gauzy tableaux of pulsing, pinpointed sunlight, I detected the smell of the sea, strong and heavy with salt and fish and other mingled fragrances so sharp I half-expected to taste something tart and pungent on my tongue. I stood immobile on the platform, observing and sniffing and wondering why and how and what it was that seemed so – well, so altogether unusual – till then I heard, faintly at first, the sound of engines, boat engines, on the water, their growling plainsong rising to join the tincture of salt and fish and the diaphanous morning light and the pale yellow sun in the clear crystal-blue sky, and the whole of it coiling within me then, tightening, like a violin's string drawn taut to the breaking point, like a single high note held and held and pulling the listener to the edge of some precipice – till abruptly, without warning, it all broke, with something like a tearing sensation, and I blinked and exhaled and the feathery curtain parted, and it was simply another plain and ordinary day, and my father and I were simply lingering idly on the platform as people collected their bags and ambled along, and the unremarkable world plodded along its mundane way.

I glanced up at my father. Perhaps he too had been dazzled by the morning's brilliant incandescence, the squadrons of shrieking birds, the fecund mingling of ocean and salt and fish, and the wet steam-smell pouring from the train; we exchanged no words, but I saw his expressive eyes wide and alert, scanning left to right, up and down. We stood without speaking, therefore, watching and waiting while our fellow travelers gathered their belongings, greeted their friends or families, and departed the station.

Soon, we were alone on the platform. My father began to purse his lips and tap his foot. I wondered if something might have gone awry, perhaps a scheduling mishap with the person who was supposed to meet us, and hoped not. My father's foot tapped harder. I was growing a bit anxious myself; for the tapping of the foot was often followed by the bulging of a particular vein on his forehead, at which point things could turn stormy. Just then, however, just as the staccato of shoe upon platform began to accelerate disconcertingly, a figure in a gray hat emerged from the station house and peered about with a frown. I saw him first; then he spotted my father, waved and smiled, and strode briskly in our direction. The tapping of the shoe ceased as my father returned the wave.

The two men exchanged greetings and my father introduced me, but my mind was still lagging and I merely nodded perfunctorily. Our new acquaintance helped my father carry our bags across the parking lot to his car. I climbed into the back seat, where I closed my eyes as the engine fired and we began to back away. Suddenly, I heard anew the frantic beat of lush, abundant wings, turned to look out the rear window and, as we departed the station, watched the mass of white birds flee the thicket of trees across the tracks and hurtle out over the water in a noisy, flapping rush.

We were booked at the Marshal House, on Hamilton Terrace, facing the water. Named, I later learned, in honor of William Marshal, the first Earl of Pembroke. On the opposite shore, across the broad, flat surface of the channel I came to know as the Haven, like stately, enormous obelisks, rose the towers and tanks of what my father told me was the Texaco refinery. Immense numbers of birds careened over the waterway, calling and screeching, wheeling over the flats then back toward the sea. I stood staring across the broad silver expanse as my father unloaded the luggage and bade our driver goodbye, the sun reflecting brightly off the damp sidewalks. Then I followed him through a heavy red wooden door and into the cozy, compact lobby of the Marshal.

As we crossed the hotel's threshold, cobwebs were still cluttering my fuzzy head, and I felt a beat or two behind. The moment we passed through the door, however, my ears perked up to the clatter of dishes and cutlery and voices ricocheting back and forth, and my nose caught the aroma of food, wafting like a cloud. I became aware my feet had sunk into a thick carpet, which, as I cast my eyes downward, struck me as some indefinable combination of red and purple. I stood mute and disconnected, only partly present. And thus I might have remained – had not a grinning woman suddenly materialized before us, bobbing her head and chattering, swirling her hands about in circles as if working spells, the combined effect of which was to suggest to my disoriented mind that perhaps she had been secreting herself behind a curtain, awaiting our arrival, and had now leapt out to accost us in some odd manner.

Fortunately, no accosting was underway.

It quickly became evident this animated lady had something to do with the Marshal. She was speaking at an extreme rate of speed, however, and endeavoring to follow her words was like racing hopelessly after a bus pulling away from its stop. I kept at it though, attempting, with a concentrated frown, to follow the gush of words.

"…jolly, jolly well … morning, a fine fine morning … must be the Americans," she exclaimed. "… Zelinski, by the post, yes … welcome, a double, indeed a double … right, all set and ready … our best room, view of the water … my favorite!"

My father attempted to get a word in, with no luck, as the woman – by now obviously the landlady, Mrs. Zelinski – had taken complete charge of matters.

"Bags over there," pointing to a corner; "Hurry along, dear," to a young girl carrying an armload of bedclothes toward the stairs; "What a handsome lad, what's your age?" directed to me, while simultaneously gesticulating to someone in the dining area; "Just fill in the blanks, sir, if you don't mind," handing a paper of some kind to my father, before calling out a *Good Luck* to a portly gentleman passing out the doorway; then back again to my father, "Delighted, just delighted … don't get many Americans here, I must say … you'll enjoy the prospect over the water, you will … anything at all, don't hesitate to ask …"

As she pressed her energetic campaign of patter and motion, her husband – for thus was he identified by the bustling proprietress - emerged with ghostly silent footsteps from an adjacent sitting room. Following his wife's crisp, efficient introduction, the so-named Mr. Zelinski nodded his head ever so slightly toward my father and exchanged handshakes, then shook my hand as well. He spoke with an accent of some sort, seemed several years older than Mrs. Zelinski, and had a distant, unsettled look in a pair of unnaturally pale blue eyes, set wide apart. Thin strands of silver-grey hair lay combed flat against his head. Whereas his wife was a minor cyclone of commotion, Mr. Zelinski seemed a pool of quiet reserve. He lingered for a few moments making niceties, then politely excused himself and retired back to the sitting room from whence he had appeared; as he turned and exited the lobby, I noticed his gait revealed a slight limp, listing almost imperceptibly to the left.

All the while, Mrs. Zelinski sustained her birdlike clucking – much of it escaped me, but the gist seemed to be that nothing could possibly give her greater pleasure than our presence in her simple establishment, except perhaps if we might now proceed to the dining room and permit ourselves to partake of breakfast, which she described with vivid fanfare.

"Every morning 7 to 9," she said with emphasis, suggesting strict attention to the clock was important. "Eggs how you like them, ham, bacon, toast the way you like it – I don't know what Americans eat for breakfast, though, do I?" she reflected bemusedly, chortling gaily. "We'll fix you right up, though, whatever you like – porridge, oatmeal, our cook's a dream, she worked at a hotel in Bristol and wasn't it our good fortune when she married a local chap! You'll be wanting a bite now, won't you? "

Breakfast struck me as a wonderful proposition, as the close, warm hotel had made me ravenous. My father must have felt the same, for we dashed our luggage up to our room, then dashed back down to Mrs. Zelinski's morning repast; as to which my recollection sharpens, for bountiful platters of eggs, sausage, bacon, potatoes, and toast, and big mugs of steaming tea with thick, fresh cream, feature prominently, whenever I think back to that first morning in the Marshal House. A young server-girl with reddish hair, blue eyes, and a ruddy complexion also appears into the picture, quietly solicitous, and I will attest till the final minute of my final day that she even smiled at me several times when my father wasn't looking. Mrs. Zelinski gabbled and kept tabs on us – "Anything you want, speak up – don't be shy!" - Mr. Zelinski remained out of sight, and when finally we finished I felt immensely content, the cobwebs now transmuted into a general fatigue and listlessness.

After the plates were cleared, we meandered outside, to look at the water and smell the air. Mr. Zelinski was out there as well, smoking a cigarette and staring flatly across the Haven. He smiled politely and my father said our breakfast had been excellent.

"Yes, that is good," said Mr. Zelinski, nodding somewhat stiffly. "My wife will be very pleased to hear it." He lifted his head toward the water. "It is a lovely day."

Again, I noticed his accent, and also, in the bright sunlight, a thin scar running down the left side of his face, beginning beside his left eye and extending well down his cheek, almost to his jaw line. His gaze lay fixed across the Haven.

"We have a boy too," he said then, motioning with his cigarette in my direction, but keeping his eyes on the water. "He is at school now, but will be home at four. I will send him to your room if you wish. His name is Alan."

"Well, that would be very nice," replied my father. "Wouldn't you like that?" he inquired, looking toward me.

I nodded and agreed that would be fine, though in truth it suited me perfectly to spend the afternoon by myself exploring this new territory, where the air and light quivered and shimmered before my eyes, and the thick bouquet of salt and fish and sodden earth wafted in the wind.

My father and the strange man with the accent and the scar continued smoking their cigarettes and talking, but I listened no further. I stepped across the street to an embankment fronting the Haven and overlooking the docks, and leaned against its stone wall, still damp with dew. There, I watched the birds circle and dive, watched the boats ply slowly from their moorings out toward the mouth of the Haven, where it opened to the Atlantic, observed small puffs of smoke emerging from the stacks of the refineries in the distance, and the red jetties jutting out into the water, and a huge black and red tanker approaching slowly from the west. The breeze blew softly and a chill tarried in the air. I closed my eyes and listened again to the birds, and felt the wind slide across my face, then opened my eyes and the tanker had crept a bit closer to the jetties on the opposite shore, and the birds were still diving and climbing against the crystalline sky. Every now and then a car passed behind me, and I heard the dull hiss of tires on the slick road as it moved by. Presently, my father called, and I crossed the street again to his side.

"Well, what do you think?" he asked.

I shrugged my shoulders.

"Different from home, isn't it?"

"Yes," I said.

"I think we'll like it here."

I smiled and nodded.

The silver-haired Mr. Zelinski was gone. We reentered the Marshal and ascended the stairs to our room, where my father changed his shirt and left for work. Myself, I fell fast asleep in my bed by the window, which I had opened halfway, the breeze billowing the white lace curtain and the birds cawing as I drifted away.

# A DANDY START

In many ways, it is the curse of the average golfer to hit a good drive. In spite of himself, in spite of everything he has come to understand about the harsh and fickle core at the heart of the game, a single decent shot seduces the middling golfer into suspending reality entirely, imagining himself an accomplished shot-maker, and thus setting the stage for the next round of failure and disappointment.

Having already parred the first hole in my mind, therefore, and actually having flirted with the prospect of a birdie, I naturally followed my strong opening drive by topping my second shot – a 5-wood – and sending it whistling down the fairway, skipping a foot or two off the ground, for perhaps eighty yards. I stared with disenchantment after the ball, and felt that familiar vague foolishness at having yet again allowed a single commendable shot to skew my vision and distort my mind. Reason was such a quick and easy victim of this game, and delusion its recurring theme.

"Well," Hugh remarked in an efficient, business-like tone as he strode by, having struck a crisp four-iron approach short of the green, and not even glancing my way. "I remember that one."

What could I say? Doubtless he did. For Hugh Evans had witnessed the full, complete repertoire of my game in bygone times, each and every shot and calamity in its arsenal, every one of them.

We had been classmates at Milford Haven Grammar School, as well as neighbors, for he lived five houses down from us on Wellington Road. His father played golf, as did mine, and after receiving my McGregors and entering my apprenticeship with Mr. Flynn, Hugh and I quickly became friends and golfing companions. Hugh had taken the game up earlier than I, however, and seemed markedly better-constructed for its requirements; he was tall and slender, in a loose, athletic sort of way, and had a laconic, unbothered manner on the course even as a boy. This was in stark contrast to the militant style of play I embraced as an acolyte in Mr. Player's sect, my attitude of personal combat with the course and, more particularly, with the ball itself. Many was the time, in fact, that I detected Hugh eyeing me with a cautious, quizzical frown, as if curious about my theory of the game; wishing to venture a question, perhaps, but wary of doing so, unsure as to exactly what such a query might possibly unleash. My only response to his infuriating habit of sending one unremarkable shot after the other down the fairways and onto the greens was to grit my teeth, swing as hard as the architecture of my frame would permit, savor the occasional reward of a prodigiously long and graceful shot, and grimly accept the ugly things that happened in between. I have an image of self-flagellation with a golf club, and came to interpret the horrendous shots as unpleasant but necessary stops on a great cycle, which, in due course, would produce good shots, and even very good ones, at their special, appointed times.

It must have seemed to Hugh, however, that I was engaged in a different pursuit altogether; some arcane diversion combining a sort of hurling motion of the body, and contortions of the face, with forays into the brambles and trees, coupled with the wanton, pointless sacrifice of countless innocent golf balls. A bizarre kind of genocide. In fact, he might even have concluded that I had misconstrued the basic rules of the game to such an extreme as to have convinced myself that "winning" consisted of losing more balls than my competitor lost. If such, indeed, had been Hugh's impression – well, there may have been a grain of truth to it, or even more. To me, however, his game seemed pedestrian and boring.

They say that opposites attract. In this vein, therefore, despite our wildly different golfing personalities, Hugh and I quickly became the best of pals, and consumed hour upon hour crisscrossing the small nine-hole course that lay serenely atop the hills above the Haven. On weekends, we caddied in the morning, sometimes carrying two bags, then played in the afternoon. We caddied in stinging, blowing rain, biting cold, and fresh, warm sunshine. We spoke not a word unless asked a question, collected our pay and pocketed our tips, ate lunch, then played golf until dark. We were young and devoted, each in our separate ways. And never, in later years, did I regret a moment of the time, for without question it had been a splendid manner in which to spend many a happy youthful hour.

Those lazy, light-hearted days lay deep in the past, however. We were grown men now, well along into life. It could be stated with absolute and ringing certainty that today was not yesterday, and that much had changed. It was also indisputable, however, that, on this excellent Saturday in May, we two old friends had somehow found ourselves together again on this oft-trod terrain; a delightful turn of serendipity, which easily trumped any niggling malaise over the passage of time.

Side by side, therefore, we headed up the fairway, our carts clattering over the gently undulating turf. Content to stroll, we dallied along, idling without care. The reunion dinner was set for the evening, but it was only just past noon and the entire afternoon – the whole blue, balmy, Saturday afternoon – stretched before us, with no reason in the world to hurry. The ageless hedgerow loomed menacingly along the right; the pasture still rose and stretched beyond, barren and empty as ever. The clouds still billowed and blew overhead, the wind still raced and rose and fell. Hugh was still tall and lanky. And his eyes were still clear and sharp and mischievous, I noted with satisfaction, as we followed our shots down the first fairway and toward the green.

"We played a bit of golf here, didn't we?" Hugh commented wistfully.

"That we did," I replied.

The breeze lifted Hugh's hair – a bit grayed and thinner, it must be said - off his brow, and he turned toward me smiling softly. "Well, I'm glad you came back," he said. "No one here plays entertaining golf."

I smiled. "Certainly not you," I observed.

I delivered a deft 6-iron to the front of the green and did, in fact, manage to par the first hole. Hugh inexplicably took three putts – I could barely remember him three-putting even as a boy – and carded a bogey. We were playing match play, over nine holes, as had been our habit; I was one-up, and off to a dandy start.

# UP AND OVER

As we approached the second tee, Hugh swiveled toward me with the most transparently wooden simper ever affixed to a human countenance. It was his intention, I believe, to simulate benign goodwill and collegiality. If such was his aim, however, it failed miserably – for I immediately perceived the malignant expectancy lurking behind his grotesque facsimile of a smile. The second hole and I had a long and tortured history.

It was an uphill par-3, over a wooded ravine. The tiny green nestled snug back against a weathered stone wall laced with lichen and weeds, and beyond this wall rose the Esso tank farm. One of the farm's enormous gray storage tanks loomed imposingly over the wall, and threw a broad shadow across the green. Too strong a shot would send your ball into the thick heather tight against the weedy wall, from where a five was likely, and a six not out of the question. It was preferable by far to be short. But not too short. For between the tee box and the green yawned a bottom choked with trees, vines, mud, shrubs, and nettles. A narrow path led down from the tee through this small wilderness, then wound steeply upward to the green, a vertical climb of at least thirty feet. I attributed Hugh's deceitful grin to the fact that in years past I had personally interred great numbers of golf balls into this unforgiving quagmire, and this hole had been my private, personal incubus. Every new foul curse I learned as a youth had been discharged upon the second hole. No doubt, Hugh expected that my vocabulary of abuse would have increased with time. He was, therefore, looking forward with great anticipation – not well hidden by his makeshift grin – to my performance.

All of this, I deduced the very moment I observed the expression on his face, that horrible smirk.

Unfazed, however, I confidently conjured up a winning smile of my own.

"Ah, I remember this hole," I announced.

"Do you?" Hugh replied distantly. "There's not much to it, really."

I had the honors and stepped swiftly – nervously? - upon the tee. In truth, I had not really expected to win the first hole, after topping my 5-wood, and was therefore just the slightest bit unready. It was essential, however, to disguise my lack of preparedness and get down to business. I stood atop the tee in the pose of a conqueror, therefore, and judged the direction and speed of the wind. The elevated green appeared farther away than it actually was, which had always made it seem necessary to hit the ball very hard; the vagaries of the wind complicated things further, and would easily lead the novice into making flawed decisions.

Once long ago I had stood upon this very same tee, jaded from observing my 5 and 6-irons rise against the currents, hang briefly in the sky as if suspended by invisible strings, then plummet down into the dense, woody thicket, and had impulsively yanked my driver out of my bag. Hugh's eyebrows had shot up in alarm. "What are you doing?" he asked sharply. "Getting the ball to the green," I had replied calmly. "Well, I expect you'll do that," he muttered trenchantly, as I turned a hard stare upon the ball – the type of stare, I had imagined briefly, in a narrow corner of my immature mind, that Mr. Player himself might fix upon a contemptible white pellet in need of discipline. Then I had hardened my stare even further, tightened my jaw, and unleashed an angry, brutal swing. And my ball did, indeed, clear the woods – that much could not be denied, for it soared high over the leafy thicket, cleared the green while on the rise, and was still gaining altitude above the nasty rock wall behind the green, before clanging thunderously into the huge gray Esso tank that sat solemnly overlooking the hole. The vile little orb then ricocheted off in some unknown direction, landing in some unknown place. I had lost track of its flight in the drooping sun, but hoped the detestable and unworthy ball would die a painful death, perhaps gnawed to bits by a famished goat.

Following this rash and shocking exhibition in the early years of my association with Milford's second hole, neither Hugh nor I had uttered a word. As the metallic reverberation from the ball's violent impact against the Esso tank died away, I had stepped quietly aside and watched meekly as Hugh lofted a smooth mid-iron slightly to the right of the green, near pin-high. Then up the path we had trudged, Hugh forging a few paces ahead. I trailed silently behind, wool-headed, and considering that smashing a driver on a par-3 was probably not, actually, what Mr. Player would have counseled.

Poised on this identical second tee again now, thirty-five years later, and gazing up over the same brush-choked gulley to the same small green – *has it shrunk … I don't remember it this small!* - I disliked the fact that this bleak memory had percolated to the surface of my mind. Why was that insignificant bout of recklessness from the past still lurking in my brain at all? What tiny handhold, what minute crevice in the ledge over which a myriad other memories had tipped and fallen, had this particular incident been doggedly gripping for all this time? And for what possible reason? It was baffling. And should not be dwelt upon. For history would not repeat itself today. Of that, I promised myself. Oh no - I was a wise and mature player now, seasoned by time and experience.

I bent over and teed my ball, but caught just a glance of Hugh's face as I straightened up; which was quite unfortunate, as I had not intended to acknowledge his presence at all. He wore a blank expression, however, and revealed no trace of the huge excitement I knew was burbling inside; his expectation, perhaps even his certainty, that fate would laughingly compel me yet one more time to lash some grotesque shot deep into the dark and tangled abyss.

These were the thoughts I knew Hugh was harboring, savoring even, like a tasty bun, at that very moment. These were also the kinds of thoughts I needed urgently to banish, lest … well, lest history, indeed, repeat itself. Which most assuredly would not occur, not in any way, shape, or form. History was dead, I lectured myself sternly; dead, gone, and forgotten.

Before realizing what I was doing, however, I stepped away from the ball and found myself squinting narrow-eyed at Hugh. "I know what you're thinking," I said curtly.

"What's that?" he asked distractedly, his countenance a mask of innocent disinterest. "I was just wondering if you were ever going to hit the ball."

I addressed my ball again, horrified to have taken notice of his existence, much less exchanged words.

"You don't want the wind to turn," he noted nonchalantly.

I set my feet and concentrated on relaxing my arms and shoulders. "There isn't any wind," I said.

"Oh," he replied, again in that same faraway tone. "Sorry."

I flung one final look at my target, the green draped invitingly yet precariously on the knoll above the woods, the flag motionless – and suddenly wondered if a 7-iron was enough club. At the moment, I felt not even a whisper of a breeze; but the wind could swirl up from nowhere, gusts could shoot in from the sea without the slightest warning. I had seen it many times. If such were to happen now, a 7 would be far too little, and a 4 or 5 would be better. I detected not the faintest stir, however, not the slightest draft or zephyr, and a 4-iron struck well on a windless day would surely rocket back against the merciless stone wall, and leave an impossible second shot. Moreover, it was unthinkable to switch clubs now, with Hugh loitering indolently and watching, his irritating veil of placidity hiding what I knew to be his hungry presentiment of my doom. I had the right club. The 7 was perfect, I assured myself grimly. But it was only perfect if I actually swung the bloody thing – and now it was time to swing.

I commenced the takeaway, slow and smooth, arms loose, my breathing even and unhurried. All was off to a good start. Arriving at the top of my backswing, everything remained in good order. For the briefest of moments, a mere sliver of a second, I looked ahead to the soft contact at impact, the ball elevating effortlessly into the air, riding blithely over the woods, then drawing slightly before landing with a neat plop near the pin. It was a beautiful vision, in which playfully chirping songbirds and rays of warm sunshine also seemed to play a part, and I smiled inwardly, much as I knew Mr. Flynn would be smiling, somewhere, when my ball dropped sweetly beside the fluttering flag. Surely, I stood upon the cusp of a shot of sublime beauty, certain to capture my old friend Hugh's admiration! Surely that, and more, a birdie putt – a string of birdies – and why not an eagle too on one of the par-5's waiting ahead, just for the fun of it? A happy chorus of songbirds sounded melody in my ears! What cheer! What joy!

But no, alas no – it was not to be.

The songbirds ceased their singing and began, instead, to scream like winged and flesh-devouring banshees; the trilling birds and the drowsy sunshine evaporated in a blink, and I – well, it had come time for me to move to the next position on my endless circle of golfing fate. For, as I commenced my downswing, without the faintest glimmer of warning, my charming dream dissolved, and I was seized, deep amid the bowels, by the glorious desire – no, the absolute necessity, the absolute rampant compulsion, overtly carnivorous in nature - to blast the puny, impudent white golf ball cowering at my feet far, far beyond the wooded depression, high over the grey Esso tanks, high across the glistening Haven, out into and across the Atlantic Ocean and toward the rocky shores of Greenland – to which mad and frothy purpose I accelerated with all the violence my frame could muster, barely nicked the top of the ball, and watched in horror as it skipped merrily down the grassy slope into the tree-filled gulley, there to disappear.

My eyelids fluttered briefly in the radiant sun.

Had I just scuffed my ball down the hill, into the briars and muck?

Really?

I furrowed my brow, hopeful I had just imagined the entire ghastly thing; hopeful I was still paused at the top of my backswing, and had not, in fact, slipped unknowingly through a slit in time where my old neuroses ran loose like dogs off their leads. But no, no, it was true, too true. I had somehow lost complete control of myself before even realizing it. And by the time my senses had returned, the deed had been done. My ball lay buried in the wooded bog, nowhere near the green, the Esso tanks, or indeed the coast of Greenland. Buried and lost yet again, in the damnable quagmire; another sacrificial victim, sustenance for another starving goat. Hugh stood observing it all, his gray eyes flat and unblinking. The fates had won. To which I could only remark, in my mind, "Well, of course."

Nothing to do but carry on.

"Your shot," I murmured casually to Hugh as I backed slowly off the tee, moving just a bit like an old man might move, stiff in the joints and a little foggy in the head. I thought my voice might have quivered a tad, most undesirably. I discreetly cleared my throat. The raucous jeering of the crows seemed to be fading away in the distance, and the luminous sun – which had seen it all - had crept, perhaps with disappointment, behind the clouds.

"My pleasure," he responded politely.

Efficiently, and without further ado, Hugh drew a 5-iron from his bag and dropped his shot just short of the front of the green. Once again, I scaled the tee. There was still no wind. This time I took my aim, gave a single waggle, and struck a 6-iron long and to the left. We trudged soundlessly down the path into the clough, where I had put to rest an entire generation of golf balls, and had just now interred a new one, out of the daylight and into the deep and suddenly cool shade, then up toward the green and the great looming Esso tank, sere and commanding beyond the old stone wall.

I had a recurring dream. Three or four times a year, I dreamt that I was returning to Milford Haven. Sometimes I returned on the train, and craned my head out the window as we approached the little platform, smiling, silly with anticipation, the station hazy in the distance but sharpening into focus as we neared - then suddenly my friends waving and calling, surrounding me as the train huffed to a halt and I stepped off into the happy swarm. On other occasions I simply found myself in Milford, in some restaurant or shop, at school, on the golf course, strolling along the street with my chums, riding the bus, hiking a rocky coastal trail amid wildflowers, butterflies, cliffs, and clover. Always, I was serene and contented.

Waking after one of these idylls, I would dally in bed, close my eyes, and bask briefly in the reverie that I remained, indeed, in Milford; that I had cheated time, and resided yet among my special circle of boon mates in the carefree flush of youth, and would never have to leave. If the dream had been particularly deep and strong, I would spend the morning in a downcast funk, puttering through paperwork, busy-work, vaguely sad, full of longing. As the years passed and I resigned myself to never returning, the intensity of the pining lessened, but never entirely vanished. And the dreams never went away.

Finding myself in a bookstore, I was prone to wandering into the *Travel* section, there to leaf through travel guides, searching for any mention of Milford. Once, with great melancholy, I read a passage in a Fromers or Fodors, to the effect that *"This once-bustling fishing port, which boasts the deepest natural waterway in Europe, has declined precipitously since the oil refineries closed in the early 80's. The town now presents a rather drab appearance, and no industries have arisen to take the place of the departed oil industry. An effort is underway to transform the marina into a tourism center, and the town's proximity to the stunning Pembrokeshire Coast should make it a convenient base from which to explore this uncrowded and unspoiled region."*

Such gloomy words conjured up unwanted visions of my old confederates dragging about the streets in shabby, dirty overcoats, sallow, poorly fed, and drained of color. I felt as if someone had lifted the cover off an object which I remembered as being beautiful and sparkling, revealing it now, scrutinized with the cold realism of adulthood instead of the soft and impressionable faculties of adolescence, as dreary and ordinary; as if I'd suddenly learned that something I valued greatly actually had no value at all, and that I was foolish for having so misjudged its true worth. But this feeling never lasted. A paragraph in a guidebook was but a wee pellet against the fortress of my youthful memories, and Milford Haven remained, in my memory, a golden place, where I had spent a golden time.

Hugh won the second hole, of course. I gave but a cursory glance toward the waterlogged debris at the bottom of the shadowy ravine as we passed through on our way up to the green, and a curt "No" when Hugh inquired if I wished to stop and search for my ball. It was enough that I had again dismembered myself on this miserable hole; why chance unearthing some dirty, scarred, mummified artifact left over from some other horrible shot three decades earlier? I declined, therefore, to look for my ball – in fact, steadfastly refused even to think about it – and marched stoically up to the green.

Once there, I sighed quietly and muttered a fresh foul oath as Hugh chipped to within three feet of the pin, sank the putt, and squared the match.

"That's hard luck," he remarked sympathetically, as he strode to retrieve his ball from the cup. "Do you want to stretch a bit before the next hole?"

# BASE CAMP

We shared a room in the Marshal House, my father and I, during our first month in Milford. The family remained behind in London, packing up the home we had leased as our initial encampment in the U.K. My father thought it important to enroll me in my new school as early in the term as possible, however, so brought me along to his new posting, to the boulder-strewn Pembroke coast. On Sundays, we called from a telephone in a small kiosk adjacent to the front desk. My father would ask my mother how the packing-up was coming and tell my brothers and sister he couldn't wait to see them. Then I would make my hellos as well.

We set up quarters on the second floor, in a cozy room decorated with faintly dingy, flowered wallpaper, and a big window that faced the Haven. Our furnishings consisted of two beds, a chest of drawers, a dusty wardrobe, a small desk that wobbled slightly, and two old wooden chairs. The desk sat beside the window and afforded an unencumbered view across the broad, blue vista of water, toward the west, where the sun faded into the sea and fans of color unfurled in the evenings. I believe there was also a chamber pot, which we did not use.

In no time at all, we established a simple routine. My father woke first in the morning, and showered while I dozed. Upon finishing, he cracked the window open and, in my semi-slumber, I would first sense, then smell, then feel, the heavy stream of fresh, bracing air pouring in from off the Haven. I would become aware of my father moving lightly about the room, the cries of the birds drifting softly on the cool currents, and, floating placidly between sleep and consciousness, pull the blanket tight around my neck – till shortly he shook me awake, and I rose reluctantly from my warm sheets to dress; after which we trotted downstairs for another one of Mrs. Zelinski's staunch and stalwart breakfasts, before launching off into the day.

As the month progressed, we watched the lodgers come and go, struck up acquaintances with those who stayed a few days or more, began to adopt a vaguely proprietary attitude, and generally settled in. We rarely saw the secretive Mr. Zelinski in the mornings. His wife was in constant sight and motion, however, sweeping in and out of the kitchen, checking old guests out, checking new ones in, superintending the help, refilling empty tea or coffee cups, wiping up, refolding newspapers, answering the telephone, and making jovial chatter all around. It seemed to be a matter of special importance that her lodgers should enjoy their meals. Every morning, therefore, she interrogated each guest as to their satisfaction with the fare.

"Are the eggs to your liking today, Mr. Barnes?"

"The bacon crisp enough for you, is it, Mr. Anthony? I know that's how you like it."

"More tea, Miss Fox? Care for some more cream?"

"The strawberry jam is quite nice, isn't it, Mr. Crowson? We had a new lot in from London on Monday!"

The questions were unnecessary, however, as the answers were always the same, the lodgers thumping their midriffs and pronouncing themselves well pleased indeed. And how could it be otherwise, I would wonder, stuffing another forkful of bangers into my mouth? Nonetheless, as if performing a ritual, Mrs. Zelinski propounded her entreaties every morning; the slightest frown shadowing her brow, a wary look creeping into her eyes, as if each new guest might be that fated one who would finally deliver a damning verdict in the negative, presaged perhaps by a moment's hesitation, signaling disapproval of the eggs – were they too runny? Or the bacon – too soft? Or the service – inexcusably tardy? Never, however, did I hear uttered anything remotely resembling a grievance. All was well, always, when it came to Mrs. Zelinski's morning victuals.

After breakfast, my father headed off to work at the refinery site, in Waterston, a small, nondescript village of stone buildings situated upon a bluff two miles east of Milford's boundary-proper. The first weekend following our arrival, he had driven me out for a look. We made the short trip in a four-speed grey Austin sedan he had acquired from somewhere, and I remember noticing that manhandling the gears of the manual transmission seemed to be providing him unusual enjoyment – we had never before owned a stick shift, nor had I ever ridden in one, or even seen one operated. I had no idea how it worked, and so observed carefully, hoping to memorize the arcane manipulations, sensing that skill with such an apparatus might be a thing worth showing off some day. Thus, we banged along the narrow road winding up from the Haven, the gears churning under my father's enthusiastic touch, his eyes bright and shining, to the site.

In truth, however, there was at this early point little of consequence to observe, for construction was barely underway. From one standpoint, the site was nothing more than a huge dirt clearing stretched out above the water, surrounded by a random assortment of colorless, age-worn structures, which appeared to be small, abandoned residences, and a ragged collection of sickly trees. Indeed, such was my initial impression; unimpressed, underwhelmed.

The more we toured about, however, a different perspective began to form. A realization crept over me – an awareness of something seething behind the flat and uninteresting scene, of huge reserves of machinery and manpower poised to leap into action, and I perceived in my father his excitement at the transformation soon to commence, as if the refinery's massive edifices were already ascending from the ground before his gaze. His eyes grew wide as he described what was to be built where, guided me over the muddy site toward the cliff overlooking the Haven, there to explain how the giant tankers would eventually dock and unload their enormous cargoes of crude oil, refill with cargoes of refined oil, and set off again on their endless journeys.

"See there," he pointed across a bluff. "That's where they'll offload. Then," tracing an imaginary line with his finger, "the pipes will run all the way up there, that's where the refinery's going to be. Then back out," tracing another line back toward the bluff, where the refined oil would be loaded into new tankers, bound for new destinations.

We sat in the car and a dreamy look entered his eye. "Think about it," he said. "First they have to find it. Then they have to get it out of the ground. Then they have to get it refined so people can use it. So they ship it here. Then we make it useable, then it goes out again, all over the world, constantly in motion. Keeping everything else in motion." He turned to me. "It's an amazing thing, isn't it, when you think about it!"

And I nodded and said *Yes*, it was – for it truly was a stirring proposition, with a certain technician's romance, this notion of being at the center of a machinery, a spider-web, that spun literally across the globe. It fired my father's imagination, and my own as well.

So, dirt was being turned, small mountains of steel and wood and iron and piping lay piled on the ground keen to be erected, straining almost palpably to be stood up, measured, fit together, and then rise into the sky. Men were moving and doing, and it seemed to me the more my father spoke that something fantastic was, indeed, going to take place, and that I, through him, was going to be part of it - and the light flashing in my father's face, the vibration in his voice, drew me into that prospect too. Already, emerging sleepily from our train that first morning of our arrival, I had felt something electrical, magnetic, chemical, sweeping through my every nerve and every sense. Now it seemed as if my father was charged too, and me in his wake, breathing in his ardor. His pleasure became my own, and I must have intuited that if something in this place could bring my father such happiness, then surely I would find felicity here as well.

From the very beginning, therefore – from that dreamlike emergence out of our berth on the Great Western express, from my first glimpse of the Haven's waters calm and quiet as a sheet of silver glass, the cathedral-like spires of the refineries framing the hills on the southern shore, from my first hearing of the gulls' wild cacophony – I opened myself completely to our new home, because that was what I saw and sensed my father doing too. And during this first month, lodging at the Marshal House as if it were a sort of base camp, I felt as if we were explorers together, on a private mission, and that every day brought new discoveries to us both.

After school, I walked. The refinery site connected to the main railway line by a fresh-laid spur, and this spur ran alongside the Haven down below the embankment; which itself ran along Hamilton Terrace, in front of the Marshal House. In the afternoons during that first month as boarders, while my father was still at work, I would walk this spur as it curved along the north side of the Haven, above what I came later to know as Scotch Bay. The tankers would float slowly in the tranquil shelter of the waterway, surrounded by coveys of tugboats painted red and blue, and smaller craft would dart about, skirting the larger boats, ferrying people on various tasks from ship to shore, and from shore to shore across the Haven. Then, as dusk approached, the trawlers crept in from the sea, eased tiredly into the docks, and discharged crews of rugged-looking men, to unload the day's catch and scrub down their boats. Always, vast numbers of birds arced overhead, crying plaintively and carving great, graceful figures in the sky. Always there was the thick salt-smell of the water, the seaweed, the mud, the fish, and always the wind turning and shifting, rising and falling. I rarely encountered anyone on the tracks, and enjoyed the solitude, a little cocoon of discovery, within which I was able to absorb and reflect without interruption upon the fresh and unfamiliar sights and sounds.

I viewed these excursions as a kind of reconnoitering. Taking stock of this new place. And, as befitted a reliable scout, I paid close attention and made mental notes of everything I saw, cataloging new findings in order to recount them to my father over dinner.

I threw rocks into the water, or sat on grassy mounds observing with quiet pleasure the changing colors on the water's surface as the sun descended in the west, beyond the cliffs at St. Anne's Head, where the purple twilight seemed to rush in like a fast tide. When an engine happened to shunt along the spur, I hopped off the tracks and scrambled up the hillside, and the crewmen and I stared at each other as they passed, their visages unreadable. Always, without fail, I found something new and interesting on each of my daily jaunts.

Occasionally, my forays took me almost all the way to the Gulf site, where around a long bend in the tracks I could make out foundations being laid, and the vast tangle of pipes spilling over the top of the escarpment, to tie eventually into the offloading facilities. By then, however, the shadows would be creeping up the hills and the day's warmth fading, and I would turn and head back to the Marshal. Passing the docks on my return, the fishing crews had finished their work and were drifting off home, or lounging and talking, smoking cigarettes and flicking the butts into the water. The watercraft were tying up for the night, the few tugboats still on the water had turned on their lights, and the tankers were lit up like floating cities. Flocks of white birds tip-toed daintily along the mudflats and rock-pools, joined occasionally by orange-billed oystercatchers, pecking at whatever special debris the day's tide had left behind. The spur ran slightly downhill as it exited town, so my return to the Marshal required an uphill climb, which left me breathing heavily, and just as the sharp air began to chaff the back of my throat, the hotel's lights would come into view and I would clamber up from the rail line, jump the wall of the embankment along Hamilton Terrace, and another afternoon's rambling would be done. Then my father and I would eat dinner together in the warm, cheerful dining room, and he would quiz me about what I had seen and done that day, where I had gone, who I had met; then regale me, in something of a conspiratorial manner, with what had transpired at the refinery site – sharing our discoveries together as it grew dark outside – and then it was up the stairs to our snug and spartan quarters, and off to sleep.

And how could I not have arrived in Milford a vessel waiting to be filled with adventures? From earliest childhood, my father had filled us with tales of travel and discovery. He himself had been raised on an apple farm in northern Virginia, during the Depression, but was seized hard and early by a thirst to see the world; an impulse of unknown origin, with no particular precedent among his stolid predecessors, but an impulse that proved strong and demanding. By the time he was twenty-two, he had indeed departed the apple farm, departed Virginia, departed the United States even, and was serving as Engineering Officer aboard the USS Greenwich Bay, sailing the ports of the Mediterranean and the Indian Ocean. Altogether, my father spent three years in the Navy – and I always had the feeling they may have been his happiest.

As a consequence of his nautical ramblings, settled much later into the staid routines of middle-class civilian life, our family dinners often revolved around recitations from his rich and perhaps-embellished collection of exotic memories. Vivid descriptions of the officers dining in a tent somewhere on the Arabian Peninsula, invited guests of some dignitary, seated around a lavish meal featuring healthy helpings of memorable local delicacies, such as goat's eyes, wet and dripping in some delicate, slippery juice. Or the crew foregoing sleep three days straight, evacuating desperate survivors from tiny villages on the eastern coast of Greece that had been flattened by an earthquake, ferrying old men and woman and children to temporary shelters along the mainland to the south. Or the unspeakably filthy ports of India, the awful poverty and wretchedness he had witnessed there; yet, too, the sublime beauty, the timbre of his voice shimmering, as he painted for us a picture of the Taj Mahal's floating domes, or endeavored to describe the sight of thousands of pilgrims and devotees lowering themselves into the Ganges, rippling and stinking in the red morning sun. And then, the subject of India never failed to summon forth rousing lines from Kipling, their martial beat evident even to my young ears, my father declaiming verse after memorized verse as the light sifted away outside our window. In this way, we ate wide-eyed at our little table, listening to stories, my imagination roaming free and unfettered, following my father in his explorations across the world.

Many was the time, in the evening after dinner, that he would rummage in the hallway closet and pull out an old blue bag, decorated with a faded tartan pattern, turn it upside down, and pour out a stack of coins and bills which he had collected and brought home from these faraway places. We gathered around the table as the foreign objects came spilling forth, a whiff of must and dust exuding from the upturned bag. We examined the strange writings, the peculiar faces and inscriptions, and I would muse with a kind of childish wonder that the coin I was rubbing between my fingers had, at some time in the past, rested in the pocket of some unknown person in Calcutta or Cairo. I would imagine the coin passing from hand to hand, through infinite numbers of exchanges, between infinitely mysterious people, from the foothills of the Himalayas to the sands of Egypt – all a mere prelude to its final exchange with a young American naval officer, who would then carry the coin across the sea to its final resting place in a faded tartan pouch on the upper shelf of a crowded hallway closet; a sad and undignified sort of end, I would reflect with a wistful pang, for a thing that had enjoyed a life of such freedom and abandon.

Then, there were other occasions, when my father would fish out a collection of slides from his Navy years, hang a sheet on the wall, and narrate a two-hour guided tour through the Mediterranean Sea, starting at Gibraltar, stopping at Naples, passing Malta, through the Suez Canal, down the Red Sea, around Arabia, across the Indian Ocean, to a colorful termination in Bombay. There were slides and slides and slides displaying nothing but blue-gray vistas of water, and an endless parade of docks and ships that all looked the same. The crickets chirped outside in the hot, humid Florida night, the images flashed brightly onto the sheet in the darkness, and my father, immersed in his memories, described every detail of the ships, the routes, the sights, the sounds, his friends among the other officers, the antics of the enlisted men, the escapades and travails. And the images I had seen flashing across the sheet on our living room wall would play endlessly through my imagination later as I lay in bed and drifted off to sleep and to dream.

So how, indeed, could I myself not have arrived on the rocky coast of southwest Wales as a willing vessel, eager and ready to be filled with adventures of my own?

There were times, that first month in Milford, when I brought Alan, the Zelinski's son, along on my excursions above Scotch Bay. He was a solemn sort of boy, an only child, and spoke little; which suited well my own contemplative nature, as I had no desire to spend my walks nattering, when I should be watching and weighing. And thus, Alan and I would stroll along the tracks and toss stones and scrutinize the activity on the docks below, while the shadows crept across the Haven and the soft breeze washed over the town and the water and the hills, the lowering sun casting a pale orange light upon the undersides of the clouds that scurried overhead. Occasionally we discussed some event at school, or he would ask about life in America, but mainly we walked in silence.

"How did your father get that scar?" I asked him once, however, on one of our larks. Every time I saw Mr. Zelinski, I wondered about the scar, and it nagged at my curiosity.

"I don't know," Alan had shrugged disinterestedly. "Something in the war, I think. I know he was in the war."

"What did he do?"

Alan shrugged again. "Don't know, I never asked."

One evening, returning to the Marshal just as night fell and the sky was turning a dark, deep blue, Alan went to the kitchen to speak with his mother and I continued on my way toward the stairs, when I caught sight of Mr. Zelinski sitting in a wooden chair in the parlor, staring out a window. He was alone, and something drew me to enter the room and approach his seated figure. He was dressed in a black suit and white shirt, with a thin sky-blue tie, and had his head turned gazing through and beyond the window. His thin gray hair was combed impeccably back, and seemed to shimmer. The pool of light from a lamp on a nearby table illuminated the left side of his face, and again I saw clearly the thin white scar running the length of his cheek. He turned slowly as I approached and his pale blue eyes were eerily flat, his face bereft of expression. Neither of us spoke for a moment, till I said, "Hello, Mr. Zelinski."

He sat silently for another moment, then replied, somewhat formally, "Good evening. May I help you?"

I had no idea why I had entered the dim room, much less ventured near his chair, and replied awkwardly, "No sir." I paused and stood before him, unsure whether to leave or to speak. "I just wondered what you were looking at," I continued hesitantly.

He lifted his lips almost imperceptibly and turned his face again towards the window. The evening now was black as pitch; lights sparkled from the jetties across the Haven, but all else lay in blackness. Peering intently out the darkened glass, in which his reflection from the lone lamp quivered, Mr. Zelinski seemed to have forgotten my presence.

I prepared to back away and continue on to our room. Just then, however, he said, "Nothing. I'm not looking at anything, just remembering when I was a boy, like you." He paused. "My brother and I used to help my father plant in the springtime. I was thinking about the planting in the springtime. It was always warm in the springtime, after the cold winter, and it was good to get started with the planting."

Again, he was silent.

"I met some Americans in the war," he said then, absently, followed again by silence.

I fidgeted uncomfortably.

"Was your father in the war?" he resumed, looking not at me, but beyond the window.

"No sir."

"I didn't believe so," he nodded. "Just a little too young perhaps. A young man, safe in America."

I lingered a moment longer, thinking he might say more, or that I should offer some comment myself. I wanted to ask how and where he had gotten the scar on his face, which seemed almost pulsing and alive in the illumination from the little lamp. And if it was connected to his limp. I wanted to ask what he had done in the war, and how he came to Milford. But he said nothing further. His eyes remained fixed on the lights twinkling in the darkness outside the window, and he again seemed unaware of my presence, so I slowly turned and left and tiptoed up to our room.

# THE JUNIOR XV

As a result of my deeply deflating performance on the second hole, Hugh had the honors on the third tee. Perhaps it was my fundamental unpredictability with the driver, but this particular tee shot had always bedeviled me. The tee box itself was elevated well above the fairway, and required a drive back across the same swathe of trees and gorse that lay between the tee and the green on the second hole – that brush and tangle into which I had just buried yet another traitorous ball.

Considerable menace loomed in view. The drive had to enter the fairway at a 45-degree angle, so that a fade was called for; but a thin stream ran across the fairway some 230 yards out, and a gentle fade that turned into a slice could easily drift into the water. The bold player might go for smashing his ball completely over the stream, in which case the green lay a mere 80 yards away, just a simple uphill pitching wedge. But any attempt to carry the stream was, of course, fraught with its own danger. Straining for that extra measure of power, it was dreadfully easy to over-swing and send your shot awry; duck-hooking down into the ravine, flaring wildly to the right and into deeper thickets, or simply dribbling ignominiously down the slope that ran off the hill upon which the tee sat, and into the valley of thorns and brush.

"I've always had a hard time with this shot," observed Hugh as he teed his ball and scratched his chin.

I suppose it could have been an innocent remark – certainly, the words themselves were neutral and unobjectionable. I thought otherwise, however. I had no doubt his bland comment actually masked some ulterior purpose – for, thinking back upon our countless hours on the course, I never recalled him having the slightest difficulty here. In fact, it was just the opposite. I was, therefore, immediately suspicious, and determined to ferret out his plot. "What do you mean?" I queried tartly.

"Well, I always wanted to have a wedge into the green like you big hitters, but I guess it's not to be."

The clumsiness of his stratagem made me smile.

He struck a 3-iron carefully to the middle of the fairway, away from the bend of the stream, but it drew more than he had intended, leaving him well short of the hazard and, I thought, some considerable distance from the green. He observed his shot phlegmatically, however, and smiled sweetly, as if to say that this day, and all things connected with it, were perfect.

Now it was my turn. In my youth, I would have unsheathed my driver in petulant anger, the better to banish and bury my sad showing on the previous hole. Such, I knew, was my opponent's expectation. That was a long time ago, however. I was a grown man now, and a rational thinker. Hugh's transparent attempt at provocation had been a waste.

"How many balls did I lose on this hole?" I asked Hugh as I took my stance and readied my drive.

"Well," he replied, "I don't believe I kept count."

I smiled agreeably, then struck a boring 5-wood that faded slightly and ran up the fairway just short of the stream, perfectly positioned, a delicious riposte to his sarcasm.

"That's for being clever," I said.

Together we laughed, and retraced the muddy trail back down through the gloomy ravine and up onto the third fairway. I forgot about the second hole, the casual golfer's essential skill being a capacity for amnesia – or, to put it more accurately, for a kind of selective amnesia, remembering with great clarity all the good shots, perhaps even exaggerating their supereminence, while consigning the rest to the dustbin of history. I felt happy and content. I had never really expected to return to Milford; simply standing once more upon this ground, therefore, particularly on a warm and sunny May afternoon full with the rich fragrance of grass and wildflowers, was a more-than ample benefaction.

We ambled along side-by-side beneath the high blue sky. Hugh told me about his work and asked about mine.

"Lumber brokering?" I asked. "Like, wood for houses?"

"Yeh, residential and commercial both. And specialty woods for custom jobs, furniture, cabinets, whatever's popular and people want."

"Is it steady?"

"Steady enough," he said. "I've been fortunate." He paused and grinned. "I didn't figure you for a lawyer, though!"

"Oh? What then?"

"Well, something useless, I suppose – I mean, the way you'd go about all dreamy-eyed talking books and the like, you know. Your books and memorizing poetry and all, seriously! I'm surprised you ended up doing anything people would pay you for, much less anything with some logical thinking to it. If finding golf balls in the gorse was something you could get paid for, I guess that might have worked out for you."

"Are you asking me to recite some poetry now?" I laughed.

"No, please!

"There was a young lad from the Haven, whose wits were well beyond savin'; made his living from wood, 'cause that's all he could; with the pitiful brains that God gave 'im."

Hugh shook his head. "You haven't changed a bit," he sighed. "Not one bit."

We waved at two old men in argyle sweaters pulling their carts up the opposite fairway, the eighth. Wisps of clouds billowed in from the west, streaming toward the shelter of the Haven, and it was all just as I had remembered and could have wished.

Our conversation drew us back to old friends and old memories, and soon we wandered into the subject of our days playing junior rugby - both of us having been stalwarts of the Junior XV at the grammar school, and, in this capacity, having consumed many stern hours slogging through the muddy practice fields, in bitter, biting cold, preparing for weekend contests against the schools in Haverfordwest, or Tenby, or Fishguard, or rivals farther inland, deep between the hills up near, or even beyond, the Landsker Line; that invisible linguistic demarcation which people said ran through Pembrokeshire, and separated its soft English south from its true, hard, Welsh north.

There, in these matches in the north, the pitches were flinty and the wind raged furiously, so furiously it hurt awfully to run, much less to play rugby, much less to smash flesh and bone against other hurtling bodies. And the boys from these landlocked towns, steeped in a harsh, proud, Celtic heritage, seemed so grimly severe about their rugby, and went about it with such implacable fixedness, as to give me the unsettling sensation of being in an uncomfortable embrace with some blind, stubborn force of great antiquity. In a way that eluded my facility with words, it seemed to me these boys were different; that they went about their rugby not as a lark or a pastime - or even to impress the girls, or to gain status in that invisible hierarchy which governs the world of the boys, motivations I could easily have understood and respected – but, rather, under some rough, unyielding prod that escaped my ken altogether. It was disconcerting, in an undefinable way. What sort of men might these hard, stony creatures possibly become? From what sort of men did they issue? I tried not to look at the wraith-like figures roaming the sidelines, shrouded in thick grey overcoats – their fathers, no doubt, uncles, grandfathers – fevered, red-rimmed eyes gleaming beneath woolen caps, deep-lined faces covered with grey-black stubble. Instead, I chased and cursed the hard boys from the hard inland villages as they bore relentlessly forward.

Our team, however, the Milford Junior XV, was different. Something about living by the sea, and the lightness of spirit that derives from proximity to the water, seemed to infuse our collective personality, so that while we always played gamely, never were we fanatical about winning or overly concerned with results. The ride back to Milford was warm and languid; the bus wound down through the rolling coast, back to our homes on the hills above the Haven, and we laughed and joked and sang, and the match itself would recede, leaving us simply with its pleasant residue, our shared effort and our shared fatigue. Come Monday, we would return to the muddy pitch for yet more practice, the gray clouds scuttling overhead, the wind lacerating our pallid arms and legs, our coach exhorting us anew to run faster and tackle harder, slam and bang with greater gusto, give it more, because – especially if we had suffered a grievous thumping in last Saturday's match - we owed the school a victory after our shameful, gutless performance.

Sauntering down the fairway – like two *boulevardiers* with time on our hands, I suggested to Hugh's amusement - we agreed that any reminiscence of our bygone rugby careers would be incomplete without special attention to the memory of our old coach - for indeed the coach of the Junior XV had carved a unique impression, unabraded by time.

The man's name was Jack Brown – a nondescript enough tag, calling to mind absolutely nothing of note or interest.

In his ordinary, daily incarnation, Mr. Brown served as the school's Geography teacher, relegated to a musty classroom hung with large, faded maps depicting obscure regions of the globe. Looking back, I suspect several were likely obsolete – but no matter. He was clipped and concise in his lectures, and stuck vigilantly to his lesson plans; developed, no doubt, over years, and completely impervious to change. No commotion, no ruckus; steady, ordered, and dry. Cloaked in this wholly unprepossessing demeanor, he discharged his teaching duties.

Behind the unremarkable curtain of his flat workaday guise, however, lurked something far different – something with which we boys on the Junior XV became intimately familiar. For, once the day's final bell had rung the end of classes, after we had changed into our kit and stretched and assembled on the field behind the school, it was some wildly unrecognizable rendition of our tepid and forgettable Geography teacher who materialized on the rugby pitch, mutated through some Hyde-like alchemy into an absolute dervish, one foot already sunk into the well of madness.

He screamed, he shouted, he ranted, he leapt up and down, he glowered, he spat black curses, he spun in circles, he kicked savagely at the ground (digging divots larger than any I ever carved into the golf course), made ghoulish faces, and threw vicious punches at sprites in the air. It was like a soda bottle shaken hard then uncorked, froth cascading out uncontrollably, spilling and foaming over everything. And, in the grip of this bizarre persona, he possessed a remarkable verve with invective. "Run, lad, or I'll have your guts for garters!" the maniac bawled at any poor wretch lagging behind the play or pausing to catch his breath. "Aha, show me more of that, you spineless pissers!" the cross-eyed crackpot cackled as we collided in heaving scrums and launched ourselves recklessly into bone-crunching tackles. "Bloody, worthless bloody bloody idiot!" howled the hysteric as some miscreant dropped the ball or slipped in the mire.

As Hugh and I strolled toward our shots and reminisced, the figure of our schizophrenic Geography teacher and rugby coach took shape again before my eyes, red-faced and puffing, shrouded in the wet mist that seemed to hover forever above the practice pitch, roaring "Well, there's a Yank who wants to play rugby! Take a lesson, you miserable cretins!" as one afternoon, in some long-vanished twilight, I raced past a pack of would-be tacklers and left them sprawling in the mud.

An involuntary shiver shook me head-to-toe, as again the soaked and clammy jersey clung to my skin, again the incessant wind cut me to ribbons, again my hands and feet throbbed as we slid in the muck, piled on top of one another, chased the bouncing ball, grabbed at one other's arms and legs, shouted and laughed, the day waning and gray dusk descending over the pitch, till finally we drag ourselves frigid and exhausted to the changing room.

As we poked around the remnants of memories concerning our mad and farcical coach, Hugh remarked, almost as an afterthought, "Rugby's a complicated game to understand."

It seemed a cryptic utterance. I offered no reply, awaiting some sort of clarification or elaboration. None followed, however. As we continued strolling the fairway, Hugh seemed momentarily lost in thought. I wondered if he was thinking back to his own days on the pitch – he had been a wonderful young player, lithe and elusive, with great endurance and spirit. He was also, I remembered, an ardent fan who followed the game very seriously – and, like every Welshman, nothing surpassed his devotion to the national team, the Wales XV.

Once, late in the springtime – it would have been April or May - Hugh had organized a group of schoolmates to charter a cheap bus to Cardiff for the Wales v. England match. The event meant nothing to me, other than the prospect of a fun-filled outing with my friends. I had clearly misread the occasion, however, for it soon became obvious that larger and deeper forces were at play, twisting my friends into tight coils of anticipation. And this bubbling excitement among my mates proved so contagious that shortly I too found myself caught up in its hot boil. This Wales v. England affair, I surmised, must be something important, and a thing worth seeing.

As dawn began to tiptoe in early on the appointed Saturday morning, the sky faintly streaked with strands of pink and yellow, the rented coach lumbered up and gasped to a halt in front of Johnson's candy shop on Waterloo Square. There, the twenty or thirty of us who had paid our share of the cost stood waiting, our breath smoky in the clear, cold air. Unceremoniously, addled by having risen at daybreak, we all piled in, and the bus rumbled noisily away, heaving and coughing like a tubercular case.

As we rode, the nervous energy intensified, and our early morning daze evaporated. Everyone's wits sharpened; the chatter and banter amplified with each mile passed. Great events loomed ahead - of that, we were certain, the entire day opening up, adventures and escapades in Wales' capitol city beckoning, parents abandoned far behind. Before us lay the promise of a fine and splendid occasion on which to be young and carefree, and a long way from home. In high spirits, therefore, we rattled happily along, and the morning lengthened.

Finally, after three hours of clunking, clanking twists and turns, from what I had by then concluded was our severely underpowered conveyance, we crept to a halt outside stately Cardiff Arms stadium, the day now brilliantly bright and sunny – and the sensation of stepping off the bus into a surging swarm of many thousand fully-steamed, fully-charged, fully-fired devotees of the Welsh National Team struck like electricity.

Energy and fervor not only sizzled through the air – energy and fervor made up every atom of the air itself. Every superheated breath singed my lungs with an unseen force, which, like some supernatural current, was crackling across and between the mass of bodies into which we had descended. It was a huge hubbub, a maelstrom of galvanized, concentrated emotion. I felt as if within a teeming, fevered, school of fish – animated and united by a single-minded focus which, I rapidly deduced, boiled down to the annihilation of the Englishmen, spawns of the underworld. I saw two men in dirty jackets fighting outside a loo. Two pals and I endeavored to chat up three rose-cheeked girls in line for fish and chips.

Our efforts proved woefully short-lived, however, as a couple of older toughs smoking cigarettes shoved us off the sidewalk and glared threateningly - as if we might seriously entertain the notion of mixing it up with them. The rapid failure of our romantic sorties did nothing to dampen our moods, however – we moved along and mingled into the throng, sank into it, bought lunch and match programs, wandered, pointed, joined in chants full of dirty words exalting all things Welsh and condemning the English as lower than buggers, and eventually found our way into the stands.

Barely in time did we locate and wedge into our places in the terrace – the pitted, weather-beaten stone steps smelling ever so faintly of urine, or stale beer – or possibly both, against a subtle finish of ripened vomitus. The teams were introduced, the national anthems played, and then, amid a tremendous, bellowing roar, the match was on.

I had no real grasp of the contest's history or meaning, of course, but the entire epic character of the clash was tangible, and I felt its waves drenching everyone in the stadium, including me, soaking every soul in hot, wet, fervor for Wales. Before my wondering eyes, laconic, diffident Hugh became transformed, churning with intensity, concentrating on every run, contorting with every tackle, crying passionately and crudely with every eddy in the twisting swirl of the game. In contrast – for although I experienced the tide of collective zeal, I could not help but also stand a bit apart - I observed as if peering in through a window, enjoying the crowd and the setting, the atmosphere, contemplating what a nice souvenir my Wales roseate was going to make.

It was quickly apparent that out of all the mortal beings stuffed into Cardiff Arms that day, only I had control of myself. The stands beat and throbbed with stomping, arm-waving, wide-eyed, flush-faced Welshmen. The reek of ale and cigarettes gathered above the crowd like a sour fog, and the entire mass swayed to and fro, delivering up one full-throated song after another, brawny and buoyant. Every spectator sported a Wales button or flag, and the strong young Welshmen on the field of battle were heroes, whose heroism resided in their sheer effort and pluck against the overbearing English, and not the actual results, as to which I gathered the crowd had no real expectation.

The match ebbed and flowed, rose and fell, and the score seemed incidental as a Welsh halfback was kicked in the head and stumbled to the sideline, only to return with a bloody bandage around his skull, and the men in the stands swelled, and their voices rang ever louder, and the brave Welshman's return seemed to ignite the lads, who surged nine points ahead with only five minutes to go. I sensed the tension tightening, close and palpable, thousands of hopes mingling with a sort of collective fatalistic anxiety rooted in history.

Then suddenly, the referee blew his whistle, and Wales had held on to claim the victory! The crowd exploded in wild jubilation, everyone hugged everyone, and the flags with their red dragons bright against green-and-white backgrounds flapped majestically against the brilliant blue sky, and my head spun from this intimate immersion in a passion, a drama, with historic, ethnic, martial, socio-economic, personal, familial, caste, and cultural substance I could not begin to comprehend, and of which I understood but a sliver.

And so, if I was unable to comprehend rugby in its fullness when living in Wales back then, a heartland and cauldron of the sport, certainly I did not understand it now, and did not understand Hugh's strange comment.

"What do you mean? I asked.

"You have to be Welsh to understand rugby," he replied in a definitive, dismissive sort of way.

I laughed. "Well, I guess that's why I never really got it, "I said. "I just played it."

"And not too bad for a Yank, I have to admit," Hugh ventured, gazing ahead down the fairway as we approached his ball.

Quite a compliment indeed, from my old, laconic, rugby-mad friend.

Following an extended period of deliberation, Hugh extracted a 5-iron from his bag. A sudden ripple of concern creased his brow.

"Is that enough club?" I inquired solicitously. Although monotonously accurate, Hugh had never been a long hitter. And he needed to clear the stream as well as the rise to the green.

"Well, what do you recommend?" he replied tersely, lifting an eyebrow.

I remained silent and thoughtful, according his inquiry the serious consideration it deserved. I narrowed my eyes and squinted analytically toward the target. "I couldn't say, really," I finally responded, professorially, as if speaking of grave and weighty matters, full of serious philosophical implications. "Whatever you think, you know better than me."

Hugh surveyed me with what seemed like disappointment in his eyes - although it might have been something more malign - then addressed his ball and waggled his club. His preparations bespoke an uncharacteristic hesitancy. He waggled again, then abruptly stepped away. "You don't think I can get there with a 5, do you?" he snapped accusingly.

"No, no," I replied quickly. "You've gotten too suspicious. I'm sure a 5 is fine. Perfect."

Again, he addressed the ball.

"It's only a bit uphill," I observed helpfully. "And the wind's behind you."

Hugh's shot sailed easily over the stream, but then seemed to catch in the air, fluttered and faltered above the fairway like a broken kite, then fell to ground well short of the green and to the left, buried deep in a nasty mound of thatch.

I uttered not a word. Nor did Hugh.

Up the fairway we trod, to my ball. I punched a solid 9-iron to the center of the green, from where I two-putted to win the hole. As we departed, Hugh gazed wistfully back down the fairway, then at me, then upwards towards the sky and the unpredictable, ever-shifting wind.

"One up," I announced in a firm voice. "No help up there."

He glanced again toward the heavens. "I didn't know you'd become an atheist," he said. "I'm not surprised."

# LORD NELSON'S HARBORAGE

We slipped easily into the early days of autumn. The leaves colored and flared yellow and red and fell from the trees to gather thick and wet upon the ground, and the sky became a radiant jigsaw of blue and pink and grey, alternating sun and rain, all against the smoky, piquant redolence of the changing season. Summer mounted a valiant resistance – each dawn emblazoned by hopeful shafts of bold and rosy light, small, isolated sallies of warmth – but gradually retreated, ebbed, and finally gave way. And then we fell full into the late days of autumn, and the rains picked up and the sky bled itself of color, and the Haven turned flat and dull.

As planned, the family arrived from London. We established permanent quarters in a drafty, two-story brick house on Wellington Road, in the little village of Hakin, directly across the short Victoria Bridge from the town of Milford proper. My afternoon wanderings were done, along with that secret sense of exploration I had shared with my father during the month we bivouacked together at the Marshal. Our interlude as scouts, as trailblazers, had come to an end.

The family's reassembly quickly resurrected a meshwork of familiar routines, and the resettlement to Wellington Road brought a host of new practical problems as well - reconfiguring the plumbing in the kitchen, installing new heaters and cabinets, plugging the surprising number of holes we found in the floors, and carpeting the dank, clammy, downstairs bathroom. No longer was it only myself and my father, alone and finding our way in a new and mysterious land.

The deepening autumn also brought another kind of change – for I had settled in at school and begun to make friends. Every weekday morning, at 7:30 on the button, the big, red, double-decked school bus braked to a halt at the stop located just down the sidewalk from our front gate. Before long – within a week of our taking occupancy, in fact - an assortment of boys and girls from the neighborhood began calling early at our door to collect me, stealing glances inside our house as if Martians might be lurking within its exotic walls. It was clear we were objects of deep curiosity, but I didn't mind.

Ah, from the mists they appear now once again, banging the door, ringing the bell, calling for me to hurry along: Mickey Dunn, an athletic, blondish, gap-toothed boy from down the hill, a wholly uncomplicated fellow given to an easy laugh and harmless jokes; John Jenkins, tall, ruddy, and rugged, with a mild stammer that worsened when he got excited, a set of jug ears that turned red in the process, and the kind of demeanor that advised diplomacy; Duncan McAllister, from a family of relocated Scots, hopeless devotee of Rangers football, owner of a sharp, slicing wit, who lived on that edge between keeping people in stitches and inflaming their ire. Then finally there was urbane Lewis Morgan, whose hair, to my envy, resembled John Lennon's, and around whom there circled a cool and worldly air, as if he was already half an adult, and above tomfoolery and hijinks.

Each morning we gathered at the stop, shivering as the days grew steadily cooler. When the bus arrived, we clambered up to the top deck, hopped into our seats, and – with the exception of Morgan, who observed distantly - clowned and japed and bothered the girls as we made the thirty-minute ride to school. No longer was my father shaking me awake in the mornings. No longer were we feasting upon Mrs. Zelinski's abundance. Things had changed. And I began to feel less like an explorer in a new terrain, and more like a settler with a claim – a very small one perhaps, barely discernable, but a claim nonetheless.

Our daily destination – the Milford Haven Grammar School – sat at the top of Steynton Road, the long, steep road that exited Milford, rose toward the hills, and curved inland to the county seat of Haverfordwest. Noteworthy to me – because it had no precedent in my experience - was the fact that every student was required to wear a uniform.

Every day, therefore, along with all the other boys, I donned a black blazer and cap, both bearing a yellow insignia depicting a ship bobbing atop the waves, a black and yellow striped tie, and a black and yellow scarf as the weather turned cold.

The ship jouncing upon the waves conveyed a two-fold meaning. First, it spoke of Milford's unbreakable connection to the sea, upon which the town had always depended in one form or another. And second, its historic infatuation with the great Lord Horatio Nelson, hero of Trafalgar, who visited briefly in 1803, pronounced the waterway one of the two fairest such concourses in the world, and thereafter was appropriated as Milford's perpetual beloved patron saint, his distinguished name destined to adorn all manner of storefronts posh and seedy, advertisements, promotional flyers, street signs, and commercial and benevolent enterprises. The badge sewn onto our caps and the breast-pockets of our jackets, therefore, bore faithful testimony both to our bond with the great ocean at our doorstep, and our fealty to the memory of Lord Nelson, proud master of the waves, Milford's adopted icon.

Milford – really, the entire Pembrokeshire coast, of which Milford was but a small part – did indeed have a long, deep relationship with the surrounding waters. They existed, the land and the sea, in a convoluted kind of marriage - the most tempestuous yet also most pacific of marriages. Indifferent, even, at times – for regardless of whatever guise or aspect the sea might display on any given day – soothing, angry, pensive, ominous - it was always simply there, omnipresent, and incapable of not being there. Incapable of not registering in some recess of one's daily consciousness. The longer I lived in Pembrokeshire, therefore, the more dug-in I became, the more I sensed this ever-presence of the sea infiltrating my consciousness as well, and began to feel its strange power.

I found it made me think about history, as London had, though in something of a different way. An even bigger, broader, more complicated way.

A Saturday road trip with the family to the massive Neolithic dolmen of Pentre Ifan, for example, or the stones circled in the boggy moorland of Gors Fawt – and I, only recently arrived from a city of virtually no historical vintage at all, suddenly able to rest my palm upon a monument hewn, carved, and fixed in place with some forgotten intensity of purpose thousands of years ago. *Thousands*. The staggering span rolled back and forth in my limber, pulsating mind. *Thousands!* It made me ask new questions – like a shut-in who has spent his life in a narrow room with no windows, suddenly allowed to leave, venturing out into a vast world. In just this way, the questions came, the boundaries of my world expanded.

Here, throughout the Pembrokeshire countryside, I could see, stand before, run my hand across, all manner of ancient works made in times beyond when I had imagined time even existing. Intricately carved stone-works, barrows, runes, blue-grey Preseli slabs planted upright in patterns of meaning. Why? What made them do it? What were they saying? And how incredibly long must history actually be, after all! So long, so very very long, was the obvious answer now presented before my eyes, and freshly-sprouting in my inner conceptions. *Thousands of years ago? Thousands! How is that possible? How could there be that much history in the world? Where could it come from?*

It came upon me like a sonic boom – I had heard one, once, awed and shaken by its fearsome reverberation. And I sensed its mighty impact – dolmens, ruins, hillforts, centuries! – now again.

Even beginning to juggle and play with such notions entailed a complete recalibration of perspective. Astonishing notions, they were – but laden too with paradox, which brought to me a subtle, humbling unease; my first vague, sketchy, inkling that, although weighed against the literally numberless swarm of humankind-past, we each, individually, count for nothing, and represent mere worm-food in the end, within us beats some desperate compulsion to cast our shadows across the chasm of time, to strike our best blows against its annihilating evanescence.

These people here in ancient times, I mused with my hand upon the cool, hard surface of some ancient, pock-marked relic, on some windy hill or heath in sight of the sea, had known this impulse – or such, at least, was the message I took from the myriad markers of pre-history that dotted the coast and the countryside. This need, this demand, to resist the march of time, this aspiration for even the smallest shred of permanence, if only a grouping of rocks bravely facing the wind. It was an impulse, my ruminations lead me to conclude, surely derived from, or at least focused and refined by, the all-encompassing proximity of the ocean; which, with every beating moment, every endlessly breaking wave, day-in and day-out, with the fixedness of immortality, must have seemed a form of mockery – mockery of the quicksilver brevity of mere mortal life, the triviality of its pains and struggles, the smallness of its accomplishments and cares.

It would have been more surprising, I speculated, had these early people, so wound into the endless, undying sea, not been inspired to fashion some sort of testament to their own existence. Full-well, they knew their pillars and columns would not last – but built them nonetheless. And yes, here they were, beneath my touch, after spans of time the scope of which I was only just beginning to comprehend. I saw them with my eyes, with my fingers felt their weathered faces.

In a way, I decided, the ancient builders had won. And, like a tiny flame being lit, therefore, with the barest flicker of thought, I began to wonder what mark, if any, it might be possible for me to leave upon the world myself.

Such were the reflections our weekend tours ignited in my mind.

If, indeed, the sea had always been a source of symbolic inspiration, it had also played a more utilitarian role, a less ethereal role, involving trade and commerce. Pembrokeshire sat squarely along trade routes which, by the Bronze Age, had developed from the Continent, across the Channel, and through the south of England, west to Ireland – routes which eventually saw communities of chandlers, tanners, caulkers, carpenters, blacksmiths, weavers, net-makers, sail-makers, rope-makers, and boat-tenders of all manner and kind sprouting up in the little villages sprinkled along the shores. The Tudor period in particular witnessed a major expansion of coastal trading and professional ship-building in the Haven; which, in turn, attracted ever-more skilled specialists and gave rise to early organized shipyards. Here and there, a relic from that age could still be found, such as the picturesque remains of the forgotten vessel resting tipped onto its side at Lawrenny Quay, decayed and evocative, half-buried in the sand, as if waiting patiently for its master to return and take once again to the glorious and rolling sea.

My father, of course, took us to it, one windy Sunday afternoon. Naturally, it set my imagination to churning.

The trade routes also served as pilgrimage routes. In the chaotic aftermath of the Romans packing up and departing the British Isles in the 400's, growing numbers of Christian ascetics began following these routes deep into western Wales and, in particular, to the isolated tranquility of Pembrokeshire. These rigorous souls tended to congregate in remote, secluded spots, where they could practice their devotions untroubled, and seemed to favor locations close to the sea, where doubtless the nearness of the elements also engendered a sense of nearness to the everlasting. These religious pilgrims left their share of footprints too, at places such as St. Daniel's Hill in Pembroke, St. Govan's Chapel, and, most famously, the cathedral town of St. David's, Patron Saint of Wales.

All of which we visited on our weekend ramblings.

The sea had always been a causeway, bringing new people to Pembrokeshire and the Haven. This was another theme I came to recognize, and of which, in fact, my family and I were examples. In the 400's, for example, a tribe known as the Desai staged a massive migration from southeast Ireland across the Irish Sea, establishing in what later became Pembrokeshire the kingdom of Dyfed. Then, of course, there were the Vikings – Norse incursions into Wales began in earnest in the first part of the 800's, and a chief named Hubba is known to have wintered in what became the Milford suburb of Hubberston in 858, along with 23 of his warships. For all I know, his men may have camped squarely in our new backyard.

The Norse raiders bedeviled coastal Wales for years, but eventually established permanent encampments along the sheltered rivers and harbors; which, over their own slow unfurling of time, transformed into settled communities and villages and crossroads of rural commerce. Place-names of hamlets and crossings throughout the county bore continuing witness to their Nordic origins; Dale, Angle, Caldey, Fishguard, Stackpole, Gateholm, Grassholm, Carew, Hubberston, Ramsey, Hasguard, just some of many. The name of our own town – Milford Haven – was itself one such example, echoing the old Norse words "Melr" – meaning "sandbank" - and "Fjord" - meaning "inlet."

Over time, the raiders simply assimilated. Their settlements became simple placid country towns, their fields extending monotonously across hills sewn with crops, their watercraft quietly fishing the Haven and the bays as the relentless Atlantic winds continued blowing day by day, week by week, year by year, as ever, forever driving vast grey cloudbanks across the sky to drench endlessly the greening lands.

Spiritual inspiration, avenue of trade, conveyer of people. And more. The sea had always made of the Haven an important point of both embarkation and arrival; a place which both sent forth and received ships on significant undertakings. In 1171, for example, Henry II assembled an army and 400 warships in Pembrokeshire, from which to launch a full-scale attack on Ireland, commencing the long and dreary infliction of the English upon the Irish. In 1405, French mercenaries from across the English Channel docked in the Haven to assist the Welsh patriot Owain Glyndwr in his doomed uprising against the English – and even succeeded in setting fire to the English stronghold of Haverfordwest. In 1457, a child named Henry was born within Pembroke Castle's cold stone walls, unnoticed and of no apparent consequence. In 1485, however, this same Henry – by then carrying the Tudor name - sailed a fleet mustered in France into the Haven, disembarked at Dale, rested and resupplied in Pembroke, then marched and made war against Richard III, ultimately seizing the English throne and founding the Tudor dynasty as Henry VII – his son, of course, acquiring lasting renown as Henry VIII. In 1649, Oliver Cromwell launched another invasion of Ireland from Milford, this one bearing his own particularly vicious stamp, extending and deepening the scabrous scourge of the English upon the Irish.

By the mid-1700's, a group of enterprising Quaker whaling families from the whaling island of Nantucket, off the Massachusetts coast, had somehow been lured to Milford by the prospect of founding a vast new center for what was, at the time, the burgeoning whale oil industry; a bold vision which never came close to fruition – but which, perhaps, dimly prefigured the arrival two hundred years later of a real and much more serious oil industry.

Finally, by Act of Parliament in 1790, the town of Milford Haven itself was formally chartered. The Navy Board built a permanent dockyard along the Haven. Schools and dwellings and official buildings rose from the ground, and commerce expanded. Believing it had muscles to flex, Milford developed ambitions in the 1800's – more akin to fantasies, most believed – of establishing itself as a major trans-Atlantic trading port and distribution depot. Visionaries imagined elaborate modern docks and grand hotels, fat-bellied trading vessels stuffed with rich trade goods from exotic, faraway locales unloading into warehouses, and trains steaming pell-mell back and forth between Milford and London.

Like all grand and overheated chimeras, these quixotic notions exerted a formidable seductive power, so that a goodly number of people ended up investing substantial sums of money in the wild designs. These schemes did, it must be said, have a certain geographic logic – but that was all. For, by this time, Milford had been greatly outpaced by Liverpool, Southampton, and Bristol; cities less remote and isolated, and far better capitalized. Indeed, Milford had the superior waterway. That was all it had, however, and scheme after scheme, plan after plan, to develop the Haven for trading vessels, ocean liners, or mail packets, failed miserably. By the middle of the 1900's, the swell of trade and commerce had ebbed away, and Milford had settled comfortably into life as a picturesque fishing village on the shores of a vast expanse of deep, calm, and tranquil water, surrounded by farms and even smaller villages; rich in bucolic appeal, but of commercial interest to no one. No one, that is, except those people who were, by the middle of the 20th century, scouring the world in search of the ideal environs for the transport, storage, and refining of enormous quantities of crude oil.

And so, in 1966, my family and a little corps of Americans and others arrived to build an oil refinery along Lord Nelson's much-praised harborage. Where I, like the rest of my schoolmates, wore the emblem sewn onto my jacket – the ship upon the waves, the influence of the sea old, unchanging, and ever-present.

# THE CADDY

The days had now gone damp and drizzly, and a fine mist hovered monotonously in the nipping, cutting air. The waters of the Haven ran sooty like lead and the wind blew continually from the west. Great banks of rain emerged from over the horizon, swept across the tall limestone crags of St. Anne's Head and The Stacks, over the sodden farms in Dale and Johnston, pelted the beaches at Marloes, Broad Haven, and Newgale, then bore hard into Milford, drenching schoolchildren waiting miserably for their buses, workmen on the docks, and housewives hurrying home from shopping. It was only tolerable, barely, because the daily downpours were inevitably interrupted at some point by tantalizing breaks in the clouds, glimpses of blue to brighten the spirit - but then thick new walls of rain would lumber ashore and linger and pour and soak us for days, foggy, dreary, endless.

Through it all, of course, we played rugby, and golf in the short respites. Up and down the length of the puddled pitch, we chased and ran and tackled. Into the sopping turf, we tumbled and dove. We rolled in the mud, slid in the mud, stumbled in the mud, were driven into the mud, wiped it from our mouths and hair and eyes, then staggered dripping into the warm and womb-like changing room, to shower and dress, before climbing aboard the big red bus, which delivered us groggily home; only to repeat it all again the following day.

On weekends, if the rain relented, I caddied for my father or his friends, then played golf with Hugh. My father possessed a vicious hook; most likely the product of his violent, ruthless swing. He was, he liked to confide proudly, with a knowing look, completely self-taught; as if self-instruction had opened the door to some esoteric body of layman's wisdom, unavailable to those unfortunate enough to have learned the game at the hand of a professional. It appeared to me, however, that the basic lesson my father had divined was identical to the lesson I, myself, had gleaned from my Gary Player guide as the distilled essence of the game: *hit the ball as hard as you possibly can.* The difference was that he implemented this edict to a degree and at a level I could never hope to emulate. Thus, my father lashed at every ball with supersonic velocity, every time, then stared with disbelieving consternation at every wild hook, oblivious to the relationship between the savagery with which he wielded the club and its horrible results. And, because patience was not first – nor second nor third - among my father's many virtues, caddying for him was much like watching pressure build inside a volcano, while the volcano endeavored admirably to keep its cap on tight.

In general, most of the time, he succeeded. When he was playing unusually poorly, however, the black clouds would descend upon my father's face, his mouth would tighten into a line, the tendons and ligaments of his neck would grow taut, his eyes would begin to bulge, and the volcanic gasses would seethe and fume, threatening to explode for any niggling, inconsequential, or perhaps even non-existent reason at all. And at these times, were I to find myself caddying for him, I simply hefted the bag and chased the wayward balls – evil, mocking, little devils - tended the pin, and said nothing. For I knew it would eventually pass; that soon enough, he would be enjoying a pint in the bar with his friends, the hot gasses receding, the softening expression upon his face confirming that, as the day reshaped itself in his imagination, he had once again struggled mightily with the course, taken some punishing blows, but, in the end, through endurance, grit, and the wile of a cool and fearless competitor, salvaged another triumph. I have already pointed out that the recurring theme of golf is, after all, delusion.

A caddie sees much of the human personality. I have described the silent, unspoken partnership I enjoyed with Mr. Flynn. Our natures seemed to mesh with perfect ease on the course. But I also caddied for loud, showy men who seemed to fancy themselves on display, eager for notice and applause. I caddied for unprepossessing men bereft of talent, who nonetheless felt it necessary to ponder ponderously and pointlessly over every single shot, before making a mess of it. I caddied for good players who were very serious and took their rounds quite seriously, which made me nervous about losing count of their score or leading them unknowingly into some obscure technical infraction, thereby costing them a precious stroke. I caddied for men more interested in chatting than playing golf, and did the best I could to make engaging palaver. I caddied for men with awful tempers, and men with no tempers at all. While it was illuminating to make this tour of the human temperament, I really had just two essential objectives. The first was to get a good tip. The second was to incline my player to request my services again in the future, so I might then garner another good tip. Observing human nature is interesting – but it doesn't jingle in your pocket the way a handsome tip does, and the latter remained always of more immediate concern.

I particularly enjoyed caddying for my father's friend, Tom Kellar. Mr. Kellar was a big, friendly Canadian who had himself worked in Texas before oil and the Gulf refinery brought him to Milford. He had a smooth, easy swing, and I liked carrying his bag because he paid well and rarely hit stray shots that required me to blaze trails into the weedy wastes. His easy swing was matched by an easy, comfortable demeanor. Mr. Kellar always strolled genially through his round, not talking a great deal, but making small observations or comments here and there with a deep, slow voice and the beginnings of a smile, evidently simply enjoying playing golf and cool-headed about its results. Of course, he was quite a good golfer, and thus had no cause for agitation concerning his play. My father had also started his career in the oil business in Texas – his first stop in a career that, in retrospect, bore some passing resemblance to a walkabout - and he and Mr. Kellar seemed to have many of the same interests. They often played together, therefore, forming sort of an odd pair with their vastly contrasting sporting dispositions.

There was another Texan of a different sort, however; a slender, lined, and wiry man called Melvin Beeker, a discontented soul who seemed to spend every waking moment complaining about the paucity of hamburgers, the cramped houses, the absence of sunshine and confounded abundance of rain, the ridiculous puny size of the automobiles, Wednesday afternoon shop-closings, again the damnable shortage of hamburgers, the warm beer, the incomprehensible refusal of television and newspapers to cover the Dallas Cowboys, and whatever else struck him as particularly unlike Texas. On top of having a personality like old vinegar, he was also an abominable golfer. Caddying for him consisted of watching him flail murderously at the ball, then cry "Goddamn it!" Whereupon, it became my duty to trek into the wilderness in search of the vagrant shot as Beeker stewed on the fairway hand-on-hips, glaring in fury as if he would gladly walk back to Texas that very moment if only God would grant him the power to traverse the waves, working his jaw as if bearing down mercilessly upon a thick, fresh plug of spleen. My father considered him a dreadfully sour man, and while at one time or another all the other Americans came to our house for dinner, the Beekers never did.

Our little coterie haled from an assortment of places; its members included Texans, my father from Florida, Project Manager Mr. Wendt from California, and others from places like Oklahoma and Colorado, oil places. We also counted the Canadians as part of the American squad, though they may have disagreed. They were all men who knew about oil, who had studied oil, whose careers were built on oil, who bought houses, cars, and paid their bills from oil, intended to send their children to college on oil, and whom oil, and more particularly the construction of facilities for refining oil in colossal quantities, had now brought to the sheltered Haven. Some of them actively disliked Milford; most patiently tolerated it. A few embraced it. The attitudes of the parents were usually manifest in their children, and so my American friends split into two main camps: those who were simply passing their time in the town, counting the days till they could return to America the way an inmate tallies the days till the prison gates swing open; and those who dove headlong into the life of the place and, by the end, by the time the refinery was complete down to the final turn of the final screw, and Queen Elizabeth herself miraculously arrived on the royal train, to celebrate its opening at a gala ceremony in the summer of 1968, never wanted to leave at all.

I was in the latter category. It was a small group; in retrospect, I suspect, just me – and perhaps, upon further reflection, my father too; though I never asked, but wish I had.

The fourth hole is a straightaway par 3, approximately 170 yards in length, climbing gradually uphill so that the green is elevated slightly above the tee-box. It is a tiny green, bunkered left and right and shaped somewhat like an upturned bowl. There is, to the untrained eye, no real danger at hand. Nothing to trouble an equable mind. Par seems a virtual certainty. To my knowledgeable sensibilities, however, arriving now at the tee, danger cried out all about. The terrain drops sharply off to the right past the bunker, inviting a wild slice into oblivion. To the left of the green crouches a dense, gloomy carpet of matted gorse, purgatory to a hook. Beyond the green runs a low stone wall, with a narrow gap which leads to the fifth tee box. A veritable multitude of subtle perils elude the careless eye. In days gone by I had encountered and been undone by each and every one of them, however, and discerned them clearly before me now; only rarely had I enjoyed any success on this sly fourth hole.

I was caddying for Beeker once, when he flared his tee shot into the deep declivity to the right; then yanked his second ball far left into the thick gorse, from where he hacked it over the green into the trap. By which point his face was bright red as if badly wind-burned, the way it might look if he had just returned from a grueling Arctic exploration, or spent a day on a sun-scorched beach, buried in sand up to his neck. Two blasts from the bunker later he was finally on the green, whereupon he four-putted, spun fast around two times like a discus-thrower, then hurled his putter high and far into the blackness of the gulley, accompanied by an extended epistle of the most foul words, while I watched mute and wide-eyed.

For some reason, as I now prepared to hit my tee shot, this calamitous incident oozed to the surface of my mind, in a kind of technicolor, as it might appear in a movie.

I glanced at Hugh, who was lifting his face up slightly into the breeze, his eyes half closed.

"I'll be glad to wait if you feel like a nap," I said.

"I'm just not sure I want to watch," he replied after a brief pause, eyes still half-closed, enjoying the peaceful currents.

The problem was that the fourth hole might as well have been custom-designed for my irritating companion. It required nothing more than a straight shot of middling distance; which, of course, perfectly described his prosaic, uninspiring game. But not mine, not by any stretch of the imagination. I therefore decided this particular hole did not offer the best venue for a penetrating retort on my part; better to tiptoe humbly past the fourth hole, I concluded, and skewer him later on one of the long par fives. I ignored his provocative commentary, therefore, and concentrated on club selection.

# THE LONG TREE-
# LINED HILL

As Christmas neared, my focus narrowed. It was now too raw and dismal for golf, the short days so bleak as to have compelled even a brief adjournment from rugby. The pitch was a drowned moonscape of soupy dirt, more suitable for raising barnyard stock than for scrums and tackles. We woke each day to thick, hard frosts. From off the black ocean, the wind careened with piercing dagger-points. No longer was there loose and easy conviviality as we gathered at the bus stop outside our gate; now we pressed our arms close to our bodies, hunched our shoulders, and begged silently for the bus to arrive. When finally it appeared, we gratefully rushed aboard, to luxuriate in its warmth. Then, thirty minutes later, as we crawled into the parking lot beside the Grammar School, we wound our scarves tight around our necks, screwed our caps down around our ears, and poured out again into the cold.

It was at this point that the ordeal of winter truly began – for thus has it shaped itself in my memory.

As we exited our buses, the schoolmasters funneled the boys peremptorily around behind the main building, where we collected and milled about waiting for the doors to open. The girls, on the other hand, proceeded directly inside, where we could see them through the windows of their cloakroom, laughing at us pitilessly as we froze.

It was an agonizing ritual, repeated every morning. We waited and waited in the Siberian freeze, huddled closer and closer against the cutting wind, shivering and stamping and snorting like a congregation of elk or musk ox stranded on the tundra. The girls – brutal, merciless creatures - made faces at us from the sanctuary of their cloakroom, folded their arms around their chests in mock shivers, stuck out their lips and rubbed their eyes as if weeping in sympathy. Meanwhile, we boys clumped ever closer together and stared dumbly, our mental functions slowing. The cessation of life approached. We began to bid our private, personal goodbyes to this wretched world. We grew numb in the extremities of our limbs. The afterlife beckoned – maybe it would be warm, warm, warm, however ... such a dreamy, tantalizing prospect. Then finally, at the last possible moment before the flicker of life expired, the schoolmasters flung open the doors and the mass of freezing flesh surged mindless-ly toward the warmth, ears red and burning, noses runny and crusty, teeth chattering like castanets, eyes glazed and stupid. Once inside, we wandered and stumbled like mummies to our classes. Eventually, after the passage of an hour or so, our senses returned, and we remembered those who had made such sport of our torment, whereupon we glared hatefully at the girls who, from the coziness of their cloakroom, had found such high mirth and glee in our suffering.

It would be cruel and indefensible under all accepted norms were this barbarous scene to occur one time only. But no, oh no – the fiendish regimen repeated itself throughout the long, desolate winter. The bus ground to a halt in the parking lot. The girls marched smugly inside the school. We boys scurried like rodents around the back. The wind howled savagely. We hugged ourselves and turned blue in the face, as the girls chortled from their windows, until we became simply one large, insensate organism, desperate for a single spark of heat. There was no talk. No horseplay. Not an ounce of gaiety could be heard, nor the slightest wisp of jocularity. There was, in fact, scarcely any sign of life at all, other than a collective husky wheezing and the malignant drone of low, steady curses, more slurred than spoken, for our frozen lips could barely move.

Then, just as the weaker stock began to fail, the doors burst open, and the entire gelid blob quivered into motion, squeezed itself into the building, then broke apart and dissipated as we lumbered, each to our different classrooms, and slowly regained once more the capacity to think some thought other than simply surviving the next five seconds of glacial cold - colder, it seemed, than the embrace of death could possibly be, colder than the coldest water at the deepest bottom of the deep, deep Haven itself, colder than any place on the Earth or above or beneath it – but not as cold as the ghastly cold hearts of the girls, who warmed themselves in comfort each morning in their cloakroom and gloated at our misery.

Such was our morning ritual as autumn gave way to winter, and winter deepened.

End-of-term exams were approaching – but I gave them precious little thought. As I have mentioned, my focus was narrowing. I must confess, however - "narrowing" is a grossly inadequate word, far too clinical and dry. I should also be more specific, for my "narrowing" focus had a definite cause and object, in a very human form. The truth is that by December, I had become blindly and unreservedly consumed with a girl whose desk in our Third Form class sat one row to my left and two seats back. And "consumed" is still too bloodless and tame a word; it will have to suffice, however, for I do not know that a word exists for the single-minded fixation, near-demonic possession, that ruled me now, in the grip of which I was as limp and helpless as a rag in a hurricane.

I search now in the clouds for some sublime phrase, some magical trick of language – my efforts bear no fruit, however, and yield only flailing, flaccid characterizations, extracted from the imagination of a worldly adult more than thirty years removed, who is striving, but failing, to convey the howling wind, so hot it burned like fire, louder than a hundred cannons, which had once enveloped a young boy captured by his first serious attraction to a pretty girl.

We stole glances during class and contrived to find each other during the lunch break. If I observed her talking to another boy in the hallway, I was devastated. We found reasons to exchange words between classes, or walking to the bus after school. If we missed each other, I bitterly surmised that she secretly despised me and was probably at that very moment locked in carnal embrace (of which I had only the vaguest picture) with one of my imagined oafish competitors. Her hair was a shade of amber, with a lucent underglow of blonde, in something of an elfin cut, and she had an elusive way of looking me in the eye then glancing down, with a dimpled smile faint upon her lips, timorous at times, ironic at others. As if she was carrying on some amusing private conversation with herself, or perceiving some double-meaning in whatever I happened to be saying. Never could I figure it out, and it worked upon me like a spell. I felt her eyes – which were unusually blue and bright - tickling on my back. I turned and smiled when the teacher called her name aloud – Adelyn Anderson - and she stood to answer. I sought her aid with math problems and French grammar, and thought about her constantly. One day, in a bold move, I sat down beside her at lunch. After a wary moment, she asked about my life in Florida.

"Is it very hot?"

"Very," I assured her. "Very hot."

"Do you know how to surf? I saw it on the telly, it looked great fun."

"Well, a little. I was just learning when we left."

"Do you like it here? Everything must be so different."

"Yes," I said, "it is different. But I like it, so far anyway."

"What does your Dad do?"

I told her he worked on the Gulf project, and she said her father worked for a fish brokerage.

"Do you have a telephone?" I asked, aflame with the notion of calling her.

"No," she shook her head. "My Mum wants one but my Dad says we don't need it."

She seemed embarrassed, and I changed the subject, because I didn't want her to think I was one of those Americans who believes himself better than people who aren't Americans. My father had told me about those kinds of Americans. I dropped the subject of the telephone, therefore, and we chatted about which teachers we liked and which we didn't, and I said I wished she could help me with math because I didn't understand a bit of it, nor French either.

"And you're so good at French!" I exclaimed. "You always know the answers! How did you get so good?"

She smiled in what I had come to recognize as her ambiguous, secretive way. "I just like it. I want to live in France one day. That's my dream. I wouldn't mind helping you, though I don't know I would be any good."

"Well, you couldn't make me any worse, could you?"

"No," she smiled, shaking her head playfully. "You do have the worst accent I've ever heard! Quite the worst! Dreadful, really!"

We agreed to begin meeting in the library. She made me promise to take the work seriously, however, which I did promise. Of course, I would have agreed to recite verb declinations backwards, on my head, had she so demanded.

As we spent more time together, my absorption deepened. I took to laboring obsessively before the mirror in the morning, desperately attempting to craft my wayward hair into just the right dapper configuration – no small task, given my unruly thatch. I cultivated support among her friends, and sought to divine the true meaning behind every word that fell from her lips, every random wave of her hand, the most minute movements of her eyebrows, and generally poured enormous quantities of time, and vast mental resources, into plotting strategies within strategies for winning her affections; daring to hope I might kindle in her something like the red-hot inferno that was searing me within from top to bottom.

Then, as the end of the term approached, the entirety of my feverish fixation concentrated itself upon one single event; an event so large as to blot out and render utterly meaningless all other matters – the Grammar School's annual Christmas dance, held every year on the final Friday of the term, just before the holiday. And I approach the subject reverently even today, for still do I experience the remnants of its tug upon my emotions, feel the residue of its gravitational pull, and recall with a kind of wonderment the way it drew in the whole of my being back then.

These mundane school events come and go, of course. I had convinced myself, however, that this particular occasion, this one Christmas dance, presented a rare and unique opportunity, a special confluence of circumstances, which would never again present itself – and which I would rue forever should it pass.

It had dawned upon me that Adelyn would doubtless be walking home after the dance - and it therefore might be possible, just the slightest bit possible, if fortune smiled and all benign forces aligned harmoniously, to approach as she emerged from the girl's cloakroom and ask if I could walk her home – and Yes, Yes, there was even a chance she might smile shyly and glance to the ground and nod her assent, at which point I might be able, actually, even, God-willing, gloriously, to take and hold her hand. And at this juncture in my speculations, everything dissolved into a kind of dreamy delirium, as my imagination wallowed voluptuously in the vision of the two of us walking hand-in-hand beneath the cold, starry sky, walking and walking, walking and walking, and the dream did not end but simply resolved itself into something like a puffy cloud, drifting in a warm sky.

It was a prospect, a reverie, to which I submitted completely.

In the fullness of time, the final day of the term did at last arrive. I had swept through my exams barely conscious of whether the subject at hand was biology, history, or English literature. Why would I care? Why would anyone care? She sat behind me, one row over to the left, wearing a tight navy blue sweater over a fresh white shirt open at the collar. If I glanced back, I could discern the light playing on her heathered hair and her brow pursed in a frown, as she pondered the process of photosynthesis, explicated the origins of the War of the Roses, or the psychological depravity of Lady Macbeth. Perhaps, if I glanced back often enough, she might raise her eyes from her paper and meet my gaze – a breathtaking possibility, which loosed an electric jolt!

If I glanced back too often, however, the teacher could suspect me of some clever form of cheating. And that kind of thing would result forthwith in a trip to the Headmaster and several swift strokes of the cane upon the palms of the hand – a painful outcome much to be avoided. Indeed, my palms throbbed with the mere thought – three other miscreants and myself having had an unfortunate experience with the cane just recently, on wholly trumped-up charges.

It was vital, therefore, my still-tingling digits warned, to be wily and careful, and to peek back at my young siren as often as possible, but pull up just short of the danger point. Perhaps it would help if I glanced back in a different manner each time – once with a quick backward jerk of my head, another time gradually raising my arm as if stretching and then peering through my armpit; the next time by just barely turning my head but swiveling my eyes to the side until they hurt. Followed by feigning a cough and flailing my head in her direction while hacking and spewing - mayhaps to catch her gaze.

At some point, I would have to scribble something down on my exam paper. Till then, however, there was plenty of time to devise new means of stealing a glimpse of her angelic visage without drawing undue attention. The days were truly dwindling till the great event, and I was not about to permit all my hopes and plans to founder on something as meaningless as school exams – it certainly wasn't Shakespeare who I was desperate to walk home from the Christmas dance!

I counted down the seconds, minutes, hours, and days. The twist and turn and churn of the waiting grew excruciating.

Then, however, suddenly, with a frightening swiftness – the day was here, it had arrived, full upon me, staring me in the face! And I was unprepared! Somehow, it had completely snuck up on me! I trembled with the sick and queasy certainty that something was bound to go wrong, that surely I must have overlooked some vital detail in the labyrinthine workings of my designs. I spent the afternoon in a dither, reviewing my plans again, front-to-back, and making certain all the accoutrements were ready. Once more, I went through all the possibilities and permutations, this time back-to-front. As evening approached, I showered, washed my hair, brushed my teeth, applied the merest dash of cologne with an insouciant flick of the wrist – such as I imagined a practiced roué might employ - carefully assembled and reassembled my infuriating and insubordinate hair, donned my reliably stylish black turtleneck and brown corduroy jacket, and convened at half-past six with a small cadre of friends and confederates - McAllister, Dunn, Hugh, Morgan, and Jenkins - in front of Johnson's store on Waterloo Square.

The hour was nigh.

Night had not yet fallen full, and the weak remnant of the departing sun was like a stubborn stain on dirty fabric. The waters of the Haven were a film of gray, and the surrounding docks and warehouses loomed and rose around us as indistinct and hulking outlines. It was a rare windless evening, but crisp already, so we hunched our shoulders, wrapped our scarves, and set off briskly for the Grammar School.

I was marching toward a destiny – or so I felt to be true, hyper-alert and tingling in every cell, with every stride, with every breath.

As we advanced, our footsteps resounded on the damp pavement. My companions yammered and chattered, but I had no interest. Whatever it was they were going on about – well, I could not have cared less. And I had no intention of speaking, myself. Should I open my mouth, I feared, only her name would emerge – and I dared not lay her name before this assemblage, knowing their talents for crass insult and mockery as I did. It was a rigid silence, therefore, which I kept. We crossed Victoria Bridge over Hubberston Pill, into Milford, and the prattle receded momentarily as I heard the gentle lap and murmur of the waters flowing below. We climbed Hamilton Terrace as it rose above the berthed trawlers and above the docks, passed the War Monument, picked up Alan Zelinski at the Marshal (I glimpsed his spectral father through an open ground-floor window, bent over a table and scrutinizing something), then turned left onto the Great North Road, following it out of town till it became Steynton Road. The temperature was dropping. My breath clouded in the air. We were buzzing with excitement, all of us, whirring like little engines, yet, at the same time, terrified; for one of the great secrets of the world is that there is nothing more tender and vulnerable than the heart of a boy before the crust of age begins to form.

The grand talk of my cohorts in hope and folly grew ever more ridiculous, the better to cloak their escalating trepidation, their terror of failing abysmally at whatever romantic fancies were throbbing within their own addled minds. Still, I held my tongue. They prodded my ribs and banged me with their shoulders, cackling and croaking like a pack of crows. The entire trek, however, I maintained a mute and monkish discipline – a reverential and adoring hush, her image hovering in the frosty twilight before my eyes.

Finally, at long last, we arrived at the Grammar School; warm and panting from our exertions, red-cheeked and flushed and, in my case at any rate, a bit woozy. In fact, as we entered the building, I suddenly felt slightly faint, as if I might pass out. Several deep breaths, however – and I had righted the ship.

"Ready, lads?" queried Morgan. "Let's not make fools of ourselves."

Together we hung our coats and smoothed our hair, preparing to enter the arena of the great Christmas gala, steeling ourselves for a desperate, adolescent, Darwinian struggle for female favor.

And what followed was an evening of glittering youthful glory, which remains vivid and brilliant in remembrance, undoubtedly because such moments come so few and far between, and contrast so against the drab humdrum which congeals as the years wear on. And words are, for those rare times, an inadequate medium.

When I was younger, I aspired to be a writer. Two or three years after leaving Milford, I began to pen stories and sketches of my time there. Looking back now, I came upon several short sentences written during that period, a few years after this evening which occupied so much territory in the land of my memory: *Above all, it was a place of first things. A girl's hand in his. After the Christmas dance, he had waited for Adelyn outside the girl's cloakroom. He felt giddy and unsteady. She emerged out the door and glanced at him for a moment, then turned her head away. Stiffly, he walked to her and mumbled, "Can I walk you home?" She smiled, nodded shyly, and then they were holding hands and walking down the long tree-lined hill. It was very cold and she had her mittens on, but one was loose. "Your mitten's falling off," he said, and she pulled it off and shoved it into the pocket of her coat. Then he held her real hand, soft and warm. And later, when they reached her house, he pulled a tiny bud of mistletoe from his pocket and, beneath the yellow porch-light, brushed her lips with his.*

I never became a writer. I became something else, went a different way. In this brief snippet, however, I captured as true as I ever could the girl who first unlocked the door of my affections, the first girl who opened to me the door of her affections, the first girl I ever kissed. And in capturing it - my lips brushing hers in the pool of yellow light, my huge, fragile, boyish anxiety dissolving into something new and calm and ardent - I somehow preserved it unmarked and inviolate in my memory, while a thousand other events have long been forgotten and slipped away into nothing.

All of this – the odious Beeker, our daily winter ordeal outside the school, my first girlfriend, the magnificent holiday dance – sloshed around my mind as I stood upon the tee-box of this sly and duplicitous fourth hole. I felt giddy beyond words to have returned, and briefly considered telling Hugh so – till out of the corner of my eye I saw him yawning a cavernous yawn. *You'll be seeing her tonight*, I told myself - and struck a smooth 5-iron to the middle of the green – a neat and tidy shot. *Well*, I thought, *maybe all this mushy meditation is good for your game?*

Unaccountably, Hugh then hooked his 4-iron left into the tangled purgatory of gorse. I stared impassively after his ball. It was really quite a poor shot. Any mistake by Hugh on the course was unusual; an error of this magnitude, however, was almost incomprehensible, as unlikely as his three-putt on the first green. The immensity of the blunder immediately refocused my attention. Had my luck on this unkind hole inverted itself? Beneath his mask of unnatural tranquility, was the rekindling of our competition rattling old, imperturbable Hugh? Had the magnetic poles of the Earth reversed? Were all the fixed patterns of life unraveling?

Hugh threw me a quick glance, evidently expecting some sort of smart quip. I had resolved, however, to tiptoe passively past this sinister hole, and feared that remarking upon the peculiar fact that my ball was on the green while his was not might tempt fate too far, and cause me to four-putt like the star-crossed Beeker. I merely shrugged my shoulders, therefore, and kept my silence as we trod to the green, where I two-putted and, in contravention of all precedent, won the hole to go two up.

# RABBITS

The fog and mist and flat gray skies of winter passed, and suddenly the breezes blew warm and wildflowers began to blossom in the hedges, over and across the greening countryside, and along the narrow one-lane roads that wove and rose and fell along the coast. We cleaned our golf clubs, Hugh and I, and headed back to the course; only this time, with a purpose, and a new-found sense of duty weighing upon our shoulders. For we had been selected, the two of us, to join the club's "Rabbits" team.

The origin and meaning of the odd moniker is unknown to me, but the idea was simple enough. The Rabbits consisted of twelve golfers, each carrying a handicap over 18, who would contest the Rabbits of the other clubs in the tri-county region of Pembrokeshire, Carmarthenshire, and Cardiganshire, in match-play tournaments at their home courses, then likewise host these teams in return matches at our home course in Milford.

It was no trivial matter. Indeed, both Hugh and I considered it a significant undertaking, imbued with a vaguely martial aspect, as we were to wear vests with the colors and insignia of the Milford Club and had received, from the Rabbits' Captain – a portly man with unruly, sandy hair, and a bulbous, red-veined nose - a stern lecture in deportment, fealty to the rules, and the honor of the club.

In addition to upholding Milford's stature and reputation, we were expected to add youth and flair and vigor to the team – which otherwise consisted of three overweight duffers with pudgy hands and receding hairlines, four middle-aged men of varied but inconsistent proficiency, plus three stick-thin men of pallid complexion, lonely strands of hair waving on their noggins like isolated weeds in a bare field. We were the youngest and newest Milford Rabbits. And surely the most anxious. Without question, however, we were also the most optimistic of the bunch, so fresh and trusting were we then, in the early days of our enchantment with golf.

It was our misfortune, however, to have drawn the Rabbits of the Tenby club for our first match of the season. Tenby was a larger operation, a city with glamour and verve and punch in southwest Wales, and overall a more prestigious outfit. On the invisible pecking order of recognition and renown, the Tenby Rabbits occupied a higher realm, and a frown of concern crossed my brow when I learned of the fixture. It promised to be a daunting opening competition.

Sobered by the weight of our responsibilities, Hugh and I prepared like fanatics the week preceding the match. Between classes and over lunch, we rehearsed our swings, critiquing one another. After school, we rushed to the course. We parried back and forth the question of whether being the juniors of the team amounted to an advantage or a disadvantage. Every side of the matter was discussed and debated; the issue, however, remained undecided. As a hedge against uncertainty, however, I decided the most effective way to offset any demerits associated with my tender years would be to demonstrate ferocious power and icy fearlessness off the tee. In practice, therefore, I widened my stance, hardened myself to the results, and whirled my driver like the hammer of Thor, toying around the very edges of the sound barrier and anatomical physics. And occasionally, at unpredictable intervals, I indeed succeeded in launching mighty hurtling rockets straight and high down the fairway, and rejoiced inwardly with the certainty that such an exhibition would cow any opponent and erase any difference in years. Why work on putting or chipping? By the time he staggered to the green, my adversary would be an empty shell, awestruck, unable to concentrate, flapping in the wind, vaguely ashamed of his own effeminate game. Driving was the thing; long, powerful driving, the ball smacking off the face of the driver, hissing like a deadly projectile, my foe averting his eyes or licking his lips or squinting at his nails. Such was my vision of the upcoming contest.

Hugh seemed to have a somewhat lesser grasp upon the true scope of the drama that lay before us, however, for he ignored his driver, focused on rehearsing his tiresome, straight shots, and even spent extra time on putting. Putting! The most tiresome part of the game – to my mind, barely even part of the game. On the green, my attention forever wandered, like a stray dog or a lost child. I experimented with locking my knees like Palmer, cocking my wrists like Player, hunching behind the ball and staring coldly at the hole like Nicklaus; but nothing held my interest. I wanted to hit my driver. With Hugh, it was a different matter - he grew grave and quiet on the green, slinked stealthily around his ball like a feline, reading the line, then stroked it smoothly toward the hole. It was artful to watch, I admit. Especially in contrast to my general technique – which was to saunter up to the ball, take a glance, then swat it.

I knew I should pay more attention to my putting – every instructional book told me so, and Mr. Flynn as well – but it just didn't suit me. It was much like the fact that I did not like asparagus. A dozen scientific studies and nutritional consultants could have recommended that I eat asparagus. I might even have accepted, as a matter of established dietary science, that asparagus was good for me. I had no actual intention of eating asparagus, however, because I didn't like it. And if the central feature of golf had been nothing but putting – well, it would never have interested me. And certainly wouldn't have made me its captive. Luckily, however, the monotonous interludes spent on and around the green were but brief distractions from the deep pleasures of thrashing at the ball with my driver.

The match day arrived, overcast and colorless. Standard conditions for springtime golf in southwest Wales – winter was fading, but fitfully so. Early in the morning, my father drove us to the club and dropped us off with two of the older

Rabbits, with whom we then rode on to the Tenby course. I had carefully cleaned my clubs the night before, scrubbed the mud and dirt off my shoes, and packed a goodly supply of balls. I felt smart and neat in my bright new Milford Rabbits' vest, warm and dry beneath my rain jacket.

The two Rabbits in the front seat chatted and smoked as we wound along the twisted two-lane road on the northern boundary of the Haven, up through the center of the county, then down to Tenby on the coast of Carmarthen Bay. I noticed that neither of them had shaved, patchy gray stubble dotting their faces. They seemed to have something to do with fish, for they talked about recent catches and prices and trawlers and various boats that were having a difficult time. Hugh and I listened only a little, however, wrapped solemnly within our own thoughts as we were - when suddenly, the car turned off the road, ran up a gravel path toward a capacious two-story brick clubhouse perched on a promontory overlooking a broad beach, and ground to a halt. The gale off the bay assaulted us the moment we exited. Shortly thereafter, the matches were on.

As my adversary, I had drawn a white-haired man with eyebrows resembling untrimmed hedges and a large, well-groomed mustache, set off strikingly against a kit of brown knickers, a brown tweed jacket, and a brown plaid cap. In his eye as we headed to the first tee was something of a startled look – or maybe it was bemusement, I couldn't tell. Following our brief introduction, he had spoken not a word, and seemed either to regard conversation as extraneous to the matter at hand, which was golf, or as something unnecessary or unseemly between a person of his age and a person of mine. At first, I felt vaguely self-conscious, as if I should be carrying on some sort of banter and exchanging pleasantries. Since the white-haired fellow seemed uninterested, however, I simply hitched up my corduroy trousers like Palmer and pulled my cart ahead to the tee, where I surveyed the first hole a bit ostentatiously and awaited his arrival.

My bushy-browed foe had the honors. "A bit of wind today, eh boy?" he remarked finally, as he teed up. Indeed, there was a veritable tempest blasting across the course; above the dunes, I saw whitecaps bursting on the sea, and overhead the clouds fled past like speeding vessels racing in the air. A boat or two bobbed in the distance, but otherwise the water was empty, dull-green and forbidding. It was, I mused, not an ideal day for golf. Particularly my style of golf, for today's conditions demanded low, controlled, running shots hit beneath the wind, and steady putting, and great patience - none of which described my game in the slightest.

The Tenby man struck a low, short drive straight down the middle of the fairway, then stepped quickly away, manifestly pleased with himself. I noted that he had hit a fairway wood instead of his driver. I was not a disrespectful young man, but for some reason did not much care for this white-maned chap with the weathered, ruddy cheeks, overly-manicured mustache, and eyebrows spiked in permanent shock. I made something of a show, therefore, of drawing my driver from my bag, bending over to tee my ball, stepping away for a moment, then addressing the ball, taking my time and waggling my club as Arthur might have waggled Excalibur. To the right lay the dunes and the wide, sandy beach, urging a wild slice, but the gusts were blowing hard off the water, and suddenly I felt certain I would swing powerfully and unleash a long, straight, and flawless drive - which is precisely what I did, with no further preliminaries and not a glance at my opponent.

From that beginning, we struggled mercilessly back and forth throughout the long afternoon. I grew colder and flipped up my collar and huddled in my jacket. My white-haired opponent struck his low, controlled shots that ran down the fairways and up to the greens. Twice I played approaches from the sandy waste, and several times chipped from the dunes. I sank two putts more than twenty feet in length. I almost holed my tee shot on a short par three. I lost four balls, including three new ones my father had bought me; the poor, short-lived creatures. The sky threatened storm, at one point pelting us with a brief shower of hailstones. My rival's florid cheeks grew ever more red and rutted, and I could feel my own cheeks burning too, in the cruel, stabbing mistral. I saw the other Milford Rabbits trudging the fairways, heads down as they pulled their carts and pressed forward into the wind. Approaching the 17th tee, I spied Hugh standing doleful on the 15th green, his opponent bent over a putt. I looked at him questioningly, with raised eyebrows, but he only grimaced in reply.

We came at last to our final hole. It had been a bitter, unforgiving slugfest. Somehow, the pale-pelted gent and I were all square; he had played perfectly for the conditions, and I sensed he was astonished I was still in the match at all, much less even. It was also apparent that he was tiring. Accordingly, I made a point of striding rapidly ahead along the pebbled path running from the 17th green to the 18th tee box, which sat atop a steep mound. I pulled my cart swiftly up to the tee, meaning to goad the old-timer into hurrying his pace, and thereby further sap his fading resources, for the clever match-player seeks his advantages wherever they may be found.

It was my honors, and I was already preparing to tee-off when he slowly mounted the rise and came to rest, panting and flushed. "It's a hilly course, eh?" I observed curtly, then smashed a thunderous drive, which flew high and long into a momentary lull in the wind, before dropping softly onto the right side of the fairway – a superb drive, best of the day. I lingered a moment, accentuating the point. Without ado, my weary competitor then struck another of his short, straight drives, drilled beneath the gales, which had resumed in a fury. I set off up the fairway before his ball ceased rolling, speaking not a word and walking fast. The tight-mouthed codger lagged and dragged behind, mustache wilting.

We arrived at his ball, which sat nicely – rather primly, to my thinking, for I believed proper golf balls liked to be thumped hard, not swatted daintily - in the middle of the fairway. He calmly punched a 4-wood that landed short of the green and should have checked in the damp ground but, instead, skipped and rolled all the way to the back edge. Normally, this would have lifted my spirits and brought forth an inner smile. As fortune had it, however, today the pin was situated on the very back of the green, and thus his ball came to rest a mere 10 feet from the hole. It was a brilliant shot. Certainly, the Tenby Rabbit would make his par, and could even sink the birdie putt with no great difficulty. The irksome geezer gave me a brief and supercilious half-glance, in which I read more than a trace of smugness.

My big drive had come to rest on the right shoulder of the fairway, affording a perfect angle into the pin. Without hesitation, I pulled a 7-iron. It was a club in which I had great confidence. It was the first club I had hit under Mr. Flynn's tutelage. It hefted with a natural fit in my hands and had, over time, favored me with many a lovely strike. Settling over the shot, however, I was unable to shake the picture of my adversary's ball reposing so serenely near the pin, panicked on my downswing, and caught too much turf – then watched in quiet anguish as my ball took flight like a dying goose, droopy and weak, and barely made it to the front of the green before plummeting to earth. I could tell from where I stood on the fairway that I was at least 40 feet from the pin. I glared out over the heaving bay and swore hotly under my breath.

It was a wordless advance to the putting surface. The Tenby man circled around to the back, marked his ball with what struck me as an unseemly flourish, then went to tend the pin while I lined up my putt. It was a long one, indeed, forty feet if an inch, over humps and swales, across what seemed like acres of sodden grassland. The brick clubhouse stood on the overlook behind the green and the deserted beach lay below to the right, and the dark sea churned beyond. The wind blustered with such careless violence it was all I could do to remain upright over the ball, and through the misty sea-spray I discerned the faint glimmer of a lighthouse winking in the distance.

I blinked my eyes once and struck my putt – and watched – and, by the time the ball was halfway to the hole, I knew it was good. The muddy ball, the brave, beautiful, lion-hearted ball, scarred but unbroken by its forced march through the harsh seaside landscape, rolled and turned and tracked to the hole as calmly as if walking a familiar route to home, and my ruddy-faced foe lifted the pin, and the ball dropped neatly, with a flat, solid echo, dead into the center of the cup, just as I knew it would.

A deep and august silence followed, in which I seemed to take leave of my body and observe the miraculous tableaux from above. Suddenly, then, I was terribly tired. My snow-haired opponent's wooly eyebrows shot up to the top of his head and he gawked with disbelief or wrath – which, I could not tell – then, stunned, proceeded to miss his own birdie putt, thus losing the match. I smiled generously and shook his hand, replying, "Thank you, Sir," when he remarked (with a distinctly brittle edge?) upon my lucky winning stroke.

Then Hugh and I rode back to Milford in the twilight, warm and exhausted, having defeated the Tenby Rabbits 7 to 5, giving Milford an upset victory in its first match of the season. I dozed off on the way and only woke when we slowed and turned into the parking lot at the Milford club, where I saw my father standing in the fog, waiting to meet us, leaning against his car and smoking, illuminated by our headlights in the swirling gloom.

"How'd you do?" he asked, as I loaded my bag into the boot.

"We won," I said, and we shared a smile.

# A SHORT MESSAGE

L ate one dreary January evening I was at my computer, doing some research for a matter at work, when I decided to take a break and google "Milford Haven" once again. Every few months, I skimmed the internet in a perfunctory sort of way, generally turning up the same travel articles extolling the natural beauty of the Pembrokeshire Coast, the *Milford Mercury* webpage, government reports on shipping activity, agricultural production, council housing expansion projects, unemployment rates, or, in the way of variety, the latest official inquiries into the *Sea Empress* oil spill disaster and reports on the progress of clean-up efforts. Occasionally I might stumble across the site of a business with offices in Milford, a property agent or solicitor. Rarely, though, did I encounter anything of any real interest.

This evening, however, my searching lead me somewhere new; a bulletin board service containing a long list of towns throughout the United Kingdom. I ran through the list and located the Milford board. The concept was simple – if you wished to try to communicate with someone in your location of choice, or were seeking information related to that locale, you simply typed your query, clicked, and added it to the board for your location. Any reader wishing to respond was then free to do so. I was intrigued, and immediately began reading the posts.

It quickly became evident that the bulletin board served as a huge stew-pot, containing messages of almost every variety, from all kinds of people, with all manner of connections to Milford, composed in everything from the Queen's English to barely comprehensible doggerel: sailors who had manned minesweepers patrolling the Irish Sea from bases in the Haven during the war, wondering what had become of the pretty girls with whom they had danced so gaily on bright Saturday nights at the emporium; wanderers whose parents had emigrated from Milford long years past, to Australia or New Zealand or Canada, pleading hopefully for a word from an old school mate, or a neighbor, anyone at all in their unforgotten hometown; men searching for old flames, and vice versa; a woman soliciting information concerning her wayward husband, who she believed to be hiding out somewhere in Pembrokeshire, most likely with a red-headed slattern called Rita; a bitter exile pouring forth buckets of bilge on account of old, imagined wrongs perpetrated upon him as a child growing up in Milford; an aging lady who had celebrated the end of the war by wantonly and repeatedly trading kisses with a complete stranger on Hamilton Terrace, inquiring whether the monument stood there still, she having relocated to Portsmouth in 1954, but her brief moment of joyous public passion having survived in her memory with the freshness of the morning dew. I spent nearly an hour poring over all the posts, and all the responses, fascinated, then entered a brief message of my own – a message stating that I was one of the Americans who had lived in Milford during the construction of the Gulf refinery, and had attended the Grammar School. Then I listed several of my old friends, and invited anyone who remembered me to please respond.

It was late and I was tired, so I logged off after posting my missive.

I was feeling quite cheery about the way my little competition with Hugh was shaping up. It seemed churlish, however, to hoard my agreeable spirits as a purely private pleasure. Arriving at the fifth hole, therefore, I decided to elevate Hugh's sagging morale with some friendly conversation, and began by hurling in his direction a wide and hearty grin.

"Well," I announced amiably, prominently displaying my best smile, "If my memory is correct, this is two drives and a 4-wood for you."

I referred, of course, to my playing partner's lamentable lack of distance off the tee; for this was a full-blooded par-5, not one of his bland par-3's, or an uncomplicated par-4 easily subdued with a middling drive and an accurate approach. No, we were on my turf now. How many times had I humbled Hugh on this 5th hole with a booming drive, followed by a scorching fairway wood to the green? How many times had I observed with delight my second shot descending from the clouds to make landfall nearly pin high, within easy chipping distance – leaving poor Hugh abandoned forlornly back in the fairway, sizing up a 6-iron approach for his third? Many times, was the answer, many times indeed. Now all the tables were turned. It was time for his clever sarcasm on the previous holes to come home to roost. Accounts were about to be settled. I was two up and brimming with confidence.

Hugh declined to reciprocate my goodwill – perhaps questioning its sincerity, age having planted the seed of cynicism in his heart.

I was enjoying myself, however, and ignored the sour shadow upon his face. I loitered a bit on the tee, savoring the mental picture of my drive winging down the middle of the fairway and rising like a hawk, like an arrow, against the backdrop of the bright blue sky. The wind was still and I sensed a chance to seize complete command of the match.

"Ah well, three straight shots still beats two crooked ones," Hugh suddenly remarked casually, as if talking to himself, or thinking out loud.

I paused in my preparations; then, without a hint of warning, things went wobbly before my eyes. Aghast, I realized precisely what was happening, recognized the unmistakable signs of the spinning wheel of my golfing fortunes in motion. I should have stepped away, right then, and regrouped, allowed the disturbance to pass. My bravado, however, had rendered retreat from the tee impossible. And thus, despite knowing full well that I should on no account swing my club, I swung it anyway, and launched a hideous but immensely powerful hook high over the rough lining the left side of the 5th fairway, and well into the adjacent 6th fairway, where an old man wearing a gray sweater and pulling a small, rickety cart watched my ball roll past his, then stop. The elderly gentleman stared at my ball for a moment, then turned to gaze foggily back toward us on the 5th tee. In my shock, I had neglected to shout "Fore!" and so belatedly waved my hand in apology. The phlegmatic fellow replied with a wave of his own, then hunched his shoulders and shuffled on, pulling his cart behind.

Had a witness not been present, I would have assaulted Hugh then and there with my driver – a loose, languid backswing followed by a powerful blow to the center of the cranium. A delicious thought! And so just and fair! Three straight shots beating two crooked ones indeed, the sarcastic conniver!

As I was prevented by circumstances from committing the crime, however, I politely yielded the tee to Hugh, without acknowledging his presence. I uttered no word, nor the slightest sound. Instead, I stepped silently aside and devoted my attention to adjusting my belt. Hugh coughed and cleared his throat, as if something had lodged unexpectedly in his gullet – intending, no doubt, to voice some sardonic comment - then prepared to hit his drive. I turned my head and watched the old man in the gray sweater swat limply at his ball on the sixth fairway, as Hugh nudged his ball 200 yards or so straight down our fairway, then stalked off in pursuit of my errant and treacherous shot.

In the end, I had always been able to tolerate my grotesqueries – as I had come to think of them - because I knew that eventually I would advance to the next stop, a much happier stop, on the great transit of my golf game. This knowledge gave me peace and fortitude. And thus, upon arriving at my grossly disobedient ball, I saw that I had both a good lie and a perfectly clear shot to the green; and sensed that I had, in fact, moved on to the next station on that ever-revolving circuit. Patience, I had learned, always paid off. And my intuition proved correct – for after watching Hugh poke a 4-wood some 100 yards short of the green, I nonchalantly blistered a 3-wood that rode high into the now-windless sky, hung still at its apex like a photograph against a brilliant azure canvas, then dropped delicately to the earth just short of the front of the green. Thoughts of mayhem receded, as I perceived a renewed opportunity to put a stranglehold on the match.

"You get a better angle from over there," I informed Hugh, when we met back on the fairway. He lay 3, just off the green, after his wedge approach had carried long and faded a tad. "If I had to hit the ball straight every time I'd quit this game. I wouldn't be able to stay awake."

"Well, I did fancy a lay-down while you took your hike," he said.

"You didn't miss that shot while you were sleeping, though, did you?"

"Not too bad, I agree," he said. "I forgot you do manage a good shot every now and then. I guess I'd remember it better if it had happened more often."

I smiled at my friend's tart humor. The seedling of his laconic nature had grown into a mighty oak of ironic bemusement toward all events. Hugh had been born in Milford, grown up in Milford, been schooled in Milford, married in Milford, raised his children in Milford, made his business and career in Milford and, barring some dramatic and unforeseen deviation, would die, be eulogized at a funeral attended by lifelong friends, be buried in familiar ground, then repose contentedly forever in Milford. He was one of those individuals who belongs completely – mind, body, heart, and soul - to one single place, and can scarcely be imagined existing elsewhere; a plant adapted for one soil only, thriving heartily in its favored setting. His life, so I imagined, had been a clean, straight line; no smudges, no detours left or right, no curves, no angles, no hills, and certainly no dangerous precipices. It suited him perfectly, this fixedness, this smooth synchronicity, into which he dovetailed with absolute precision.

Yet again, my thoughts turned to what my course might have been had I contrived somehow to remain; if Milford had also been my home for all these many years. I wondered whether my restless, seeking nature could have found satisfaction in its placid, recurrent routines, or whether its true appeal had always been that it represented a world I could never actually inhabit, and which served mainly as a concept, a construct of some idyllic, unattainable existence. Why had I never been able to escape its tug upon my memory? Or simply put it away on a shelf in the cupboard, along with the myriad other memories of my youth, memories of other places I had lived, other people I had known, other things I had seen and done? Such questions led nowhere, however. Whatever the cause, for whatever reason, I returned always, in my mind, to the deep and tranquil waters of the Haven, and my little band of friends who took me in as if I were a native, born and bred.

I arrived at my ball, which lay a mere five feet short of the green and seemed to radiate a transcendent aura; so placid, so untroubled, that it might have been placed there by a pair of tender, loving hands, rather than having flown sizzling through the air like a bullet. What a shot! I reflected, congratulating myself on my golfing prowess.

I glanced at Hugh, but his gaze was turned in the other direction. I had a perfect lie, more suited for a putt than a chip, and therefore proceeded insouciantly to putt the ball to within a foot of the flagstick. Hugh's chip ran well past the cup, and I tapped in for a birdie, to win the hole and go three up. I announced the score in a loud, clear voice, but Hugh pretended to pay no attention – it was evident I had inflicted a telling wound.

We dropped our putters back into our bags and grabbed our carts. As we departed the fifth green and made our way along the lumpy path toward the 6th tee, he gave a mischievous little laugh.

"I had to let you win that one, you know" he said. "You wouldn't have thought it worth coming back if you didn't win that hole."

"You don't begrudge me a birdie on my favorite hole, do you?" I asked. "You sound jealous. You shouldn't be jealous after all this time."

Hugh laughed again. "Jealous? But does everyone in America play golf like you?"

"We have short attention spans," I said. "We need constant stimulation."

He nodded as if pondering a sage observation. "Then why play golf? Why not auto racing, or bungee jumping, or something like that?"

"Ah well, maybe you're right, I've been playing the wrong game. But think of all the entertainment you would have missed. You should thank me for having broadened your horizons."

We both laughed together. It was a bit of a stroll to the 6th tee and we trod slowly along the path, pulling our carts side by side.

"Will Alan Zelinski be coming tonight, do you think?" I asked.

"I don't know," Hugh said. "I haven't seen Alan in ages. I'm not sure he even lives here anymore. Why?"

"No reason, really. He was just the first friend I had when we moved here, and I'd like to see him again."

"I think he got into something with computers," Hugh said, frowning. "I think I remember he went away to work, then came back when his mother got ill. Then she died and the hotel closed down, and I don't know what he did then. He always kept to himself, you know."

I nodded. It wasn't much in the way of news.

I didn't tell him I was still curious about the baffling and secretive Mr. Zelinski.

We walked on toward the next tee. The clouds rolled past overhead and the wind was gentle and warm, and a red and black tanker sat placidly in the Haven in the distance like a huge animal, a leviathan, enjoying the sun in its favorite watering hole.

# AN EAGLE REMEMBERED

Above my desk at home hangs a picture of my mother, myself, my two brothers, and my sister, gathered on a grassy outcrop high above a rocky shoreline, somewhere along the Pembrokeshire coast. My father liked to take us touring on the weekends, and we could have been near St. Anne's Head, or the Stack Rocks, or Strumble, or farther up the coast toward St. David's. It is impossible to tell, and the photograph reveals no clues, except that a small crescent of pebbles and sand is visible at the water's edge below, framed by a semi-circle of jagged crags jutting up menacingly from the foaming sea.

Each of us wears a coat, and my mother is holding my youngest brother up for the camera. An unhappy look sits upon his face - a three-year old who would rather be back home. A blue stocking cap sits crookedly atop my head and frothy whitecaps are visible in the background, crashing into the cliffs. It looks and feels like late autumn, just before winter's full onslaught. The sky is gray, the grass has lost its color, the wind tussles my mother's dark brown hair, and my sister looks pale and chilled. Likely, there was a cold wind blowing – once, years later, my mother remarked that she had never one day been warm in Milford. She never spoke poorly of our time there, and I do believe she enjoyed the adventure of it. She was not despondent when we left, however. It was, in many ways, an isolated and rugged place.

I perused this photograph once again as I logged on late one raw, rainy night in early February, checking my mail before going to bed. I was scrolling mechanically through my messages, only half-reading and preoccupied by a matter at work, when suddenly I sat up at attention and frowned. Displayed before me on the screen was a message from an unknown address, titled *'Old Mates From Milford.'* I leaned back in my chair, eyes fixed upon the words. Had someone actually responded to my inquiry of two weeks past? Who? For several moments, I remained motionless, save for the fingers of my left hand tapping as I thought. Then I opened the message: *Hello, do you remember me? You better! You knew me as Adamski but now I am Caron Nolan, and still in Milford. Do you remember us? Write me back, I can't wait to catch up with you after all this time – I've not forgotten you!*

As a result of my impressive birdie on the 5<sup>th</sup> hole, I retained the honors on the 6<sup>th</sup> tee. By this point, I was positively stuffed with confidence – and why not, three up with four to play, and having just dealt my opponent a devastating psychic blow? The augers were beaming brightly, like festive lights. Hugh, of course, maintained his air of bemused distraction. I knew, however, that he wished keenly to win the match. He kept glancing furtively toward the sky, as if hoping for rain, and perhaps a premature and inconclusive end to the contest. He couldn't lose the match if it was rained out – instead, he could claim a draw amid a quintessential Pembrokeshire downpour, and avoid the ignominy of defeat at the hands of the returning Yank. Nary a drop of moisture was in sight, however, only huge billowy clouds, like impish, airborne islands, skimming across a placid blue expanse.

The sun was climbing higher and the day was warming. As was my mood, which was altogether chipper. I considered proposing that Hugh hit his drive from the ladies' tee – the 6th was another par-5, the longest hole on the course, in fact, and uphill as well – but concluded such a gesture was unnecessary and might constitute poor form. It would more than suffice simply to thrash him sternly here, on the 6th hole, and thereby claim an irrefutable victory in our dramatic reunion match.

Bending to tee my ball, I shot him a swift look. He was staring inquisitively at the head of his driver, seemingly deep in thought. It occurred to me that I ought to be able to hit a thunderous drive, then perhaps reach the green in just two shots. For, aside from its length, hole number 6 was actually rather benign, with ample driving space, no vales of gorse and muck, no brambles, no water, no trees. Why, once upon a time, my father had even managed to eagle this hole, I recalled. My father – he of the violent, self-tutored swing! I knew the miracle had occurred because I had witnessed it with my own eyes. In fact, it stood out in my memory with its own gilded glow, like a picture preserved in a lustrous frame.

It had been a dull, pewter-skied Sunday afternoon, clouds lingering listlessly overhead, periodic rumbles of low thunder in the distance. Hugh and I had just putted out when my father, playing in a foursome behind us, struck a 3-wood from the fairway that pierced the air like a cross-bow's bolt and, incredibly, came to rest a mere three feet from the pin, where Hugh and I had just been standing. I turned back down the fairway to see my father poised in his high, contorted follow-through, held up my hands to show how close his ball lay, then remained to watch him hole the putt. Long years of awful golf were thus redeemed, and my father never forgot his eagle on the 6th hole. Whenever thereafter we spoke of golf in Milford, he resurrected the feat anew, verified that I still remembered the glorious occasion, and recounted in minute detail the weather conditions, the club choice, the purity at impact, the flight of the ball, and its slow roll toward the cup.

What if I eagled the 6th hole now myself! What a story! What a tale, if I could duplicate his wondrous feat! What a brilliant idea! And so easily within reach; one of my long drives, another fiery 3-wood to the green, then a bit of luck with the putt – yes, I could do it, of course I could do it! And bring a wonderful sort of memento back to my father in the bargain! And, furthermore, not incidentally, thereby irrevocably doom my cunning companion, who would likely be playing a middle-iron into the green for his third shot. What a dandy way to wrap up my grand triumph! Stepping up to the ball, I felt assured the happy outcome was all but pre-ordained, and must surely come to pass.

I paused for a moment, taking in the turquoise midday sky and ruminating upon its untroubled loveliness.

Abruptly, however, my serenity was punctured. "Do you remember when your father eagled this hole?" Hugh asked suddenly, just as I was taking my stance. Only a moment earlier he had been gazing sleepily at the road behind the tee, paying no attention to anything at all. What was up?

"No," I replied warily.

"No?" he cried, eyes round in shock. "Of course you re-member – he hit a 3-wood from the middle of the fairway and it almost went in the hole! We were on the green there, and his ball rolled up and you looked back and waved at him. We watched him make the putt! You must remember that!"

"Why?" I asked.

"Why what?"

"Why do you remember my father eagling this hole? What does that have to do with anything?"

"Well, I just remembered it," he said defensively. "You really don't remember your Dad's eagle?"

"Not really," I replied, perhaps a bit defensively myself, a bit clipped, then prepared again to hit my drive. What gambit was this? He was such a crafty character, subtle and conniving. Some ruse was afoot – he had no more just happened to recall my father's eagle than I might just happen to recall Newton's Third Principle of Thermodynamics before striking a putt. I was no dupe for his tricks, however - whatever they were.

But suddenly then, and inexplicably, I felt a rush of guilt over having denied any recollection of my father's greatest golfing triumph, as if I had betrayed him in some indirect and convoluted way.

My mind was wandering – had I hit my drive yet? Focus! I stepped away from the ball.

"Okay, I remember now," I said to Hugh.

"Good!" he exclaimed, sighing with relief. "Good, good, thank goodness - You don't want to forget something like your father making an eagle on the longest hole on the course!"

I fixed my gaze again upon the ball.

"That would be unforgiveable," Hugh observed.

I waggled my driver. *The heads on these things certainly are big these days*, I remarked to myself.

"Wouldn't it be something if you eagled it too!" Hugh piped up again, a quiver of excitement in his voice, as if he would enjoy the feat far more than I, or my father, possibly could. I shifted my eyes and stabbed him with a glare. "Oh yes," he mumbled, trailing off, "what a thing that would be, what a story ... oh my, yes, what a story, what a tale to tell, indeed ..."

I had been camped on the tee for some time now, looking at the ball, stepping away, looking at the ball, stepping away, waggling, glowering, hesitating. My father's eagle notwithstanding, I had to hit my shot. I set my teeth, therefore, and shoved Hugh into the background, where he seemed to continue muttering while gazing idly across the empty road behind us. I exhaled slowly, wound my left shoulder loosely beneath my chin, shifted my weight onto my right leg, cocked my wrists, followed neatly with a downswing, turning my hips and shifting my weight back onto the left, lagged the club, drove my right shoulder smoothly through, stayed behind the ball, heard a smack that was neat and precise, and produced my finest drive of the day, the small white ball jetting straight and high down the middle of the fairway, soaring like a raptor on the hunt, then daintily drawing and descending to rest, with a kind of lordly aplomb, upon the bright green sunlit expanse recumbent before us.

I stood motionless, watching the ball arc and land, and did not want to move, for I felt within a spell, balanced on a narrow ledge in a narrow space between time; the years and the people, the doings and omissions of the past mingling with the present, old stale doldrums stirred by a fresh wind, and the moldy film of loss dissolving, as the bright, round pellet rocketed with a hiss against the burnished sky, hung momentarily above the rolling course and the Haven's softly lapping waters, then fell silently onto a spot upon the lush fairway - exactly where, perhaps, my father had stood waggling his 3-wood thirty-plus years ago, preparing to swing his lashing swing and claim his great achievement.

I turned to Hugh and saw him smiling at me eyes aglow, thin hair streaming in the breeze, as if he were privy to the selfsame spell, the identical transport, and had stepped alongside me through this slit in time to experience as well its strange, nostalgic happiness.

I vacated the tee and coolly twirled my driver.

"Long and straight at the same time?" said Hugh. "Well, I am mildly impressed." He leaned forward and placed his tee, then stood back up and looked down the fairway. "I suppose I'm glad you came back, even it was just to show me up."

"I didn't need to come all the way back here just to show you up," I replied. "I did that plenty in the old days. I guess I just got stuck on this place. Don't know why." I shrugged my shoulders and smiled.

Hugh struck his drive with his typical lack of show. We departed the tee and took off strolling down the fairway. His expression turned pensive for a moment. "Bloody ridiculous place to get stuck on," he then said playfully. "We thought you Yanks would never leave, then all of a sudden here you turn up again!"

I stared at the open message on the screen. I read it again, then once again, more slowly. I recognized its sender immediately; knew her well, in fact - and had not forgotten her either. I sat at the computer thinking, remembering - pulling from a dusty file the story behind the sender, a story that wound through several families in Milford, and through the Marshal House and into my young life there as well, and this story unfolded now in my memory as if written in a book before my eyes.

Like so many things in Britain during that time, the tale that lay on the other side of the message on my screen was connected to the war. More particularly, it was connected to Hitler's decimation of Poland. That some link should exist between my days in Milford, and Germany's invasion of Poland and the ensuing great conflagration of the twentieth century, may seem perhaps more than remote – nonetheless, however, such a link existed, and was real.

Following Poland's demise, the utter destruction of the Polish Army, and the massive displacement and killing of huge numbers of civilians, the British government launched an intensive recruitment campaign among refugees and survivors. Fervor was not lacking. Large numbers of Poles flocked to join the Brits in resistance against the Nazis, and Britain put these Poles to work in all manner of roles, dangerous and mundane, throughout Eastern Europe, the Baltic, and elsewhere.

Some of these Poles had experience in aviation and became affiliated with the RAF, soon assembling into their own flying unit – which became known as the 304 Squadron. In 1942, the Polish 304 was assigned to an RAF base set up in Dale, on the Pembrokeshire waterway's northwest coast. There, the 304's mission was to hunt German submarines, protect Allied convoys, and harass enemy shipping. In this way did a sizeable cadre of Polish pilots, mechanics, and support personnel come to the Haven in the middle of the war.

Of course, the Allies eventually prevailed. But the devastation in Poland had been vast in every conceivable way.

As a consequence, thousands of the Poles who had served with the British had neither land nor home to reclaim, nor any person awaiting their return – and, in any event, not all were eager to repatriate to a country falling under the heel of the Red Army and Stalin. Thus, when peace eventually arrived, large numbers of these Poles who had made common cause with Britain found themselves completely alone and adrift, as bereft as orphans.

The Brits knew they owed a debt, however, and undertook to pay it. In 1946, the government established something called the Polish Resettlement Corps, intended to aid the relocation of these now-rootless Polish soldiers into various communities throughout the United Kingdom, and assist them in fashioning new lives. Thousands took part in the program. By the time it was cancelled, the record-keepers estimate as many as 150,000 Poles had been resettled throughout the UK – including in Milford Haven.

One of the Poles who made his way to the quiet little fishing village was Stefan Zelinski, my friend Alan Zelinski's brooding step-father. When I later learned the story of the Poles in Milford, I formed at least a small sense of what that grave, haunted figure perhaps saw, or thought he saw, or wanted to see, staring out the windows of the Marshal on dark nights, alone in the sitting room with only a small lamp burning, and the possible origin of the long, thin scar that marked his face.

I recall particularly one of our afternoon forays along the tracks above Scotch Bay – it was late on a lovely September day, and I had once again asked Alan Zelinski what his father had done in the war. "I told you I don't really know," he had replied testily. "He doesn't talk about it and we don't really ask him," then returning his gaze across the bay's unruffled waters. Indifferent Alan seemed to lack any deeper interest in the matter. Persistent as I was when something snagged my imagination, however, I wasn't about to abandon my investigation so easily.

A few days later, therefore, after school, I arranged to find Mrs. Zelinski alone, tending her small garden back of the hotel, and turned the conversation toward the subject of the war; which, I told her untruthfully, we were studying in History. "Was Mr. Zelinski in the war?" I queried innocently. "Alan said he was." Mrs. Zelinski was examining and snipping at her roses. "Well, in a way," she replied absently. "He did something secret – he always said he took an oath not to talk about it, and he never has."

I scarcely believed my ears. It seemed inconceivable she could have lived with the man this long - his mysterious scar, the limp in his gait, his pensive, preoccupied deportment - without being driven mad by curiosity as to exactly what it was he had done that required the taking of an oath! I felt compelled, therefore, to probe a bit further. "Maybe he'd tell me what he did?" I suggested. "He probably didn't take any oaths to the Americans." Mrs. Zelinski turned from her roses to fix me with a stare. "I doubt it," she said flatly, conveying quite clearly that pursuing this line of inquiry was worse than hopeless and would, more to the point, incur her displeasure. And, indeed, something in her tone and look did persuade me to foreclose further efforts at fleshing out the shrouded wartime exploits of the veiled and enigmatic Mr. Zelinski.

It continued to baffle me, however, how she and Alan managed to restrain themselves from interrogating the cryptic gentleman until he cracked. I would have given it a try, at least.

Also relocated to Milford through the resettlement program was another Pole, a man named Pyotr Adamski. This refugee ex-soldier had been an airplane mechanic with the 304 Squadron when it operated out of Dale, before moving on to another posting. At the end of the war, however, he determined to return to the Pembroke coast. Something about it had made an impression – whether the natural beauty, the peace and tranquility of the waters, some particular person, some indefinable quality of air and light and feel, is unknown. Return, however, he did. And, while Stefan Zelinski married the widowed owner of the Marshal House – whose first husband, I later learned, had himself perished early in the conflict – and thus took up a new career as a hotelier, Pyotr Adamski rented a small room in Milford and went to work on the fishing trawlers, as the fishing industry was thriving anew and offered steady employment to any man willing to work. Pyotr was willing to work, and so work he did, on the trawlers. And once he began working, he began saving a little money. Then a little more, and a little more. And then, in 1950, Pyotr married a local girl. In 1952, they had a daughter, their only child, named Caron. And this happened to be the same year in which I was born myself, across the ocean in America.

And now, these stories – the one belonging to the crafter of the message upon my computer screen, and the other to its reader - arrive at a point of intersection. Through those cloudy currents that direct these kinds of things, it transpired that, sixteen years later, by which time Pyotr had his own boat, and my father was building the next-to-last of the great Milford refineries, I came to be idling in early spring with a cohort of lunkish pals alongside the muddy field behind the Grammar School, watching the Junior girls' field hockey team host Haverfordwest, a light rain drizzling off the brim of my cap, when my attention lit upon a lithe, brown-haired figure streaking sprite-like across the pitch, maneuvering the ball effortlessly with her stick. Something about the scene and the action caught my eye and my interest and, as I studied more closely, it was obvious no one had any chance of catching or defending this brown-haired girl. She raced and swerved and zigged and zagged at a speed and with a grace that stood out as if illuminated by a spotlight, far outclassing the other players. I stared and squinted, and forgot the drizzle. Perhaps it was the wet hair streaming out behind her shoulders. Or her dark, glinting eyes, intently tracking the ball and scouting the options, shifting left, shifting right. It doesn't matter - something drew me in, and I followed her course across the pitch as she skipped in and out and around her opponents' flailing sticks, then suddenly drove the ball hard past the goalie and threw her hands to the sky in exultation. And, as the ball distended the back of the net, I too experienced the odd sensation of wanting to throw my hands to the sky in celebration.

I concluded we must be in different classes, for I had never seen her before.

"Who is that girl?" I asked Tommy Ryan, who was standing beside me, periodically kicking me in the shins then smiling sweetly when I glowered at him.

Ryan frowned his freckled brow and peered across the field. "Which one?" he asked. I pointed at the girl with the glistening dark hair. "That one," I said. "The girl who just scored."

Ryan had lost interest, however, and was now twisting Aiden Lloyd's ear, so I turned to Mickey Dunn and asked, "Who is that girl who scored the goal?"

"Pole," said Dunn.

His response made no sense to me. "What?" I asked.

"Pole," repeated Dunn.

At that point, Ryan jumped on Dunn's back and both of them, Dunn and Ryan, fell to the ground, wrestling.

The match soon ended, but my eyes followed the girl whose nickname, I had by then deduced, was evidently 'Pole,' as she departed the field. Gone was the taut, feral intensity. Now she was all smiles and laughs with her team-mates. Tufts of grass jutted from her hair and mud streaked her face; she seemed to shimmer with a splendid, healthy glow, a luster left behind from effort and energy expended in a joyous pursuit, the happiness of a special skill flexed and spent. I stared as she passed, heading to the changing room. For some reason, I hoped she might glance my way. She didn't, however, and I watched her disappear.

Once the players were gone, and the spectators taking their leave, Dunn and Ryan finally ceased their wrestling and rose from the ground, filthy and disheveled. Ryan looked at me and asked, "What?"

My thoughts had remained upon the dark-haired girl, and I looked back at Ryan stupidly. "What?" I repeated dully.

Ryan looked at Dunn. "Americans are thick," he said.

I could only grin at his pronouncement, rendered with such certitude – for such was Tommy Ryan's playful, endearing nature that it was impossible to take serious offense at anything he said, though during the course of a typical day he said innumerable outrageous things to everyone.

The girl they called Pole was gone, along with the rest of the team. I walked home with my band of friends, alongside the Haven on Hamilton Terrace, then across the bridge to Hakin as it grew grey and cold, and home to Wellington Road, where later I climbed into my warm bed and thought about the girl I had seen and listened to the rain outside until I fell asleep.

Dumbstruck and still, I sat before my computer – as if Ryan had been spot on point and the sad truth was that Americans were, in fact, thick. My finger hovered above the mouse. The message from Caron Adamski – the girl they called 'Pole' – had instantly unleashed a tumbling torrent of images, and spirited me back: running after school on a bitter, frosty day, chasing across the playing fields behind the gymnasium, grabbing her scarf, my cap falling to the ground, our breath gusting out like clouds into the frigid air; rambling with

friends on the grass-thick cliffs above Newgale as the waves
barrel onto the wide, sandy shore and our youthful laughter
carries away on the gentle, ever-present wind; riding the bus
to a party at Sam Winter's house in Dale, where we hold
hands and watch the red and blue sailboats bob on the water
and kiss innocently when it grows dark.

Then it is late afternoon on another day, a close, cloying,
late-spring day. To celebrate the impending completion of the
refinery, after which we would all be leaving, the Americans
had organized a baseball game on a makeshift field behind
the Esso Club. Caron sits on a hill rising behind home plate,
with the sun falling red at her back. Our days in Milford are
waning and I keep glancing at her from my position at second
base with an empty feeling, so contrary to the cheeriness of
the other Americans, who are brimming with excitement at
the prospect of returning home. My youngest brother, only
four, wanders up to her clutching his Teddy Bear and briefly
plops down at her side, then wanders off, and she lifts her
hand in a wave as the scarlet sun descends and the game
comes to an end - and I sense my life in Milford ebbing away,
receding like the tide in the Haven itself.

In my helplessness and perplexity, I grow tongue-tied and
speak little as we walk to Waterloo Square after the game,
where she bears home to the left across the bridge, and I bear
home to the right. After dinner that evening, I retreat to my
room and open the window and sit looking out at the night,
smelling the waters of the Haven as a peaceful wind brushes
across my face, watching the yellow moon hover serene and
severe above the quiet countryside, and wishing we never had

to leave. I know with a harsh, brittle, certainty that I will never see these people again, never see this place again, and will suffer with my heart rooted in this little corner of the world while the rest of me travels far away.

And then, of course, before I knew it, like the sudden, too-quick fall of darkness after a drab, sluggish afternoon, we were gone from Milford. Gone, I mourned, forever. I had been sick and queasy the entire day, forcing my mind to other things, trivial things, humming, playing songs in my head, kicking a ball against the wall out back, feeling my stomach tighten and squirm and wanting – in truth – to cry discreetly. And then, just as the ragged clouds pasted across the sky began to gray, the taxi arrived. With a terrible, nightmarish clarity, I heard its tires crunch the gravel as it turned into our drive and came to a stop. I stood rigid in the foyer as the driver's knock sounded on the door and echoed loudly – too loudly, too conclusively, too final - through the empty house. Then everything happened swiftly and with cold precision.

My father opened the door and twilight flooded in. I looked outside and saw the cab. My father helped the driver load our luggage, then called for us to come. I walked out of our house and then we were in the taxi as it backed out of the drive, crunching the gravel again, turned right at Waterloo Square, descended the hill out of Hakin, crossed over Victoria Bridge, and delivered us to the station.

My father and I carried our bags onto the train. I stepped out alone then, onto the platform, where a group of my friends had gathered to see me off. I stared numbly at their faces and fumbled at words I never could recall, then boarded again and, as the train rumbled and drew away, leaned far out the window, as far as possible, as far as desperately possible into the thick, gray dusk, until my life in Milford shrank and vanished and was no more. I craned my neck, peered achingly into the distance, until there was nothing left to see, only blackness. Then I finally gave up, withdrew back into our compartment, into my seat, and sank quietly into a deep, dark pool as we sped on through the long night to London, and back to America.

No, I had not forgotten. I remembered it all, and had never forgotten.

I replied to Caron with a long message, then went to bed and dreamed again of Milford; a happy dream, in which I returned and stepped off the train on a brilliant, crisp, and shimmering morning, into the waiting arms of my smiling troupe of friends.

Of course, I proceeded to lose the 6th hole. My exemplary drive quickly became a topped 5-wood - frustratingly, my second of the day - followed by a badly sliced 8-iron, a chip into a bunker, two sand shots out and two putts, for an 8. Sadly, there would be no regaling my father with epic tales of replicating his great triumph. Instead, Hugh won the hole with a bogie and I was now just two up with three holes to play.

I sensed the tide was turning.

# A HEAVEN IN A
# WILDFLOWER

The refinery rose inexorably from the scoured ground and weeks passed into months and my life in Milford flourished and took root. There were long, languid springtime walks along the trails and farm roads winding through the hills to Little Haven, to Sandy Haven, to Broad Haven, to St. Brides, and picnics in thick, damp clover overlooking wide beaches and rolling waves. Their names, the names of these beautiful beaches, themselves roll from the tongue, as if made for speaking aloud: Whitesands, Freshwater, West Angle, Swanlake – each calling forth images of sunlight glinting off calm, untroubled water, birds and breeze and warmth. Among the verges bordering the country lanes, wildflowers ran riot: red campion, white stitchwort, bluebells and cowslip, ragged robin, spring squill – the very sounds of the beguiling words working a kind

of intoxication in my mind, the romance and transport becoming complete as Adelyn draws an aster from the banks
outside Sandy Haven and turns to me with her enigmatic
smile, quoting a poem we had studied in class that week: *To
see a world in a grain of sand and a heaven in a wildflower ...*
then releases the aster to the wind as the waves fashion a
kind of music in my ears.

"I like poetry," she told me, confiding, once we began revealing more of ourselves, that she often played at working
rhymes of her own.

"Show them to me?" I had asked. "Can I read them?"

She touched her finger to my lips and smiled. "Not yet."

"What are they about?"

"Not yet."

At lunch, we played cricket on the field behind the
school, where awaiting my turn at bat I reclined by her
side in the grass, or in a circle with my pals Dunn and
McAllister and the others, the ground soft and rich with
the sensuous fragrance of things awakening and stirring to
life. Rainy afternoons drove us to the Esso Club for snooker
and darts. We launched nighttime sorties for fish and chips
at a dim-lit shop back off Charles Street, owned by a man
who had lost an eye in the war, and pursued trysts with the
girls at the theatre or at someone's house, where the parents
took their dinner in the kitchen while we played records in
the parlor. There was walking home from school oblivious
to blustery showers, the rain being such a common thing
that only upon arriving and puddling on our front stoops
would we realize we were soaking through and through.

There were countless clever pranks perpetrated in class, and romantic fancies born and obliterated and born again, and gauzy dreams dreamt by young people just old enough to feel something impatient pushing inside, something incipient, germinating, something straining for light and air; young people reaching after things they could neither name nor even clearly discern, but still too young to know the true nature and cost of all these bright objects, or the weight that eventually bears down heavy upon every beautiful conception. And so, trodding the quiet paths beside the sea, we watched the spring rise around us from the dreadful despond of winter and dreamed and hoped and wished and wanted, agonized, despaired, and laughed and questioned, opening to the world like buds opening to the sun, and utterly, equally, defenseless.

In between rugby and cricket, we played soccer, where Tommy Ryan reigned supreme - top boy by far, and lording in his supremacy. Skills sublime – a left-footer - none able to strip him of the ball; and myself least of all, of course, new to the game. Quick-tongued Ryan's devilish blue eyes sparkle with wicked pleasure as he runs me in circles, jabs me with barbs and insults, sends me this way and that way, tripping and stumbling over my own feet with his feints and tricks till, in maddened desperation, I resort simply to kicking mindlessly at his legs. After soccer we ran track, long-jumped, high-jumped, and threw the javelin and the discus, and Mickey Dunn even pole-vaulted with an old aluminum pole so stiff no one else could even get airborne. The school's annual Games Day arrived in May, and my father left work early to watch me run the hurdles and the sprints. I repaid his interest by smashing at high speed into the very first hurdle and tumbling ignominiously to the ground, but redeemed myself later with a strong leg in the relays. Jenkins won the discus with ease and Morgan dominated the long-jump and high-jump. Caron claimed an armload of ribbons in the girl's events, and Dunn triumphed in the pole vault, as the only entrant actually managing to elevate above the earth.

In the fall we returned to rugby, as if renewing a holy ritual. A thin curtain of rain is swirling and Jenkins, red-faced and wide-eyed, charges down the pitch, fixing me with a hard stare, lowering his head and challenging me to tackle. He's the largest boy in class and a thousand calculations race through my mind as I weigh my options and their consequences. Then I shudder with the bone-clattering impact as our frames collide and collapse together to the muddy turf, from which we rise wordlessly and – for myself, at least - shaken and woozy. Sam Winter and Jenkins and McAllister battle thick in the scrum, hooker and props. Lewis Morgan cool and composed at the number eight, and stout Joe Stack, built like a beer-barrel, manning his post at scrum half, feeding the ball to the halfbacks, through Reece and Griffiths and Dunn, and finally out to me on the wing. I sprint toward the goal line, wind and raindrops spattering my face, exuberant, buzzing with youth and joy, skipping and darting and eluding a swarm of tacklers to score - *A try for the Yanks!* Our demented coach cackles gleefully, as if reproaching the locals in disgust. Then it is warm and close in the changing room, filled with steam from the showers, and the hot water washes the mud and dirt away and we are clean again and weary.

Wending our way home after practice, I stoically endure the zealot McAllister rattling on and on as usual, extolling incessantly the superior qualities of Glasgow Rangers football, giving worshipful voice yet again to his fanatical passion. Till eventually we come to Waterloo Square and all go our separate ways, to our separate homes, and I to mine.

So the days slipped by and I fell without effort into the small daily routines of the town. Of themselves, standing alone, they meant nothing, but steadily they began to accumulate into a fullness. Our youth group hikes the narrow country byways to quiet villages, where the rocks and sand and sea sweep endless to the horizon and seem outside of time and every other constraint. Without warning, ferocious squalls erupt in drenching downpours, as we dash for shelter beneath a copse of willow beside the road, or huddle tight beneath the eaves of an old stone church hidden in a grove of ash. Then the sudden downpour ceases and out we rush to renew our jaunt, while the world glows wet and green.

On Fridays we stay late after school to play soccer in the gym, then trudge home with our duffel bags over our shoulders, exhaling contrails of smoke into the crisp night air. Sometimes the girls remain behind as well and we all walk home together. Always, the lights from the tankers shimmer off the calm waters of the Haven and the tugs skim silently alongside like noiseless protectors, their red and blue lights winking and blinking.

"Where are you going when you leave?" asked McAllister one clear, still evening as we approached the War Monument on Hamilton Terrace.

I was looking across the dappled blackness of the water, and said, "I don't know."

"He's not going anywhere," declared Adelyn.

I smiled ruefully.

"He can't stay here. He can't play football," said McAllister.

"Just like Rangers," I replied, and McAllister hit me hard in the arm, in the same spot where he had hit me only the day before, and the day before that as well, in response to some other caustic comment concerning his beloved team. I am unable ever to think of him without hearing anew his gleeful chirp, arriving at my door in the mornings: *Rangers won last night!* Followed by the names of the goal-scorers, their respective goal tallies for the season, Rangers' present home and away record, their standing in the league, a comparison of their position at this point in the season relative to their position at the same point last season and the season before, the manager's prospects, and on and on without surcease, forever sporting his Rangers scarf and vigilant for another opportunity to punch me in the arm.

"Liverpool's a real team," Morgan stated, as if it were a known and established fact.

"City," retorted Jenkins.

"The Dallas Cowboys," I said, and we all chortled into the bright, cold, starry night as we climbed the hill from Victoria Bridge to Waterloo Square.

The seventh hole was a subtle masterpiece of deceit. A mere 120 yards in length, yet it always seemed to me that only blind good fortune could possibly guide a tee shot to safety upon its tiny green. A stone wall (the same weather-beaten, lichen-caked wall which separated the 4th green from the 5th tee) crossed at an angle in front of the green some 110 yards from the tee. Between the tee and this stone wall lay nothing but muck and mire. Beyond the wall the ground rose ever so slightly toward the green, and was therefore a bit drier, but only just a bit.

The tee was positioned squarely into the prevailing winds, which were fickle in the extreme. As a consequence, the choice of club varied from day to day, from hour to hour, and even from minute to minute. I had seen men slash fairway woods into gusting gales, then bite their lips in disbelieving resignation, as the wind lifted their shots high into the howling sky and short of the green, short even of the stone wall. I had observed other men, on other days, fly 9-irons deep into the prickly hawthorn beyond the green. I could testify to men skulling their balls like rifle shots, hard into the unmovable wall, striking the mottled rock with a sickening sound like thumping a melon, then careening off at wild angles.

Once, caddying for a thin, taciturn, elderly club member known to me only as Mr. Grubbin, I had witnessed a ball struck into the onrushing wind with a driver, brought to a dead halt and elevated vertically into the air, then dropped directly down on top of the old stone wall, from whence it bounced again to an incredible height, before finally splatting almost obscenely into the muck, on the muddy tee-side. Grim and gray-pallored Mr. Grubbin had followed the bizarre trajectory of his shot with narrowed eyes, but turned not so much as a glance my way when its flight reached its heart-rending finale. He merely readjusted his threadbare charcoal tweed jacket, which he habitually wore with all three buttons buttoned, and hacked wordlessly through the soggy terrain toward an ugly triple-bogey. While it was impossible to distinguish his good humor from his bad humor, this incident seemed to have soured Mr. Grubbin's round, however, for at its conclusion he dispensed a tip that was miserly even by his pinched and grudging standards.

Well-acquainted with its diabolical randomness, therefore, I perceived the seventh hole as a paradigm of unpredictability, a metaphor for the indiscernible design which inhabits the center of the world; and thus, like so many other things, completely impervious to individual will and intent. Oh yes, I warned myself, I knew the handiwork of fate, and saw its sign on this short, deceptive, seventh hole.

The inexperienced player bestrides the tee and spies the green so near, just right over there beyond the low wall – why, you could throw the ball that far! - puffs out his imagination, and envisions finessing a short iron snug up against the pin, or at least safely within two-putt range. This naïve dupe fails, however, to detect the rising, falling, ever-shifting currents, or the graveyard of sodden earth between the tee and the wall, or the bracken lurking back of the green, beckoning the ball into its embrace like a shameless, irresistible vixen. No, this prideful sport perceives only a blandly uncomplicated hole reclining open and unprotected before him, completely pliable to his desires. The myopic fool fails to comprehend that here, on this diabolical seventh hole, he can do nothing more than launch his ball, put it into flight; at which point other forces will assume control, render him a mere spectator, and toy blithely with his shot before depositing it into some resting place of their own random choosing, reducing his careful plans to tatters fluttering in the gale.

Thus do the fates of golf spin their inscrutable web.

I was no poor fool, however, no naïve dupe. I had been in this place before, and was not some callow neophyte ripe for disappointment. Nor, of course, was Hugh. He teed his ball, therefore, then stood upright, stretching his back and squinting at the green. "What do you think?" he asked, following a moment of contemplation.

"I don't think anything at all," I replied. "This hole doesn't need any thinking. Looks like a simple shot to me."

Hugh slid his eyes in my direction. I stared impassively into the distance. Just minutes earlier, on the sixth green, it had been still and quiet. Now, however, on the seventh tee, it felt as though we were standing in a wind tunnel. The howling inrush thrust our hair straight up, rippled the sleeves of our jackets, flapped our trousers.

"No more than a 9," I continued helpfully – suddenly aware I was practically shouting, so ferociously was the wind assaulting our faces. "Easy hole!"

Sheets of clouds raced past overhead as if pursued by hungry hounds.

Hugh shifted his gaze back to the green, then pulled a 4-iron from his bag. "I'm disappointed you've become such an unreliable chap," he said. "And to think I used to defend you when everyone else said bad things about the Yanks."

"Well, most of them didn't much like it here," I replied, in a weak defense.

Hugh struck a perfect shot that rode high against the incoming gusts, held its line true, then descended casually to the green, four feet from the pin. It was, under the conditions, a stunningly perfect stroke. He turned my way with a satisfied look and raised his eyebrows. "Now, what were you saying?"

I shook my head absently. "I didn't say anything."

"Well, sorry I didn't take your advice," he said, bending down to retrieve his tee. "I should take your advice more often."

"Take my advice?" I replied, feigning surprise, as if unsure I had offered any advice at all – I would never, for example, have recommended a 9-iron into this unforgiving tempest.

"Oh, yes," he said, clipped and sardonic. "Of course I should have hit the 9 – sorry. Next time I will."

I hesitated as Hugh stepped off the tee, and did not move; for suddenly a thought had struck my mind. I pondered the notion briefly – then smiled, because Hugh had just presented me, unwittingly, with an opportunity to play a subtle but potent psychological card. For his tongue-in-cheek contrition at having ignored my advice concerning club selection had caused me to recall a specific event from our past. And his mock apology for having spurned my suggestion fit precisely into the incident. Acute student of match-play and the human subconscious that I was, I perceived immediately how to turn his sarcastic retort around and, perhaps, regain my faltering footing. I chose not to reply forthwith, however, but allowed his words to float in the air. Finally, with a regretful sigh, I said "Well, but you never did take my advice, did you?"

"What do you mean?" Hugh asked quickly.

*He's become an awfully suspicious guy*, I thought cagily.

Again, I withheld any response and made him wait, to simmer and puzzle.

"Nothing really," I said finally. "Just a general observation."

I stepped to the tee and took a few practice swings. In my hands, I held a 5-iron. As I nipped the turf and gazed toward the green, I could sense Hugh's agitation.

"Well," I resumed nonchalantly, in a helpful tone, "I was just thinking about the Christmas dance that year. You remember - I kept telling you to ask Marianne Morris if you could walk her home, but you were too afraid? The prettiest girl in the class was yours for the asking, but you lost your nerve and didn't take my advice. I remembered that just now, when you said you should take my advice more often. You should have taken my advice back then, really." I concluded with a shake of my head, as if underlining the sad verity that the woeful mistakes of the past cannot be corrected, and opportunities forfeited disappear forever.

"Rubbish! Complete rubbish!" snapped Hugh peevishly, thrusting his arms skyward. "Thank God you don't live here! I'd have to listen to you itemize my failures on a daily basis."

"No, not all your failures," I replied blandly. "Just your major ones, like not walking Marianne Morris home when you had the chance. I mean, Marianne Morris, for God's sake! It might have changed your life, you never know!"

He screwed his face up in scorn.

*Excellent!* I observed; I had struck a nerve – one I knew was there because we all had it, and we all knew we all had it. Marianne Morris had been the acknowledged beauty of our class – of the entire school, in truth - and the remote object of all the boys' most keen and poignant longings. Hugh had admired her from afar, was given to speaking of her in language rosy and poetic; but had never actually exchanged with her a word of any significance, nor a glance nor a nod of greeting. In fact, there was no evidence she was even aware of his existence, or could have distinguished him from the hundred other pimply, doting louts who circled in her orbit. Somehow, however, Hugh had devised a fantastical scheme back then to ask Marianne if he could walk her home after the Christmas dance - just as I planned to approach the celestial Adelyn with the identical hopeful supplication.

His mad design had, it seemed, been a long time forming. And, as the gala approached, he expounded ever more bravely upon his prospects. It was true, in fact, that Marianne was unattached at the time, with no known favorite. It was also true, therefore, that Hugh's chances were indeed equal to anyone's, at least in a purely theoretical sense. His hypothesis had not yet been disproven, of course – but then, any hypothesis that is never tested is never disproven. And, as it is but a skip and a jump from hope to conviction, particularly among the young and feather-brained, Hugh had persuaded himself as the Yuletide jubilee neared that his success was assured. In the final days leading up to the great celebration his delusion peaked, and he became absolutely certain his odds were no longer merely level with the rest of the field; oh no, he had suddenly become the only one with any prospects at all.

His friends, of course, urged him onward toward the precipice.

I have described the volcanic gasses that bubbled through my veins and limbs and nerves as the festive soiree approached; how I gave hours to planning every angle and tactic, analyzing every variable foreseeable to the human mind, concerning my dream of walking Adelyn homeward beneath the stars. I may have brought more fervor to the exercise than the rest of my motley adolescent peers, but all the boys were in some state of agitation, each harbored some secret, unvoiced fancy, some hope like a jewel aglitter in a hidden case.

Even so, however, even measured against the general backdrop of this acute and sweaty mixture of teenage desires and fears, it is difficult to describe the extremity of Hugh's psychic condition that evening; for in truth he was beyond planning – why plan for that which is guaranteed? He was beyond that paralyzing indecision which rots the normal school-boy's amorous aspirations. He was beyond self-doubt, which is merely a waste of time for those who have already seen the future. No – Hugh now occupied some otherworldly plane of immaculate serenity as we strode through town, bore left, and climbed the long hill toward the Grammar School, huffing and puffing into the wintry air. Wrapped inside the dense cotton of unreality, he kept throwing me confident looks, bold looks, looks that cried, "I know you envy me, but it is not my fault and I cannot help it!" I thought it perhaps a bit premature, given that Marianne seemed as removed from his grasp as the moon, but made no comment. While I was cautiously hopeful I might, indeed, depart the dance with Adelyn's hand in mine, I could conceive of literally no circumstance under which Hugh's weeks-long hallucination could possibly come true. A cruel finale awaited, I felt certain. In the end, however, that was his affair. We all must take responsibility for our irrational flights, our follies, whether we be mere school-boys or far enough into our years to know better. At the time, however, I did not dwell overmuch on such notions – instead, I simply glanced his way, shook my head, then forgot him. Hugh's fate concerned me far less than my own. By the time we arrived at the Grammar School, therefore, I was giving him absolutely no thought, no thought at all.

Sifting through memories back to that night, Marianne was, indeed, extravagantly radiant and untouchable. Her halo of golden hair, which surrounded and framed, as if on display, her fresh, glowing countenance and flushed red cheeks, glistened in the reflected light. She smiled sweetly at each suitor, laughed gaily, but seemed to fix her dark eyes, her enchanting black-and-indigo eyes, on no one in particular; and least of all on poor Hugh.

And what an awful, awful transformation in my doomed companion! The assured and confident Romeo had been abandoned outside in the parking lot - while in his place some stumbling, hapless wretch had entered the holiday dance! Like a skittish feline, he prowled and circled and darted and feinted - all the while, beneath a weirdly beetled brow, his eyes never straying from the figure of his goddess. He approached then withdrew, he colored beet-red and broke out in a sweat; his feral brow gleamed with a kind of waxen, cadaverous sheen, moist and baking beneath the hot, unforgiving lights. We urged him, we prodded him – *Ask her to dance!* I implored. *Go talk to her!* I exhorted, *Ask her! This is your chance!* He was helpless, however, unnerved and turned to mush, his absurdity bared for all to see. It was slow torture; ending only when the party was over, and the girls emerged from their cloakroom into the smoky, star-filled night, and, just as I shuffled tentatively toward Adelyn to ask if I might walk her home, Marianne emerged in the center of a group of chattering girls and swept grandly past poor, ridiculous Hugh, leaving him stranded mute and forsaken in the parking lot, like an old, forgotten, fence-post.

And thus had ended Hugh's spectacular delusion, alone and forlorn outside the cloakroom, utterly unseen by the girl of his dreams.

At one time or another, to one degree of another, all of us fell under Marianne's supernatural spell; and thus, before departing Milford, inevitably, I was smitten too. We boys were like subjects drawn helplessly to this winsome sovereign. Mine, though, was only a brief bewitchment. Always, my affections returned happily to Adelyn, my first girlfriend, who seemed to fit so true; just as my memory, in later years, was to scroll back time again to the yellow light at her door, her timorous smile, her blue eyes shimmering like miniature stars as I lifted the sprig of mistletoe from my pocket, to hold above her head. And recalling Hugh's silly, paper-thin fantasies at that long-ago Christmas dance led me to ponder her again now, here on the seventh tee, and wonder what I could possibly say to her at the dinner this evening - what words could ever be the right ones? What words might she have for me?

"What are you waiting for?" Hugh barked suddenly, quashing my woolly contemplations. "It took you thirty years to come back here – is it going to take you another thirty to hit your bloody shot?"

I gave him a flat, disinterested look.

"And you're wrong with all that Marianne stuff," he added vociferously. "That's ancient history! Ancient!"

His protest barely registered, however. It was, indeed, time to hit my shot. Accordingly, without much in the way of conscious mental engagement, more-or-less automatically, I hoisted my club and skulled my ball like a bullet at the top of the stony wall, heard it strike with horrible violent force and, with a sort of clinical detachment, observed it whistle wildly off to the right into a nasty clump of bristling briars.

I gave Hugh another noncommittal look, this one conveying supreme unconcern, as if amused that some interloper had just hijacked my club and perpetrated that grotesque travesty of a golf shot. It might even have been true. In fact, it was entirely possible that I was no longer even on the course at all; for resurrecting Hugh's great failure and my great happiness at the Christmas extravaganza had unbalanced me completely. Would she remember our walk down the long tree-lined hill in the cold night air, or had she forgotten it completely with the passage of years? Was I being a fool – as big a fool in my own way as Hugh had been all those years ago – at least a pubescent teenager has an excuse for acting the fool – should I have come back at all?

"Have you been practicing that shot in America? I don't remember seeing that one before," asked Hugh, with the tone of a person keeping a checklist, peering toward the wall and frowning, as if trying to make out my ball in the patch where it had come to rest.

I smiled dully, the way a dunce might smile. My mind was in a daze. I shrugged and started forward, into the mud and muck.

Once again, of course, Hugh won the hole. After my appalling 5-iron, it was merely a formality. I was now just one up, with two holes to go, and had lost my moorings.

At some unrecognized point, the years become the color of fog, and lose definition. They pass like thin shadows in the dusk – you see them, or think you see them, but can describe none of their particulars. Traversing these years is like walking through a dim vapor, in which most things appear the same with every step, and only occasionally does something especially large or bright or immediate leap forth to command attention. What blazed so brightly is now ordinary. Infinite prospects have narrowed. Choices have been made and passage-ways have closed and destinations have been fixed.

But, ah, how different it is in the days of youth!

We read Wordsworth in English Literature that springtime, and his clouds trailing glory swept palpably before my eyes and the wind in their wake rustled my hair – and I knew these clouds because I lived beneath them in Milford. Our tiny town was but a speck amid an enormous panorama of rolling farms, green hills, narrow winding roads, shady groves, broad tawny beaches, limestone cliffs, and churning waves. The sky was filled with soaring sea-birds, crying their endless, riotous cries. The ground was thick and verdant, mossy and soft beneath the tread – the tread of our little band as we set off from the youth club, roving across the hills to some secluded spot above the sea, there to linger over a picnic lunch and loll the day away in cool springtime clover, laughing and jesting before tramping home together in the blue twilight; the tread of our feet just beyond the reach of the waves that rolled and spread across the sand at Broad Haven, as we skipped between their watery fingers and ran along the dunes. Our happiness was innocent and unforced – we did not even know it for what it was, it seemed to flow so naturally from the ground, into the atmosphere we breathed, and into and throughout our young lives. Only in retrospect does it fully reveal itself – this rare shelter, this rare time, which we inhabited as strangers to sorrow, strangers to loss and disappointment, strangers to loneliness and fear, companions together without artifice. We stood with our feet upon the stark brink marking the demise of youth, and did not know it.

At certain times, however, I sensed it, sensed something ending, something leaving, something looming – even as McAllister feverishly reported yet another Rangers score, as Adelyn took my hand to swing our arms in tandem, or as we sat silently together, watching the waves tumble while the sun sank and the moon rose like a bright signal high above the ocean. In those moments I knew, with a deepening sadness, that soon I would be crossing that ocean and entering the unknown, while my friends remained behind in the Haven.

There are many ways to look at life, if you have a mind that tends toward symbolism and metaphor. One way is to imagine that life is like a river. It is a much-used image, but for good reason. You paddle a frail dinghy along the current. At first, the paddling is easy, so effortless you barely even realize you are moving, and do not recognize the frailty of your craft. Gradually, however, it dawns upon you that the river is passing. And then, it further dawns upon you that somewhere it must end – in fact, its terminus may even be in sight. Regardless of whether you have enjoyed the passage thus far, you are now in no particular hurry for it to end. You wish to paddle more slowly. You may even experience a poignant jolt, ruminating upon the swiftness of the journey, its irreversibility, and how many things might have been done differently along the way. At the beginning, however, when first you embark in your own little boat, paddling and maneuvering amid the currents, the excitement and newness is so consuming that there is no thought at all of where, or when, or if, the river stops – you simply paddle joyfully and are convinced, if you even consider it, that all time lays ahead of you, that you will ride the river, that there is, quite simply, no end, not ever. And this is how we felt back then in Milford Haven.

Except I knew I had to leave.

Every now and then, in a bumbling way, I tried to broach the painful matter with Adelyn.

"I'm going to have to leave, you know," I would say, as the time grew closer. "Probably in July. I don't want to, but I'll have to."

She would fall quiet and squeeze my hand. "But you'll come back?"

I knew inside the only real answer was *No*, but "Yes," I said, "Yes, as soon as I can."

She would squeeze my hand again, give me a small, trusting smile, then look away.

*But how?* I thought. *How?*

There is a second photograph, which I also look at often. It hangs beside my desk in the corner. Below it, propped against the wall, stands a driver that Mr. Flynn gave me on the day before we departed Milford, when my father took us by the club to say goodbye. It was late on a scruffy afternoon, the end of a dull, sour-feeling day, and the ponderous clouds skulking overhead were like rags in need of a wash – as if the rain, when it came, would fall oily and soiled.

I stood in Mr. Flynn's dark, musty shop while he muttered and rummaged back in the shadows, among his bins of clubs. Suddenly, he pulled forth a brand new Spalding driver, a jet-black sheen gleaming on its wide, deep head. He held it out to me, told me to take it, and to remember everything he had taught me. I received the club into my hands as if receiving a holy relic, a shard of the Cross, or John the Baptist's femur. Mr. Flynn was a big, gruff man, and I knew that giving me this new driver, accompanied by his few sparse words, was a great token of affection, and I felt my throat tightening and my mind repeating the concentrated, hopeless thought, that I did not want to leave. "You've been a good caddy and have some promise if you keep at it," he said in his thick brogue, reaching to shake my hand, his own hand huge and rough and calloused. "When you win the Open, remember where you learned to play. And who taught you."

Then we stepped outside the shop, where he knelt to one knee as my sister put her arm across his enormous shoulder and my brother and I stood to either side so my father could snap a final picture. I recall him smelling of beer and cigarettes, and needing a shave. In the picture he is displaying a hearty grin, but it looks somehow forced on his creased and ruddy face, and I remember he seemed sad himself at the time, brusque and awkward.

My father took the photograph, then we stepped away as he spoke with Mr. Flynn alone. I was staring across the parking lot toward the first tee, and down the familiar fairway into the fading light.

My father called – I realized I had been clutching Mr. Flynn's driver to my chest and breathing hard - and Mr. Flynn stepped back towards his shop with his hands on his hips, his vast midriff bulging beneath a stained, white turtleneck sweater. We clambered into the car and pulled out of the parking lot. I turned my head as we eased onto the Dale Road and saw him for the last time, motionless before his shop, hands still upon his hips, feet planted wide, the shop door open behind him and his great bulk filling its entrance, the parking lot empty. And then he was gone.

As I sat down to my computer, I studied the farewell photograph, and the black Spalding driver resting beneath it in the corner. The old driver resembled now some artifact, a primitive precursor of modern golf technology - its glossy black sheen long gone dull, its deep face dry and cracking. *Why haven't you taken better care of it?* I chastised myself, feeling I owed Mr. Flynn an apology. I resolved to oil the wood more often, lest it crack beyond repair. Then I turned my attention back to the computer.

Every two or three days now, Caron and I were exchanging messages. And, through her, I was also reconnecting with more old friends. It had a distinctly miraculous quality, as if I had stumbled upon a portal through which it was possible to communicate with memory-spirits across chasms of time and distance, and not only in occasional pools of dream in the deep of sleep. Suddenly, they lived and breathed, more real each day, gaining in substance with each traded message, and their numbers ever growing: Gwen Thomas, a software designer living south of London – we had belonged to the youth group that met every other Thursday evening, rambled up and down the countryside in the summertime, and went caroling through the neighborhoods at Christmas. I remembered huddling outside a row of council houses on a freezing December night, singing carols and watching the steam escape in clouds from her mouth as she leaned into me for warmth, her blonde hair tickling my cold, numb cheek. Marie Kellar, daughter of my father's Canadian golfing partner, who had also worked on the Gulf refinery, now ensconced on a farm outside Houston; Mickey Dunn, hero of the pole-vault; Sam Winter, son of a boat-builder in Dale; and Phillip Price, my old seat-mate, now selling medical supplies in New Zealand.

Phillip and I had shared a double-desk directly behind Jenkins and Sam Winter in class, from where we devoted vast amounts of time to tweaking their ears and otherwise annoying them behind the teacher's back; Jenkins growing red with sputtering anger and threatening to beat us brutally after school, Sam maintaining his trademark silent composure and ignoring us. He had something of a sphinx-like quality, even as a boy, did Sam Winter. Imperturbable. Serene, as if he had already mapped the pathway of his life, sidestepped the welter of doubt, distraction, and second-guessing that bedevils most young people, and intended no more than to put one foot ahead of the other down that path, all else being fluff and triviality. A tweak on the ear from a prankish kid behind him in class? Nothing at all, less irritating than a bug.

After work, I hurried home to my computer. My in-box was an invisible door, opening from my ordinary life to the sweet green hills and compatriots of my youth. No longer was my time in Milford like some blurred and wrinkled snapshot buried at the bottom of a drawer, more indistinct with each passing day. Just the opposite – now it quickened nightly, before my eyes, beneath my fingertips, and Mr. Flynn observed it all from the photograph on the wall, his plaintive smile somehow not so melancholy.

The reunion was set for the last weekend in May, and the weeks passed swiftly. Winter gave way to spring and then, as suddenly as we had departed Milford on that long-ago July dusk, I was boarding an airplane for London. On a bright, breezy early morning in May, therefore, with patches of clouds dotting the sky, I landed at Gatwick. My next destination was Milford Haven.

# THE HARDY
# PEMBROKESHIRE
# CHARACTER

The eighth hole is, it must be said, a dull and uninteresting pause on the otherwise engrossing circuit of the course. Scouring the dusty corners and lint-cluttered byways of remembrance, the eighth hole yields up but a single enduring memory. It is a strong one, however, which evokes a chill even today. The signal event took place on a gray, blustery Sunday afternoon in the late reaches of winter. I can peg the point in the season with some accuracy because, although I was wearing lined trousers and a jacket over top of my sweater, my hands were not completely numb and my ears were not afire, as would have been the case in winter's spectral depths, rather than its final, dwindling days. It was cold, but no longer glacial. The course was sodden, for it had rained hard earlier, and the sky was threatening squalls as the wind drove angry clouds in from the sea.

Hugh and I were matched up with a father-and-son pair from Carmarthan, who were visiting friends in Milford for the weekend. The thing I recall with a kind of photographic clarity concerning the father, a friendly, talkative, red-faced chap, is that he had a single long fiber of black hair sprouting from the bridge of his nose; and, not surprisingly, given its eye-catching oddness, this lone and lonely filament comprised by far the most striking feature of his countenance. I struggled mightily not to gawk at this ludicrous strand of hair, as to which the gentleman himself seemed thoroughly oblivious. It must have been a full two or three inches in length, though, and fluttered merrily in the breeze. I asked Hugh if he saw it. Of course, he replied curtly, as if I had insulted his powers of observation - he wasn't blind.

The son was a dour, impassive boy with an assortment of colorful pimples, in various stages of ripeness. His sole vocalization consisted of shouting "Right!" in a cocksure military timbre, after everyone had struck their tee balls, on every hole. It was, I thought, a bit ridiculous, as if he imagined himself auditioning for a role as Sergeant Major in a movie set in some picturesque outpost of the Empire – *Zulu*, perhaps, which I had recently seen at the cinema. I concluded he must also be completely oblivious to the fact his father had a preposterously long black sprig burgeoning from the bridge of his nose. Had I been this boy, and had it been my father displaying such an outlandish peculiarity, I certainly would have brought it to his attention, and enlisted all available resources – mother, siblings, friends and neighbors, mirrors, tweezers – to do something about it. In any event, the father chatted amiably, the boy cried "Right," every time we teed off, and we progressed nicely through our round until eventually arriving at the eighth hole.

I was last to mount the tee. The other three – Hugh, the father, the son - had already hit their drives. A thin veil of fine, light drizzle hung in the air, lending the scene a vaporous and dreamlike appearance. Peering forward, I noticed a foursome making its way in our direction up the third fairway, which ran parallel to the eighth, on the left. I paid them no mind, however, as they seemed well out of harm's way, far left of where my drive should land. I flicked my gaze down our fairway, the eighth, took a final sighting, and commenced my backswing.

Just as I began to lift the club, however, I detected, from the corner of my eye, one figure from the approaching foursome veering off abruptly toward the strip of rough that ran between and separated our two fairways. This figure was striding with great purpose, and it seemed to me he might even be planning to continue marching on through the strip of rough and into the eighth fairway, our fairway. In the briefest of milliseconds, these perceptions flashed through my mind. Then suddenly I found myself into my downswing, unable to stop - despite my instant and frightening certainty that I was actually going to send my ball screaming directly at that lone approaching form.

And, of course, that is precisely what ensued. My driver struck with a thunderous crack. The ball took off like a bolt of lightning, arcing long and high and hooking steadily, inexorably, ever farther to the left, homing in like a laser on that one oncoming golfer.

I gaped, speechless – and then it got worse, exponentially worse.

For, with a shock that made my stomach go soft, I suddenly realized the target of this deadly missile was none other than Mr. Flynn himself, now well into the strip of rough and heading toward the edge of the eighth fairway, completely unaware of my golf ball bearing down upon him like an angel of death.

I saw Mr. Flynn, I saw my ball in flight, and I saw with horrid clarity their inevitable meeting point. I croaked a weak "Fore!" which accomplished nothing beyond causing the wretched Carmarthenshire boy to glance at me in puzzlement, as my throttled call drifted away on the wind. My ball continued hurtling toward its predestined encounter with Mr. Flynn, and I stood frozen with dread.

Then, just as the ball began to dip toward his lumbering frame, Mr. Flynn halted and placed his left hand upon his hip, the ball shot through the triangular opening between his bent arm and his torso, and skidded past him into the rough, as he stood over his own ball and blithely pondered his approach to the 3rd green. He never saw my ball, never heard it pass through the crook of his arm or scythe into the rough, never heard my feeble bleat of warning.

I stood paralyzed, blinking, tingling down my spine. Funny lights danced before my eyes. My legs felt weak and useless as towels. "Right!" the pimpled Carmarthan urchin grunted smartly. Then we all moved off the tee and headed down the eighth fairway.

I passed Mr. Flynn as he approached the 3rd green, and smiled wanly in his direction. I don't believe he noticed me, though; he was squinting into the sky as if trying to read some message in the clouds. I continued on by, therefore, and never mentioned the ghastly affair. But the horror of it was fixed forever in my memory, and remained the only event of note I could recall concerning the otherwise bland, unmemorable eighth hole.

Just as I had never forgotten this close encounter with disaster, neither, I was sure, had Hugh. My sad showing on the 7th hole had given him the honors on the 8th and he smiled – no, it was actually more of a leer – as he took a practice swing. "Well, two up, is it?" he inquired casually.

I gave him a flinty look. "One," I replied.

"One?" He feigned surprise. "Is that all? Are you sure?"

"Quite sure."

"Well." He waggled his driver back and forth. "Well, well," he muttered. "Well, well, well, how did that happen?"

He swung his drowsy, effortless swing and sent his ball low and straight, down the middle of the fairway but a goodly distance short of the green. Stepping off the tee, he pulled up a large grin and remarked, "What a lovely day for golf, eh?" His vapid observation sealed my certainty, my absolute certainty, that he remembered perfectly well that awful day on which I had almost decapitated Mr. Flynn with a murderous hook launched from this very same tee - and thus I resolved to ignore every syllable that fell from his mouth, and his very existence as well, if possible. I had no intention of revealing that I, too, at this very moment, was reliving once again every terrifying detail of that brush with calamity. Nothing would gift Hugh more glee than for me to acknowledge that now, today, gazing down the fairway, I again discerned, as in a morbid nightmare, the shadowy bulk of Mr. Flynn plodding toward me, blindly ignorant of that ill-struck projectile streaking his way.

"Easiest drive on the course," offered Hugh, prodding at my silence.

"By far," I replied.

I scanned the waiting fairway.

"Plenty of room to the left," Hugh continued.

I declined to renew our conversation. Instead, I set my jaw and cleared my mind, then hammered a dreadfully wayward hook that easily cleared the band of rough separating the 8th and 3rd fairways, where Mr. Flynn had escaped grievous injury those many years before, made landfall hard in the middle of the 3rd fairway, skipped and ran, and eventually rolled to a halt on its far side, at least 80 yards left of where I had been aiming. There was dead silence. I stood on the tee, empty of thought and glassy-eyed, as if sedated but not yet prone. It was a complete debacle of a shot.

"Right!" cried Hugh crisply, as he took off marching down the fairway.

Winter could be dark and gloomy in the Haven, and drive the spirit into dismal corners. It wasn't so much a matter of temperature – for a bitterly cold day beneath a brilliant, blue sky can have a bracing and even inspirational effect. And, while it certainly got quite cold enough for me – Florida-bred as I was - the fact was that the warming influence of the Gulf Stream did spare us the kinds of ferocious extremes common to other northern climes on similar latitudes. It was less an issue of where, precisely, the thermometer stood, and more a matter of the combined effects of temperature, precipitation (by which I mean rain), clouds, and wind. And the sheer constancy of it, with seemingly endless days of the same wet, penetrating bluster. It required no effort at all to be an optimist and a dreamer in the soft splendor of summer in the Haven. In the middle of winter, however, by the twelfth or fifteenth week of it, a certain grimness of mind began to accumulate.

It wasn't a total waste, however. For, as unsuitable a canvas as the winters may have been for sentimental reverie and sun-spackled daydreaming, the bleak season did provide the perfect backdrop for a different kind of experience, one with which I soon became familiar. It was an experience which even today sounds like something only a crackpot could embrace – and that is, running cross-country three times a week, regardless of the weather; which fluctuated between uncomfortable and awful, but soaked and miserable either way.

It commenced upon our return from the Christmas holiday, and required only a t-shirt, shorts, and what I learned to call plimsolls - a/k/a sneakers. No base layers, no gore-tex, no water-repellant shoes, no thermal accoutrements, all of which would be standard issue today. Accompanied, no doubt, by petitions of protest, righteous condemnation on social media, and threats of legal action, even, by outraged parents and child welfare activists. No, it was different back then in Milford – back then, it was a t-shirt, shorts, and plimsolls, nothing more. My mother swore I was going to catch pneumonia. My father's attitude was that when you live in Rome, you do as the Romans. I heard the acidic Beeker, returning a yard implement to our house one Saturday in January, remark that it was the "most dumb-assed idea" he'd ever heard, which he intended to convey directly to the Headmaster – it was an idle threat, however, voiced simply because Beeker enjoyed complaining.

Whatever it was, it was an ordeal, the memory of which time has failed to soften. Later, I came to grasp it was connected to something larger, something that had a distinct and venerable local meaning - the building of The Hardy Pembrokeshire Character. A phrase I learned was part of the vocabulary of the place, and a concept that resided in all aspects of its tough, resilient psyche.

"Well, now," the coach of the Junior XV might comment, particularly following a drubbing. "You boys are Pembrokeshire boys, and I expect a bit more in the way of the Pembrokeshire character than what I saw today."

An article in the local newspaper concerning the Haverfordwest amateur team's match against Swansea might remark upon 'that hardiness of character for which Pembrokeshire is so noted.'

Even the Captain of the Rabbits team, welcoming myself and Hugh to the team, made some allusion to the fact that as we were Pembrokeshire-bred (well, only loosely, in my case) we were required to show the proper Pembrokeshire spine.

There was, I ultimately realized, a sort of unique provincial pride tied up in the notion of ruggedness, of mind, spirit, and body – qualities which are not made lounging at warm firesides, upon soft pillows. No ... it requires something a bit different to produce The Hardy Pembrokeshire Character. Something a bit more ... extreme? Something such as ... running cross-country in the foulest of weather, in the absolute, desolate, dead of winter?

My theorizing, of course, only came later, with detachment. At the beginning, setting off into a light January sleet on my first run, there was only a kind of astonishment. It had no reference point in my background or prior life, and I can still barely describe the disbelieving state of my mind. Freezing rain, the trees stripped bare as skeletons, the sky a hopeless, colorless ash. Wind slashing our faces like glass, hands and feet like blocks of ice. Unprotected against the elements, utterly undefended, fully exposed to icy gales, through frosted pastures, up and down hills and along slick, winding roadways, under polar skies, drenched then numbed, numbed then drenched again, storm-whipped, glaciated, bone-chilled. Every other day, throughout the bleak and blasted winter, stride after punishing stride... running cross-country ... my mind staggered at the notion that civilized educators would compel young and vulnerable fellow human beings, the flower of the next generation, the hope of mankind's future, to waddle mile after mile and hour after hour through muck and waste in such dismal conditions, clad, for all practical purposes, in nothing. Surely, reason and the liberal spirit would be better served were we to remain indoors! Happily would I have put extra time into studying French verbs or working out obtuse math problems in the library, contributing to the Advancement of Knowledge! Equally gladly would I have submitted to several swats of the Headmaster's cane upon my delicate palms, as long as they were to be administered in the warmth of his office. I never adapted to this cross-country business. Even though I dutifully dragged my devitalized limbs through muddy potato fields and soggy pastures and every other manner of forlorn quagmire along with the rest of the youthful herd, through rain and rime and squall, my mind had difficulty digesting what was happening. In the end, however, slog on I did, slogging along and freezing with everyone else.

As the leaden sky drained itself, like a great wet rag wrung hard and long, we dragged across the potato fields that stretched away behind the school. A couple of boys - zealots, compulsive over-achievers - ranged ahead of the pack. Another group lagged behind. I ran with the crowd in the middle. After crossing the first set of fields, we came to an old gray rock wall and vaulted over onto a narrow road, which wound down a hill and yet farther away from the school. Inevitably, some boy or another would bang his knee on an angle of stone, fall mewling and cursing into the mire, then rise to carry on, clumps of dirt in his hair and smears on his face.

The rain dropped steadily and our feet slapped on the roadway. Voices receded to a low drone and we listened to each other exhaling and inhaling, in a kind of rhythm. Occasionally a car approached and slowed as we edged over to the side of the road, and the tires would hiss as it passed, spraying water, then we fanned out again and lumbered on. After a while, even Ryan grew quiet and gave up his joking, and McAllister left off babbling about Rangers' latest match. And then we ran in silence, cold and dogged.

At the bottom of the road we swung left, jumped another stone fence, then pounded along a dirt path through more endless, watery potato fields – home to what I later learned were the famous and prized Pembrokeshire "early potatoes."

The group in front pulled away, and the group behind fell back, and we stamped dumbly together through the sloppy landscape like a drove of ruminants embarked upon a kind of clumsy, disorganized migration. The trees rose macabre and naked, dripping branches arcing skyward like twisted limbs from tortured corpses. In the spring, these fields were carpets of green, and in late May and June, the farmers' children missed school to help with the harvest. Now, however, in the tomb of winter, the glens and hills and farmlands were nothing but soaked and sopping earth. The saturated turf sucked our plimsolls off our feet, and occasionally one of us would stumble into the slop and arise coated with mud from head to toe, like a corpse risen from beneath the ground.

Our breath misted into the air, and hung like a fog above our pack. We crossed the fields and mounted a hill to yet another wall, which we jumped to yet another road, when suddenly it began to rain harder. Some of the boys lingered behind on the wall, taking a break – Lloyd, Price, Ryan, and a few others, I recall, on one particular occasion - but we turned and shouted and they slipped down to the road and began to run again. Ryan, upon rejoining the group, cursed us viciously, and some clever boy observed that running in the rain was the only bath Ryan would have that month, to which Ryan replied with ever more exquisite oaths while the rest of us hooted and howled. Then we grew silent again and pressed forward, slapping along the road; a respite, at least, from the clinging mud.

As the running became easier along the paved surface, my mind would roam. Sometimes I wondered if I would ever be able to play golf properly, or if I would slice and hook and top the ball forever. Sometimes I imagined remaining in Milford, though I knew, of course, this was not to be. Spinning out this dream, however, I envisioned playing rugby for the Senior XV and becoming a stalwart for the Rabbits at the golf club – maybe even Captain one day. I would go to the University in Cardiff or Aberystwyth, then live beside the sea in Dale or St. David's or Tenby, writing books. In class, we were reading Dylan Thomas and Hardy, and it seemed to me that, short of working my will upon golf balls and subjugating golf courses across the globe like Mr. Player, there could be nothing as pleasing as a life of words and stories, making a sort of music of descriptions, plots, and turns of phrase. Adelyn floated in and out of the scene, sometimes in the center, sometimes on the fringe, depending on my moods. Always, however, I was by the sea, the wind whipping my face and waves crashing below, the soft green pastures rising inland to hills, the Haven protected and serene and Milford perched above its silver surface.

Once settled into a steady rhythm, I liked to survey my running mates and toy with divining their futures. I knew I was returning to America. That much was sure – to where, exactly, I did not know, but somewhere across the ocean, far away. What of my companions, however, remaining behind? Was McAllister destined to take root in Milford and devour the Scottish football results for the next fifty years, reduced in his dotage to a wizened nuisance loitering along the waterfront and pestering passersby with meaningless prattle of Rangers' latest exploits? Would Sam Winter carry on his father's boat business and contemplate the sheltered Dale waters for the entirety of his days, the embodiment of how a person may find the deepest sanctuaries of meaning and purpose in just one small but singular place, within small but singular bounds? It was only beginning to dawn on me that childhood and adolescence indeed reach an end, and that adulthood waited not too distantly ahead. Just as I crossed the bridge from Milford into Hakin every day on my way home, there was another bridge soon to cross, and I seemed to discern its outline ever more often in the quiet at the end of the day.

By this time, however, we would be rounding the bend to the foot of the hill on Steynton Road, the bottom of that long tree-lined hill that led down and away from the school and into Milford proper, the bottom of that long, steep hill which required surmounting as the final labor of our long, terrible run. In preparation, we clustered, prancing and stamping and swearing in anticipation of this last trial - then shot off up the fearsome incline.

Oblivious now to the rain and cold, our burning legs pushed hard and fast up the ascent. Every boy struggled on his endmost reserves, some edging forward, others weakening and slowing. Our mouths sagged open, incapable of words. Grimacing, gasping, we drove our legs forward. On my final cross-country, my last harrowing climb up this great and awful hill, I scampered through a deep puddle of freezing water, overtaking Lloyd just at the summit, then angled left across the parking lot and made weak-kneed toward the finish line at the entrance to the school. The rain was pouring in buckets, huge drops drumming my face; McAllister and two others pulled ahead of me and I ran hard across the parking lot, numb and flailing, straining to catch them. My legs became light and weightless; a wave of exhilaration swept over me. I saw the Games teacher grinning widely at the finish line, his hawkish blue eyes locking mine and reeling me in as if I were on a line, like a spent and yielding fish. In his expression of approval, I became exultant. McAllister's group crossed the finish line, I followed on their heels, and the teacher cried, "Now there's a Yank who wants to run!" as I fell into the crowd of exhausted boys. Then Lloyd staggered across as well, and McAllister was pounding me on the back, all of us shouting and laughing together, dazed with fatigue and effort as the rest of our friends topped the great hill and crossed the finish line to join us too, in giddy triumph.

And, as if the gray skies had abruptly brightened, there were no more melancholy thoughts, no dismal premonitions, only happiness and contentment amid my merry band of mates in this quiet village by the silent, glistening waters of the Haven.

And thus, we ran cross-country, in the numbing embrace of winter, building The Hardy Pembrokeshire Character.

# A SAD CASE

Caron and I had been trading emails over several months before I boarded the plane for Gatwick. As best she could, she caught me up on all the news. There was, of course, a great deal of it – more than thirty years' worth. As I might have expected, amid the good news there was bad. And the worst of it was learning that sweet and playful Tommy Ryan had died in a terrible accident three years after I departed Milford. The circumstances were horrible to contemplate.

One fine spring morning Ryan, with a group of pals, had made a trip to a rugby match in Cardiff – Caron said she recalled Wales was playing New Zealand's famous All Blacks, who were making a tour. It went without saying, of course, that attendance was mandatory for any fan of rugby or supporter of Wales. And it was equally necessary, of course, for any true supporter to tour the pubs in preparation for the contest.

It required no effort at all, therefore, to picture young Ryan, gabbing and jesting and joyful, cavorting from pub to pub before the match, the center of attention with his bottomless humor and inexhaustible blarney. Following his morning ramble through the public houses, he boarded a local train for a short ride to the stadium and somehow, for some unknown reason, made his way unseen out the back door of the last car. There, poor Tommy Ryan slipped or fell and, in some manner that was never understood, became entangled in the undercarriage, was dragged cruelly along the tracks as the train ran between stations, and perished young, much too young, on a blue and star-crossed Cardiff day which never should have come.

Everyone remembered Tommy Ryan, reported Caron, and the entire community mourned as if every family had lost a son. It was, she wrote, the kind of gutting thing that no person in a small town ever forgets. Ryan's father was now long deceased as well, and his brothers gone away. His mother still occupied the same modest council house where Tommy had lived as a boy. I remembered a slightly-built chap with freckles, a tousled thatch of ruddy, red- brown hair, and prancing, puckish, blue eyes, clad every day in the same grimy shirt and the same shoes, holes worn through the soles, but who also forever carried a ready smile and brandished a humor that was sharp as a needle, but filled with good feeling. I thought of all the years of life I had enjoyed and all that I had seen and done, while unknown to me poor Ryan had been sleeping in his early grave, and felt sad.

And there was more.

My old boon companion McAllister – he of the Rangers obsession – had survived a catastrophic car accident while away at university, had lingered in a coma, then spent more than a year at home in Milford, recuperating, before eventually moving away. How badly was he injured? I asked. Caron had only a spattering of details – she had seen little of McAllister after our grammar school years, and most of her information was second-hand. She understood, however, that his recovery had been less than complete. "Less than complete" - that was what people said. That was the general consensus. But exactly what, I implored, did this mean? What was "less than complete?" She was unsure, and had no answer.

I opened an old scrapbook to several photographs snapped in my final days at school, and found one of McAllister standing alone with his shoulders hunched, making a silly face into the camera, then another in a group with Dunn, Jenkins, and Morgan. His yellow and black school scarf hung around his neck and his tie was pulled carelessly to the side. Slung over his shoulder was his green kit bag. Looking at the pictures made my arm throb again in pain, as if still bruised black-and-blue from his regular and uncannily accurate punches, blunt retorts to my sarcastic commentaries concerning his team. I wondered how Rangers had fared these past thirty years. I wondered what had happened to McAllister, and worried.

Analyzing my approach to the 8$^{th}$ green, my concentration was badly askew. I had begun the round determined to defeat my old antagonist Hugh Evans, but now, awash in the memories that seemed to lurk behind every rock and tree and bush, my resolution had dissolved. Every glance around the course resurrected another emanation from the past, which then summoned forth another, followed by another. Hugh had already hit a long iron approach just short of the green, and stood with his arms folded, observing me. My thoughts were loose and roving, foraging among tidbits left over from times gone by, the way a vagrant might sift through three decades of detritus discarded but not yet decomposed, seizing upon every sparkling trinket that catches his eye. I remembered waiting to tee off in a club tournament on some brilliant blue and bitterly cold winter morning; wearing a new navy parka over a white sweater, but hands red and numb, the wind whipping like a lariat across my face. My eyes tearing in the pitiless wind, I had played a 3-iron off the tee that morning, in order to stay beneath the gusts, and the dull impact vibrated painfully through my hands as though they had been struck with a stout stick. I felt like shouting across the fairway now at Hugh and asking if he also recalled that squallish, frigid round, but knew it would seem absurd.

Something about his posture, however, immediately dredged up an image of yet another day, this one a schoolday on which Adelyn and I were huddled over a table in the library, whispering furtively as she sought to explain the proper use of the future tense before our weekly exam in

French. She had a ridiculous ease and facility with the language, which baffled me no end. She had just begun urging me yet again to take a more scholarly attitude, when we heard a scuff on the carpet and glanced up to discover Hugh approaching us, smiling a sly and crafty smile. He arrived at our table, then leaned over and said, with an insinuating leer, "Time for class, lovebirds."

Uncannily, the identical wily grin now reappeared upon his face as he stared at me from the fairway, awaiting my shot. My expression must have betrayed the dazed condition of my mind, for he suddenly waved his hands and called my name. "Still here, are we? Pay attention, you'll do better!"

His commentary barely registered, however. Scarcely made a dent; for now, I was skipping from memory to memory in a faraway time, like the needle of a phonograph skipping along an old record. The brakes on my retrospection had given way completely, and I was reliving yet another bygone incident.

"Remember that party in the Kellar's garage – I told you I walked Marianne home and you didn't believe me?" I shouted across the fairway.

Hugh stared blankly for a moment, then replied "No," in a voice more short and brittle than usual.

"Yes, you do!" I exclaimed. "You just won't admit it."

"Why would Marianne let you walk her home from a party?" he cried. "And what does that have to do with anything?"

I chose not to respond. It had nothing to do with anything. And besides, by then I had slid effortlessly back to a breezy night in autumn and skittering leaves and the smell of the water and the Kellar's garage, close and hot. On the stereo, *A Whiter Shade of Pale* swelled and crested. Beside me, clasping my hand, was Marianne, reserved and quiet in a powder-gray dress, cheeks flushed red, black eyes black as pitch. We left the little party before it ended and crept beneath the scurrying clouds and the sullen, hidden moon, through a maze of silent, windswept streets climbing up from the Haven, our footsteps echoing on the empty pavement. We came to a gate before a dark house, set back off the street and shrouded by foliage, where we stood in a pool of illumination from an overhanging streetlight. The late night mist danced in the glow from the lamp and swirled in the whispering wind, and the light rippled across her golden hair and I thought the dark house ominous and bleak for such a beauty. I ran my fingers across the back of her hand, then across her hair, and suddenly I was confused and bereft of speech; I kissed her once, quickly, then was gone, retracing my steps hurriedly through the winding streets, back to the Haven and across the bridge and home.

I teetered now above my golf ball, three decades later, gazing above the trees into the distance, as if I had glimpsed some strange object streaking in the sky. With dramatic immediacy, I experienced anew the current of disquietude that had stolen over me, standing before Marianne at her gate that long-ago night, her hand in mine. I experienced again the same inexplicable uncertainty. The shadowed house had seemed unreal, as if merely a façade. Some ethereal quality surrounded Marianne – her bronzed and burnished hair, her raven-jet eyes and knowing mien - and I recalled thinking, ridiculously, that perhaps as she passed through the door of that shadowed dwelling she would return to the realm of spirits, return from another sojourn among us sad and earth-bound creatures, among whom she did not truly belong. And I had been struck speechless, in my unfledged innocence, as we stood in the circle of light before her gate.

"You're hopeless!" cried Hugh, barging rudely into my meditations. "Thirty years later and you've still got Marianne on the brain!"

I looked at him with a silly grin, and nodded.

"Hit your bloody shot!" he exclaimed. "She graduated, went away, got married, had children, and that's it! She was able to carry on without you – hit your bloody shot!"

"Why are you so agitated?" I shouted.

"I am not agitated!"

"Of course you are," I insisted sharply, with an emphatic nod. "She's still on your brain too!"

Hugh pursed his lips, glowered, and turned away with a frown.

I pulled a 5-iron from my bag. The cloud of nostalgia began to dissipate. After all, we had a match going here, and I was only one up with two holes left. It was a thin and precarious lead. Too thin. Too precarious. And my wretched drive had left me with a dodgy second shot. Staring with new conviction at the green, and ready for another try at unsettling Hugh's psychic balance, I said, "Well, I understand why you never got over her, though," then waggled my club, awaiting a retort. All was silence, however. Again, I waggled my club, and waited. And waited some more. Hugh had turned to stone. My artful zinger, I concluded, aimed at the object of his deepest adolescent fantasy, must have struck true and done its work. I shifted my feet, flexed and swayed, all the while anticipating some sort of rebuttal, some defense or plea. Finally, however, I could delay no longer, so took an uninspired swing and swatted a limp, listless fade that wilted and dropped well short of the green, and right; a pitiful denouement to all my preparatory waggling and shifting and adjusting. And a complete waste of my clever psychological parry.

Hugh and I met in the middle of the fairway and walked together toward our shots, unspeaking. Finally, he gave a sideways glance and shook his head sympathetically. "You're a sad, sad case," he said, shaking his head the way I imagined a physician might, just before informing a favorite patient they have some incurable disease. "Grown-up and still can't face facts."

We laughed, and the remaining remnants of my sentimental haze slipped away. "The difference is that you've been living here for the last thirty years and I haven't," I said. "I've had thirty years to romanticize everything."

"Not much to romanticize, I don't think," he replied, after a moments' pause, raising his eyebrows and wrinkling his brow. "It rains and blows most of the time, not much to do, nothing to keep the young folk around. Most of us are just simple people growing older all the time. I don't see anything too romantic about that."

"In your case," I said, smiling, "you're right."

"You truly are a sad case," he muttered, and we ambled on together toward the green. "And I haven't missed you a bit," he added truculently.

By the time we arrived at our respective balls I had completely regained my focus. The lead, I reminded myself, still lay in my hands – a not-insignificant fact at this stage of the proceedings. I was away, in the short rough to the right, but my ball was sitting cleanly. I punched a smart 8-iron up the front of the green, toward the pin in back. The moment I struck the ball, I knew I had hit it well - and, sure enough, it came to rest quite pleasingly, a mere four feet from the hole. A par was now entirely possible, which would then take me to the 9th and final hole one-up; a strong position, indeed, from which to close out the match. I smiled inwardly. My excellent chip had shifted the pressure to Hugh. My momentary walkabout had not proved fatal after all. I congratulated myself on having maintained a solid grip on matters.

Hugh lay squarely in the middle of the fairway, perhaps twenty feet short of the green. He also drew an 8-iron, and surveyed his shot nonchalantly. He shrugged his shoulders a few times, as if loosening them up, with an air of vague disinterest. He swept his club at the ground two or three times, and seemed to sniff the air. Finally, he looked down at his ball. Then a gust of wind ruffled the leaves on the trees behind the green and I heard their sibilant crinkling as Hugh bent over and deftly, as if discharging a mere formality, chipped his ball directly into the cup, after two bounces, to win the hole.

He lifted his head and turned to me. I stared back at him, both our faces blank. Then he smiled innocently and stretched, somewhat like an infant waking from a nap. What could I say? It was a preposterous, preposterous, stroke of luck, at the most pivotal point of the entire match. I had no refuge but scowls and sputters, so therefore scowled and sputtered venomously. "You didn't really think you were going to win, did you?" Hugh inquired mildly, almost apologetically.

My fear, my premonition, had come to pass. With only a single hole left to play, we were suddenly all square. My comfortable lead had evaporated in a flash. I stomped to the green and pocketed my ball, while Hugh extracted his delicately from the cup.

"Still a daydreamer, eh?" he remarked casually as we headed to the final tee. "It never pays."

Hugh, the realist, the prosaic plodder, had read me true.

# THE GRIM MARAUDER

The ninth and final station on Milford's nine-hole course is a long par-4 that elevates uphill to the clubhouse, and I had never played it well. There were many paths to failure on this hole, and I had trod them all. To my eye, the tee-box seemed set at an odd, uncomfortable angle. Left and right, tangles of bracken bordered the narrow fairway, and a shallow, muddy ditch lay concealed just within reach of a well-struck drive. Beyond, the fairway narrowed further, tilted leftward, and rose steeply up to a platformed green. The green itself lay encircled amid trees and shrubs and bunkers, and its surface undulated like a tidal swell frozen into place. Perhaps it was because I was usually dragging with fatigue by this point, worn down from battling the course with the ever-changing vagaries of my mediocre game. Perhaps it was only a mental thing. For whatever reason, however, the simple fact was that the ninth hole had always brought me disappointment.

And so, inevitably, once again, my tour of the course ended with a thud. I sprayed my ball left, then right, then left again, while Hugh, without ceremony, poked his way down the middle of the fairway and neatly up onto the green. In the end, I needed to sink a thirty-foot putt to halve the hole and halve the match; too daunting a task. By the time I bent over to gauge my line, I had already resigned myself to the outcome. I missed the putt before even striking it, thus losing the hole and losing the contest; undone by an excess of intoxicating reminiscence.

Resolute Hugh had prevailed more often than not back when we were boys. It seemed fitting, therefore, that he should prevail again today. In fact, our little rivalry had resembled perfectly so many of our bygone competitions that its conclusion was entirely satisfying, in an ironic sort of way. Had I held my lead and claimed the win, some fundamental rule of the course would have been subverted, some iron verity of history shattered. Better to keep things as they were meant to be. No need to tamper. Looking into boxes of memories is one thing; rearranging their contents is another. I had returned to Milford to seek what survived from the world I had left behind those many years ago, not to upset or remake it. We smiled, therefore, shook hands, loaded our clubs into Hugh's car, and made our way to the pro shop.

I bought my father a shirt, upon the left breast-pocket of which was imprinted the club's seal (prominently featuring waves and anchors, of course), and chatted with the boy at the desk. The shop was crisp and modern, well-lit, well-stocked, even colorful, and bore not the slightest resemblance to Mr. Flynn's old cave-like nook. And of course, Mr. Flynn himself was long gone too. *Never heard of him,* the boy said flatly. *Who is he?* Hugh had told me the boy was a local sensation, an aspiring tour pro, a long hitter with nerves of steel. I examined the lad closely, and saw only a lanky teenager with curly brown hair and a raw, unlined expression. Soon enough, I reflected with a certain perverse satisfaction, time and the world would notch their marks upon that unmarred surface. As he handed over my receipt I told him I had lived here when I was young, and had learned to play golf on this course; he listened perfunctorily, with no interest. I took the shirt and thanked him.

We crossed the parking lot to the clubhouse, where we sat in the barroom overlooking the course and Hugh bought me a Guinness. Lining the walls were plaques engraved with the names of all the club's past Presidents, year by year. I located 1966, 1967, and 1968, and saw inscribed upon those markers the names of three of my father's friends and golfing partners – Arthur Pledger, Gareth Gaines, Ollie Frost – each of whom I had known, and caddied for more than once. Mr. Pledger, in particular, had been a handsome tipper; Frost less so, but a jocular gentleman with whom to pass a morning. Hugh knew nothing about them; whether they were alive or dead, or where they might reside.

Over the bar, there seemed to hang a dreary, soggy atmosphere – so unlike that place which, in memory, long ago, had rollicked with no end of laughter and good humor. Today, however, every association it evoked seemed mildewed, moth-eaten. The afternoon was deepening, the sky beginning to cloud. Finally, I located one lone patron, an elderly man in a black woolen sweater, huddled alone at a table in the corner, who remembered Mr. Flynn. I sat with him briefly, hopeful for information – but learned only that Mr. Flynn now dwelt absent-minded and doddering in a small house off the Dale Road, rarely venturing out. The man recalled him as frail and unsteady when last seen, at the chemist's on Charles Street, sometime last winter, fumbling for change at the checkout, assisted by a woman, perhaps his day-nurse. We sat silently. He had nothing more to tell. The old gentleman tapped his mug absently on the table, both of us thinking our thoughts. *Old Dick Flynn*, he then muttered softly, rising, shaking his head, and moving away. *Oh, a mighty golfer*, he continued, descending the stairs, as if reminiscing now to himself alone. *A mighty golfer indeed.*

I finished my beer and felt like leaving too. Hugh and I stared out the big bay window across the course to the Haven. A tanker eased slowly and deliberately to the west, toward the mouth of the Haven where the watercourse welcomed the sea. Two tiny tugs accompanied the giant ship. The sun was obscured, partially, by approaching clouds, and half the scene beyond the window lay in shade, the other half washed with that familiar, yellow, late-day glow. It was a panorama intimate yet remote; intimate because I had lived within it, breathed within it, walked and worked and reached and puzzled within it, and remembered it so well; but remote because now I was merely a spectator, and no longer a part of what stretched before my eyes. Watching evening settle over the Haven through the thick glass of the clubhouse window made it seem like just another one of my recurring, emotive dreams; or like watching a movie, or glancing idly through an open door into another person's life.

Hugh had fallen silent as well, gazing pensively upon the view, and I wondered what he saw. I wondered if, perhaps, he saw two carefree youths roaming the course and peering intently after their shots as they vanished in the blue gloaming. I wondered if he saw how the elements that form our lives, the people and places, the choices, the acts – those committed as well as those omitted – all the triumphs, the yearnings, the failures, which, in their immediacy, burn and sting with such ferocity, come eventually to fade and blur like the light upon the course itself was fading with the onset of night. I wondered what Hugh discerned out the window, because this was what I saw as I cradled my empty mug and stared through the glass across the expanse now divided into realms of light and dark. I saw that memory, and its meaning, and all the bits and parts from which it is stitched together, paddle furiously against the irresistible current of time. I saw Milford and its people safely encased in the eternal dream world of reminiscence – but also saw that, in the corporeal world of flesh and blood, rock and wind, memories are merely specks of dust floating in the sunlight, and the foretime dissolves and disappears like a mirage, as time ultimately devours all things past and present and future like a heartless, marauding beast. And in this grim land, under this ruthless regime, a person's history, I thought, is destined to become but a carcass gutted and abandoned by the sated monster. Only a fool would struggle against its certain disintegration, much less undertake to keep its spark alive – vain and doomed, like a cupped hand endeavoring to shield a tiny flame against a cold night gale.

Yet here I was – and this was a fact. Many years had come and gone. Time had not stood still - the mighty Mr. Flynn rendered shattered and feeble, and all but forgotten; Hugh lined and ruddy; myself gray and bespectacled. I wondered anew how this place had dug its hook so deep; and enjoyed a quiet pleasure, a quiet flush of triumph, because the little raft that carried my history here had held its heading against the cruel, decaying beat of time, and Yes, my memories endured, intact and whole and good, and undevoured yet.

We left the club for town. I was staying at The Crescent, on Hamilton Terrace. Hugh dropped me at the door and sped off to run some errands before the reunion dinner. I was still a bit weary from the trip over, and wanted to rest before the big event. On an impulse, however, I walked up the Terrace toward the Rath, to the shuttered remnants of Marshal House, and stood for some minutes on the sidewalk studying its crumbling paint and dingy trim, staring at the door, now boarded shut, through which my father and I had entered on our first morning in Milford. I circled around to the back entrance, the one through which Alan and I would rush home from school every day that first month, when the hotel had been my home, the base from which my father and I launched our explorations of this new-found territory.

It was silent and abandoned now – no laughing school-boys, no feet clambering on the pavement and clattering into the kitchen – but the old sounds and old memories hung heavy nonetheless. I remembered having dreamt once – a strong and clinging dream; my friends were waiting for me up on Charles Street, up the steep hill from the Marshal House. I had bolted out the front door and was straining to race up the hill, laboring and gasping, but my legs seemed to weigh a thousand pounds. Regardless of how I struggled, I made no progress, and they finally drifted away, faded away, one by one – and I had, I recalled, awoken bathed in disappointment, clammy and melancholy, wrapped once more in the deep, inconsolable sense of loss that inevitably followed these nighttime sojourns to the Haven.

Before long, I headed back to the hotel, and up the creaking stairs to my room. I had requested a view facing the Haven, and indeed my window opened across the old docks, the flat blue sheet of tranquil water, and the old refineries' spires against the green slope of the southern shore. A mammoth tanker lay at rest at the jetty, and a single tug plowed lazily toward the west. Three sailboats skimmed by, heading also to the west; to Dale for the evening, I supposed. The street below was quiet, but I could hear gulls squawking as they swooped and plunged above the water. I perched on the edge of my bed and looked out the window for several minutes, then grew sleepy, set the alarm, and dozed off to the cool touch of the late afternoon breeze and the rising, falling, familiar chorus of the birds.

The occasion for my return to Milford, the rope that pulled me back, was the class reunion Caron had organized. Like all things avidly awaited – perhaps too avidly awaited – the actual event itself came and went quickly, and exists now only as a fast-moving reel of episodes or frames. Many are blurred. Many run together. A few, however, stand out, like sequences of color in a black-and-white film. These, I have lodged securely in that stubborn storage bin which holds my strongest Milford memories.

The reels' opening frames commence with waking refreshed after my golfing foray, showering, changing clothes, and departing my room at The Crescent, bound for the marina, our gathering place. The reels end several hours later with a bus pulling away from a restaurant in darkness, my hands pressed against a cold glass window, staring back into the night. Here now, however, the first reel is loading, threading neatly onto its track, the projector's wheels and gears beginning to whir with a subdued metallic hum, and the frames streaming and clicking into view through the grainy lens of remembrance.

# FRAMES IN A FILM

*N*ightfall is near.

*Atop the hills, a ghostly gray-blue veil gathers. Soon enough, this veil will descend upon the town, the Haven, and the still waters. It is coming now, in fact. I feel it more than see it; and sense it more than feel it. Its moist, sensuous, suggestive stroke brushes my cheek; its wet touch presses upon my lips like a damp fingertip, urging me to silence. The air grows chill. I know that nightfall is imminent because I recognize the familiar draught welling up from the land and the sea as day becomes night on the banks above the calm-flowing Haven. The misty veil's caress across my face excites a swirl of emotions – excitement, longing, nostalgia – all mingling as the mild wind stirs, as the ever-present night-wind courses from the Atlantic.*

*Orange and crimson streaks upon the western horizon, wildly aflame just minutes earlier beyond my window at The Crescent, now deepen to indigo, salmon, and a faint half-moon peeks into view in the far distance, high above the ocean. A signal, perhaps? To me? I stare, and wonder.*

*The surface of the Haven itself turns shadowy and mottled. Glints of silver flash as splinters of dying light perish against ripples.*

*Sounds are muffled and far away. A passing boat sounds a mournful horn. Turning, I barely make it out, but envision the craft wandering doleful in the deepening twilight, calling sadly into the gloom; calling out of habit alone, perhaps, and no longer hoping for reply. Dimly, however, I discern what could be its lights, blinking on and off, and leave the lonely vessel to its search, continue on to the marina, where the bus awaits to ferry us to the site of the evening's reunion.*

*Soon the gray vapor will billow out thick across the water. For a final moment, though, the beacons from the boats and the colored lights on the jetties shine vivid and bright – but then it darkens suddenly, and a wide causeway of stars emerges overhead, arcing across the waterway to its southern strand. They fill the sky, endless tiny nodes of light, endless luminous lamps, unchanged from when I was young in this place; clear and splendid above the little town.*

*Although fully awake, indeed acutely awake, my advance to the marina has the aura of unreality; a sense of sliding toward an imaginary place, as in dreams we glide effortlessly from one scene to another, each one gripping, but none of them real – the misty veil, the incandescent arch of stars, the mysterious stillness, the low and tantalizing water-sounds, all creating a fantastic dreamscape – the journey of a fool, a hopeless dreamer, a silly, silly man.*

*The Haven's steady, stately lap, however, and the rich night-water smells, and the winking lights, and the trod of my feet upon the embankment, are all palpable enough, and indeed I am not in any mirage, so onward I press through the pale fog – and sure enough, only twenty paces further on, there appears a blurry iridescence in the haze, and, through the mist and another twenty paces, I suddenly see figures milling, windows alight, the headlamps of the waiting bus – and then my footsteps cease and miraculously, in a consuming blaze, a phosphorescent burst of light and happiness and speechless unbelief, I arrive, and it is real; engulfed by wide-eyed, joyful friends from a gilded time that did not die, the air ringing with lilting noise, my ears full of merriment, and the slow, dreamy, thoughtful walk from The Crescent and across the unseen bridge of time is over.*

At 7:00 p.m. sharp, we departed the marina for the site of our dinner, The Dragon's Claw hotel and restaurant, there to rendezvous with other classmates traveling on their own. As we board the coach, the evening's second series of frames flicks swiftly across my field of vision, and we leave the marina behind:

*Away into darkness and sharpening wind we pull, bearing inland, old friends jovial and bantering, everyone talking to everyone, loud and cheerful, the countryside rolling by as we climb the hills, up and up and away from the Haven. It is a land of giddy shades, a bus full of phantoms brought to life – names and faces, faces and names, one after another, strewn together and jumbled, materializing amid exclamations and greetings and wide-open arms, then sinking back into the general melee – Jenkins, Lloyd, Jones, Davies, Thomas, Burrell, James, Larkin, Griffiths, Llewellyn, Mullen, Duffy, all aboard the bus, all present, all in grand high spirits, all young and unmarked again within this magical conveyance, running a route not from stop to stop, but from year to year and age to age.*

Caron – who had evidently honed a latent talent for organization, and seemed to have brought to the planning of our reunion weekend all the vigor formerly applied as Captain of the girl's field hockey team – had found just the right location for our celebratory dinner. I was amused by its name; as a venue, however, The Dragon's Claw was perfect. Located not far from the Pembrokeshire Coastal Path and St. David's, a stylish boutique hotel with a cozy, well-stocked, wood-paneled bar, large windows, a spacious dining hall with high ceilings, and long oaken tables made for thumping. Reel three finds our bus arriving at The Dragon's Claw after a 30-minute ride. Already, I was hoarse and gasping for air, as if I had sprinted the entire distance.

There should be no mystery as to the person foremost on my mind as we pulled to a halt. A wave of apprehension and uncertainty swept through me, however – a reprise of the anxiety I had experienced upon arriving at the Grammar School for the Christmas gala on that wondrous bygone eve? Was this a bad idea? No telling what sort of destruction time might have worked, and why risk marring memories that sparkle so like sapphire and emerald, like silver ornaments made just for you? Would I have done better just to leave it alone? To allow glowing, haloed remembrance simply to molder peacefully away, before eventually sinking into the sands of an inevitable sunset? Perhaps – however, it is too late now for second-thoughts, for our coach has stopped and here I am, foolish or not, and reel three clicks and pops into view:

*Roaring, hot, deafening - The Dragon's Claw a hopeless wall of sound. Impossible to distinguish one voice from another. Grasping outstretched hands, shouting, clasping, lunging, hugging, slapping backs and bussing cheeks – craning my neck and inspecting the crowd, scanning and winnowing through the drove of hot, bright faces for one particular countenance, one particular set of features, one particular expression – where is she? Is she even here at all? Had some last-minute intervention kept her away? Too many people – old friends all, but so many, an overflow of commotion and not enough space, panting, sweating, perspiration slick on my brow, ears hammering – I continue scanning, however, continue searching; and suddenly there she is, wedged back into a corner, conversing intently with two other women (I recognize them too), half-shadowed. She smiles hesitantly at something uttered by one of the women, then glances to the floor, and I note the faint dimpling in her left cheek accenting her reticent smile – and then her head inclines casually in my direction, almost insouciantly, as if she had already detected my eyes upon her but wished, before engaging them, to pause, and make me wait – then finally her head lifts to catch my gaze, and our eyes meet as the clamor rises higher and fills the room. The furor crests, recedes, then masses anew with even greater intensity, like a giant wave, all simply one titanic din. I smile and shrug, as there is no chance of making my way through the throng, and she purses her lips and raises her eyebrows ever so slightly, her smile dimpling again – and then someone else is pounding my back and crying out my name, and I turn away to rasp another gleeful salutation.*

Amid all the high and happy spirits, I came upon Alan Zelinski, and finally learned the secret of his father. It was something hard and sobering, without an ounce of the romance or glamour I had once imagined. I had fought my way to the restroom. As I reached for the door it opened from the other side – and there stood Alan. For a silent moment, we looked at one other – the spindly boy grown thick and sturdy, with his mother's profile, sharp-beaked like a falcon's - then broke into delighted grins. We retreated to a corner and went through the catching-up. Then I asked him, point-blank, because I was never going to get another chance: *I was always so mystified by your father, did you ever find out what he did in the war?*

Alan frowned and bit his lip. "I did," he said. "I was never curious about it, the way you were, though. I thought if he wanted to tell people about the war, he'd tell them. If not, well, it was over, in the past."

"How did he come to tell you?"

"He was in the hospital. He had lung cancer, very advanced when he finally went to the doctor. So it was terminal by the time they found it. He told me he'd started smoking when he was ten. They sent him home for a bit – he didn't do any real treatment or anything, he wasn't interested. He was home for a month then went in the hospital and died. That was 1980."

"He did smoke like a chimney," I said. "I remember that. I hope it wasn't too hard."

Alan shook his head. "No, it was peaceful enough in the end. He was lucky."

I nodded and said that was good.

"Anyway," he resumed, "he never told my mother a thing about the war. And she never asked him. She wanted to forget the war, I think. I remember her telling me you were so interested in it because you hadn't lived through it. A day or two before he died, though, I went to see him – it was raining hard, a really dreary day. I sat with him for a while, then he said he wanted to tell me about the war. He said he'd never told anyone about it because it wasn't anyone's business, and everyone had some kind of story about the war anyway. But he said he'd decided he ought to tell someone, and since it wasn't going to be my mother, it was going to be me. 'Sure, of course,' I told him. He gave me a funny little smile – he hardly ever smiled, you remember that."

"Oh, yes, I do remember that. I was afraid of him."

"He was very gentle, never raised his voice. Treated us very politely. Not a warm man, though," said Alan. "Anyway – he told me he'd had an older brother, named Tomas. They lived on a farm in a village in western Poland. Just a little farm, they weren't rich or anything. When the Germans came they burned the village and everything else, rounded up all the animals, shot them for food. Anyone who put up a fight got shot too, men, woman. Both his parents. They put my Dad and his brother in a camp they'd set up, basically tents inside barbed wire, they were collecting people from all the villages in the area. They didn't know what was going to happen next. One night a couple of them made a run for it, they thought they'd found a gap in the wire they could get through. Of course, it didn't work, the guards heard them and started picking them off. My Dad was halfway through the wire, sliding on his back on the ground, underneath it. Tomas was behind him, waiting his turn. Then Tomas got shot and fell on the barbed wire. It pushed the wire down into my Dad's face – that's how he got the scar, sliced the side of face open. Dug a trench in his face. But he slid on through and kept running – Tomas was dead."

I shook my head slowly. "So both his parents and his brother were killed."

Alan nodded. "My Dad and one other guy got away. Then they just wandered. They hid during the day and moved at night. Eventually they split up. My father wanted to get to the west. The other fellow wanted to stay in Poland. So they went separate ways. He said he just wandered for days, trying to work his way west, to the coast – he thought if he could get to the coast he might be able to get a boat somewhere. He said it was bad – no food, sleeping wherever he could. Then it started getting cold, really cold, and his shoes falling apart. So he got frostbite on his left foot, just his toes – it got his big toe bad, and later they ended up having to amputate it."

I nodded my head again. "Hence, his limp," I said.

Again, Alan nodded.

"Eventually, he stumbled into an underground unit in the north, near the coast, working with some British agents. They took him in and got him connected with our secret services. He said we had secret service all over Eastern Europe. They trained him, and he spent the war as a sniper for us– he told me he'd always been the best shot in his family, good with a rifle, kept them in meat during the winter. He said he wasn't a battlefield sniper – they sent him after Nazi officials, money-men, politicians, that kind of thing. Very quiet stuff, behind the scenes."

"My gosh," I exclaimed, picturing the courtly, self-effacing Mr. Zelinski I had known, against the portrait Alan had just painted. "What a story!"

"He said it was the best work he did in his whole life," said Alan. "He wasn't half as good at anything else. And didn't enjoy anything else half as much."

We sat silently, reflecting. Then, for some reason, I felt compelled to lift my glass.

"To your father," I said.

Alan and I touched glasses.

Then he put his arm across my shoulder and we returned to the main crowd.

My jaw throbbed and ached from bellowing, over and over, in a croak ever-more guttural, the shorthand narrative of the past three-and-a-half decades. The tumult was just too much, and the space too small. On and on it barreled, however, glasses clinking, bodies jostling, faces reddening under the combination of heat and ale. Then, mercifully, just as it all threatened to curdle into a big, sour mess, a bell rings three times signaling dinner - and this same bell rings sharply again now, three times in the echo chamber of my memory, announcing the opening of reel number four:

*Running the length of the dining hall are three long, wide, heavily-varnished tables, and Adelyn has already taken her place. I rest my hand upon the chair next to hers and, as she glances up, arch my eyebrows inquiringly. She smiles, I smile, she rises to her feet, we open our arms and embrace, then hold one other at arms' length to smile again. At first, neither of us speaks. Then, however, we take our seats and venture a cautious handful of plain, pedestrian words; ordinary and clumsy phrases, not the flowing eloquence I had, in a part of my mind, imagined running between us smooth as stream water rippling over flat rocks. Of course, our most pleasing remembrances belong safely tucked away in the cushioning tissue of time-past, where they can float like clouds and drift on tides, coming and going according to our own subconscious rhythms and currents. It is a gross transgression of the order of things when one of your most heartfelt youthful memories sits beside you with a guarded, curious smile, and covers your hand with hers, as once she did when you were but a callow, uncertain boy. And thus now, after saying Hello, and brushing her cheek, I feel solemn and subdued – but then, she had never been a person of many words, and I remind myself that it was precisely her ease with silence that had made her presence so comfortable in the first place, when I was a newcomer here, and with a serious turn myself. Our conversation, therefore, gropes haltingly along. We keep at it, though, and soon enough the stiffness begins to fall away as the activity around us roils on, and we smile and shrug and laugh again.*

*"Say something in French," she exhorts me then, grinning like a devil.*

*In protest, I say I cannot believe her first request after 35 years of silence is that I speak French!*

*"But you speak it so beautifully," she replies innocently. "I've missed it so! I came back just to hear it.!"*

*"Tu es cruel, ma Cherie. Tu connais je parle francaise comme un Americain!"*

*Her impish eyes gleam bright and blue, and her laughter knits us back together. "It is so much worse than I remembered! So very much worse!"*

*I shrug.*

*"And it is still 'tu' and not 'vous?' Even after all this time?*

*"Certainment."*

*Our little joke undams our hesitation, and now we dive into old times, old memories and associations. It all flows free and loose, full of cheer and humor, and her hand upon mine conjures up memories of two fresh, moonstruck, puppy-lovers, and the unsullied, sweet, and poignant way in which young people become intimates in the earliest blooming of dewy-eyed innocence; all of it now residing deep in the past, of course, and better for it, but sparkling still, and not forgotten in the silty ocean of the everyday.*

*Our lives, naturally, have taken us in different directions – into our own careers, marriages, families. She teaches English Literature at a girl's school in Canterbury, and spends summers teaching in France – as close as she has come to her childhood dream of living there. And your poetry, I ask – which makes her blush, hesitate, and reveal she has drawers full of it, none of which has ever seen the light of day.*

*"Will you let me read them now?"*

*"Maybe."*

*"I'm serious!"*

*"Maybe."*

*Life has treated her fairly, she says, with her enigmatic suggestion of a smile. She has expected neither bliss nor perfection. She is happy. So too am I – certain now that indeed it has not been the errand of a fool, this keeping alive against time's onslaught our frigid trek down the long tree-lined hill after the great Christmas dance, and the pale light above her door; this having returned to sit in The Dragon's Claw to feel her hand again upon mine, a sort of silent proof that, in protecting our small, youthful affection against the giant outwash of life's experiences, I have done something good and right. And so, we sit and speak and watch the crowd and think our thoughts.*

The hours pass and we settle deeper into the evening, through food and drinks and drinks and food. Surveying the scene, I brood wistfully upon the numberless nights I had dreamed of something like the very scene unfolding before my eyes, only to awake beneath a cloud of dolor in the morning. I marvel again that I am actually here, it is all real, all true, and it covers me like a quilt stitched of warmth and belonging; edged, however, with sharp needles, reminders that fine and grand as the evening and its sentiment may be, it is also a transient thing, which will soon enough belong to the past as well. Which is, in fact, the theme of reel number five – the wicked pain and pleasure of nostalgia, from which there is no true relief, ever:

*Later, as the night lengthens and yawns begin appearing upon faces in the crowd, Mickey Dunn, flushed and apple-red, rises unsteadily to his feet – an old school cap perched crookedly atop his head – and, in his capacity as unofficial master of ceremonies, calls for silence. In a bleary kind of way, he thanks each person for coming, and recites the distant locales from whence some have journeyed – a woman from Hong Kong, another from Australia, a fellow from Vancouver, Tom Kellar's daughter from Houston, and myself. A short and maudlin speech follows, much applauded by his beer-soaked audience. He requests a moment of respect for those no longer with us – poor Ryan, plus two more of our schoolmates; one claimed by a heart attack just a month earlier, the other, a former taxi driver in Haverfordwest, dead from drink a long while past. We lower our eyes and all is still, then Mickey pronounces an Amen and the uproar kicks off again, though a bit tiredly now. Mickey gives up talking, retakes his seat with a heavy sigh, and removes his cap, as if formally disavowing all further official duties.*

*Earlier, I had located McAllister, but only for a few brief moments. Now, however, I seek him out again, find him, plop down beside him, and enquire straightaway about his injury. By this point in the evening, everyone is ready to ask the questions they really want to ask – and anyway, he is an old, old friend. Five of us were in the car, he reports dully; the drunkest one, naturally, doing the driving. Two were killed, two walked away, and I ended up somewhere in between. The left side of his face is paralyzed, and sags just a bit. He has difficulty getting his words started and they run together when he becomes excited. Two years of therapy, he says. But he kept at it, is married now, two children, lives in Reading and works for a finance company. He recounts incidents from bygone times, from rugby matches, from cross-country, from especially memorable parties, rambles to and from school and to the beaches, which I recall as well, and we take pleasure in our remembering together. To my immense relief and enjoyment, I find his shining personality and great good humor unchanged, and picture him once again ringing our doorbell in the morning, kit bag slung over his shoulder, nattering brightly all the way to school about Rangers' latest fortunes. You were always hitting me on the arm! I cry indignantly. I'll hit you again! he stammers excitedly, voice rising, and then we sit with our arms on each other's shoulders, just watching.*

*One of us – I don't remember which – brings up Ryan, Tommy Ryan. He was a sweet lad, McAllister says, both of us shaking our heads and staring at the floor. Ryan's old friends, he says, still drop by to see his elderly mother whenever they find themselves in town, and a group had called upon her earlier this very day. Ryan's family had been a poor one. I remembered visiting his home one afternoon with a company of pals, a drab row house on a back street. His mother had offered us tea as we waited for Tommy to come downstairs, which we all politely declined. In the stale, quiet parlor, dim in the faltering late-day light, I had noticed the room was filled with pictures of her children. The mantel above the fireplace was crowded with photographs of her three boys, Tommy being the youngest, the baby. More pictures of the boys hung on the walls and cluttered two mismatched tables at either end of the settee. The air was thick and still and we had nothing to say. Mrs. Ryan sat smiling, unmoving, hands clasped in her lap, and no one spoke - then Tommy came bounding down the stairs, jabbering and jesting, and we all jumped up, thanked his mother, and ran out the door to some forgotten adventure. I recalled glancing back as we leapt off the steps, and seeing Mrs. Ryan in a faded, flowered apron, leaning against the open door, smiling and waving and calling after us to be careful, strands of graying hair wafting in the breeze. Now, McAllister and I sit silently, remembering playful, life-filled Tommy Ryan, and pondering the fate that had killed him so cruelly and so young, then wounded McAllister, but had left me, thus far, and in a way, untouched. As we nurse our thoughts, the tide of nostalgia builds and withdraws, eddies and swirls. Ah, I wish he was here tonight, McAllister says. We fall silent again, then I say I wish I hadn't stayed away for so long — I wish I had come back sooner. I tell him that sometimes I even wish I could have stayed. McAllister smiles a crooked smile, his face drooping on the left, eyes moist and glinting. I wish a lot of things, mate, he says softly, don't we all? We share terse and rueful laughs, then lean against one another and return to observing our old chums.*

Somewhere around midnight, the evening stumbles to its inevitable end. The movie reel of fragmented images, dotted with gaps and illuminated only in parts by bursts of light, is nearly finished, but for a few final frames, the ones I recall most distinctly, the ones I have held most tight:

*The party is over, the hour is late, and it is time to leave. It sped by quickly, and the leaving comes quickly too. Out of The Dragon's Claw we file, subdued now, talked-out, into the parking lot, where the air is unusually crisp and chill for May. I begin my goodbyes. Marianne – ageless, elegant – beams serenely. We exchange fond hugs and wish each other well. Jenkins, Dunn, Gwen, Lloyd, and more – each of them I embrace, knowing it will not come again. Then Adelyn and I step aside, draw each other close, and, for one silent moment, enter unseen into another life, an alternate unfolding of events, in which, against all odds, I indeed remained in Milford, and our adolescent affection took root and deepened and flowered; and, in this fleeting instant beneath the stars outside The Dragon's Claw, we slipped neatly through time, inhabited a stone house amid trees, in a glen facing a broad, brown beach stroked by waves and foam, and lived a timeless, perfect life together, became of this beautiful landscape together, grew old and wise and died. The whole of this dreamy journey we traversed in the span of a single clasp, in which everything and everyone else receded and the paths we had actually carved in our lives disappeared, replaced by the simple stone house and the glen and the beach and the waves – and then it was over. Lightly, I brushed her cheek and said I had to go. She squeezed my hand a final time as I turned to board the bus, where I took a window seat, alone. When all the seats were full, the driver turned the key and the engine rumbled to life. I sat staring straight ahead, emotions from the last time I had left my friends behind in Milford slashing in sharp, cutting gales across my mind. Gales, in fact, stronger than ever had been my longing to recover this lost past. Just before we pulled away, however, I heard a knock on my window and turned to see Adelyn, poised on tiptoes in the parking lot, bathed in pallid, blue-white moonlight, a coat clutched about her shoulders and one arm out-stretched, piercing blue eyes wide and bright and fixed onto mine. I laid a hand against the cold glass and stared back hard into her fierce gaze. The bus began to draw away and I pressed both hands and my forehead flat against the cold glass and held her in my sight until the bus turned onto the main road, and she vanished into blackness. Vanished and fell away forever, into the cool May night, and gone. I will never see her again, not in this life – nor the time and place of which she was the dearest part.*

In the same way my father derived a special pleasure from rummaging in the hallway closet and dragging out the treasury of slides from his beloved Navy years, I occasionally retrieve these reels of our reunion dinner from their dusty storage place and view them again, enjoy them again, before returning them carefully to safekeeping.

# IT'S A GOOD LIFE

I t was early the next morning when I rose at The Crescent, weak gray light seeping past the curtains and into my room. I had slept deeply, without interruption. For my final day in Milford, Sam Winter had promised to carry me on one of his tour boats across the water to Skomer Island, and we needed, he said, to get an early start. Remembering the cool, sharp-edged bite of a Pembrokeshire morning, noting the overcast sky, and knowing we would be out in the elements all day, I fortified myself with a hearty break-fast and was waiting in a filmy morning mist outside The Crescent when he pulled up just after 8:00 a.m. A trip to Skomer seemed a fine and fitting way to take my leave.

The weather was dull and torpid. The air felt lifeless and the sky seemed to press low and damp upon the town. We wound leisurely along the narrow Dale Road, onward to, then through, the tiny bayside village of Dale itself, over soft, graceful hills decorated with lovely wildflowers, violet, ivory, red and blue. Along the way, Sam pointed out various landmarks – a stone church nestled into a pale yellow meadow, a pocket cemetery hidden beneath a grove of willow, in the fold of a shaded rise – and related how he had gone away to school in Glasgow, then returned to take on the family business and live by the water; which, he said simply, was all he ever really wanted to do. Just live by the water – smiling mildly as he spoke the words.

Fifteen minutes beyond Dale we mounted a long grade above a small, pebbly cove, turned onto a gravel path past a small, weathered sign that read "St. Martin's," descended, and parked. From there we clambered down a slippery footpath to a wooden dock, where *The Minerva* lay tied at rest, loading passengers for the trip to Skomer, across the choppy waters of Jack Sound.

Skomer Island lay three miles to the west, off Marloes Peninsula, where the Atlantic mingles with the Irish Sea and both pour into the wide mouth of the Milford waterway. Like so many places in Pembrokeshire, its name has a Viking origin. The archeologists tell us that Skomer served as something of a way-station, or stopover, when the Norsemen had the run of the coast. Excavations have uncovered remnants of cooking utensils, burial sites, encampments, and runes. Of course, Pembrokeshire is full of such works. Skomer, however, unquestionably provides the most dramatic setting.

At first glance, the island appears not at all an inviting place of repose. In fact, it more readily suggests the exact opposite – a place of high danger and hardship. Its steep cliffs rise dramatically and forbiddingly out of the stormy sea. Waves bash and break like thunderous explosions against its countless jagged outcroppings, arrayed angrily at the island's base like rows of serrated teeth, making landfall difficult and frightening for the unskilled. Perhaps, however, it was precisely its intrinsic peril which had made Skomer such an appealing resting-place for the Norse seafarers. Their dexterity on the waters being unmatched, they were able to rest and sleep without worry on the island, secure in the certainty that any unwanted intruders were sure to be thwarted by the natural defenses of wind and waves and rocks.

But that was long ago. "No Vikings around today?" I inquired of Sam, who was recounting brief snippets of the island's history. "Well, they're probably all around," he laughed. "They just don't advertise themselves as such anymore."

We made our way slowly across the sound, puttering through the bucking, foaming, white-topped rise and fall. Against the backdrop of the thrumming motor and the boat's hypnotic swell, I pondered my friend Sam's connection to the place. In school, I had known him as a studious and deliberate boy. It was not at all surprising that, after taking a degree in Marine Engineering in Glasgow, he had returned to Dale and transformed the modest family operation into a robust and far-flung enterprise, one of the largest businesses in the county. West Haven Marine Outfitters – which in the 60's had occupied itself with repairing dents and dings and motors for the small local fishing fleet, or the occasional pleasure craft – was today a custom designer and builder of yachts for discriminating and affluent clients throughout Europe, owned a large warehouse and dock, stored and refurbished recreational boats in another warehouse during the winter, operated sailing and diving classes out of Dale during the summer, and ran sightseeing boats to the two nearby offshore islands – Skomer and its sister, Skokholm – under a long-term contract with the Pembrokeshire Wildlife Trust. The previous evening, in the same contained, self-effacing manner which had been his hallmark as a boy, Sam had described his small empire to me. When I asked whether it might be possible to visit Skomer before returning home, he said he needed to attend to some business with the caretaker on the island himself, and proposed we make the trip together – as a result of which, we were now bouncing our way across the sound on *The Minerva*, Skomer Island looming before us in a sort of grave, stark isolation.

I found the setting – ancient, ominous, wild – full of drama.

The island neared and the boat began to slow, approaching a narrow stone shelf, which served as a landing. I stood in the cabin with Sam and the pilot, who was maneuvering the boat in the choppy sea as it closed upon the sheer rock cliffs. The sky was dull as lead. Bound for a day of hiking or bird-watching, the passengers were attired in all manner of raingear, headgear, boots and coats, binoculars and baskets slung from their shoulders, walking sticks clutched in their hands. The pilot edged the craft delicately into place against a flat slab of rock. The mate leapt off and tied a rope to a rusty metal post embedded in the shelf. *The Minerva* heaved and bobbed in the swells. The passengers gathered up their rucksacks and bags and disembarked, hopping onto the slick stone platform as the waves tossed up flecks of foam, then edging gingerly up a tall, narrow stairway cut roughly into the side of the cliff above the sea. "Mind your step," called the mate. "Careful now, careful." Up the cliffside, the passengers filed. Then lastly, Sam and I ascended as well, climbing high above the rolling blue-green water, up to the very crown of the cliff and onto Skomer Island.

During our approach, I had spied what seemed like thousands and thousands of birds nested in little nooks beneath the brows of the crags. Before flying over for the reunion, I had read a bit about the almost unparalleled diversity of Skomer seabirds; gannets, razorbills, puffins, gulls, falcons, shearwaters, comorants, and stormpetrels – and delighted now in witnessing them in their huge numbers, curled up and snug in countless holes dug into the mossy loam, strolling carelessly along the precipices, or spiraling across the sky. Immense flocks soared off the island and assembled into giant formations, wheeling in enormous arcs above the sea, while other vast flocks lit upon the island, landing delicately in sheltered crevices in the cliffs or among the wildflowers, uncountable numbers of seabirds crying and cawing and diving in the powerful draughts and currents streaming up off the ocean.

As Sam and I paused to catch our breath following the climb, my gaze circled the island's summit in all directions, taking fully-in the breathtaking sight; the prodigious, undulating table – even more undulating than the 9th green, I reflected – nearly treeless, bare, save for expansive carpets of dazzling wildflowers, wild gorse, bracken, and the occasional rock mound ornamented with green and rust-orange lichen; the entirety of it arrayed against a mammoth canvas, brutal yet ethereal, of sea and sky. The wind gusted without remittance. *Not much shelter here*, I thought. Indeed, following the terrors of the open northern seas, the smooth waters of the Haven must have seemed a sacred blessing to the intrepid ancient seafarers, its welcoming marshes and protected inlets offering tranquil harbor and rest.

We stood wordless and surveyed the panorama, till Sam raised his arm and pointed into the distance, toward the island's interior. Squinting into the glare, I discerned a dark wooden structure huddled in a depression, facing out to sea.

"The caretaker's house," he announced.

I stared at the solitary edifice, which itself stared blankly through its empty windows across the ocean.

"He doesn't live there all the time, does he?" I asked dubiously, the setting striking me as more than remote.

"Most of the time," Sam said. "They send them up here for a few years at a time. This ones' almost done. He'll be leaving soon."

I studied the isolated house and the naked, austere landscape, utterly undefended against the Atlantic's tempests, utterly exposed to all its capricious ferocity. "Years," I repeated with a sigh, and grimaced.

Sam smiled and nodded again. "Well, he likes the work," he said.

"I guess he better. What's he like?"

"We might run into him. He gets all about. He's supposed to make sure everything's kept up, so he looks after everything. Sometimes people get lost and he finds them." He paused. "Not really a job for me."

In silence we stood, watching the birds cut figures in the sky and white-bearded rollers surge against the rocks.

"I like this one," Sam continued. "Some of them I haven't been too keen on, but this one's alright. I'll miss him when he goes." We gazed across the tangled bracken at the care-taker's residence. "Actually, he doesn't even want to leave," he added with a shrug.

We struck off along one of the many footpaths crosscutting the thick groundcover, leaving behind a large assembly of red-and-black puffins strutting and fussing about their lodges at the brink of a nearby precipice. The dense, wet grass dampened our pant legs and the breeze rippled our jackets. We separated from those who had accompanied us on *The Minerva*, and soon were alone. I kept shifting my gaze from left to right, back to front, and saw only an impenetrable sheet of gray from one horizon to the other, as if a pewter blanket had been drawn across the sky. To the west stretched only ocean. To the east, the Pembrokeshire coast. Beneath our feet, thick brown gorse, a network of muddy footpaths, and the occasional rabbit scampering from one burrow to another. Separated from the world, I felt we were. Separated altogether.

Sam stepped ahead on the narrow path, hands stuck in his pockets. The sense of isolation was broken only by the rustlings of hares scurrying in the brush, or flocks of black shearwaters racing past, screaming and flapping, as though terrified by some awful horror. Both of us bearing a residue of fatigue from the previous evening, we were in no hurry. We traded words idly, but mainly just walked. Overhead, clouds whisked away against a pallid, grayish screen. The ocean had become a distant, muffled growl, and the wind was strong and fresh, and for some reason I wanted to close my eyes and lift my face in order to feel its rippling rush across my skin and through my hair. As we ambled along the footpath, against the background of the sea and the ashen sky, I reflected that Sam – and Hugh and Caron and most of my other friends, for that matter – seemed to fit here within the Haven as snugly as the comorants and puffins fit into their nests atop Skomer's outcroppings; and wondered again if I could ever have slipped so neatly and naturally into this life.

I knew, of course, the answer was *No* – the entire idea was fantasy, and there was no explanation for how and why I had continued indulging the notion, continued resurrecting it over and over. The fancy, however, spinning it through my mind, embellishing it with people, events, and encounters, gave me pleasure in some way. Fulfilled some purpose. So I had kept it alive, even nurtured it, like a unique sort of tree or flower, and refused to extinguish it – which would have been the pragmatic thing to do.

Musing in this way, I suddenly heard a noise to our rear and turned to see a thin, bearded man striding up the path toward us, his face surrounded by a thick mop of disheveled hair billowing and puffing in the wind. Sam had also turned at the sound, and now smiled broadly. "Here he is," he cried.

"Terry Gabriel! I knew you would find us if we wandered long enough!"

The new arrival halted before us, extended his hand energetically, and exclaimed "Hello, Sam Winter – I haven't seen you for too long! Welcome back!"

"How are you, Terry?" Sam replied, smiling and shaking the proffered palm. "You look excellent! I've been busy."

"Well, typical, eh? You should slow down a bit ... you know, *the world is too much with you ...*"

"That's true," said Sam, shrugging. "But meet my friend – an old schoolmate from America, came back for our reunion last night."

"All the way from America!" the caretaker effused, stepping closer and offering me his hand as well. I saw a face finely lined, and eyes unnaturally pale and penetrating. A nest of blonde hair hinted at grey around the edges, and he had the kind of lean, wiry frame that brings to mind an ascetic lifestyle; although humor played around his lips and his limpid eyes danced mischievously. "Well then, welcome to my kingdom by the sea," he declared expansively, raising his eyebrows and spreading his arms to encompass the ocean to the west and the shoreline to the east. "All my world is at your feet!"

I laughed, thanked him, and said I supposed that if he was king, then Sam must be a lowly serf, at which we all laughed together, then turned to continue along the trail, winding deeper into the heather amid the infinitude of rabbits.

We chatted as we walked, the caretaker and me, as we had aroused each other's curiosity. He asked how I had come to Milford in the first place, and the reason for my return. He had the kind of demeanor that invites disclosure and honesty, so I told him it had been a special place for me when I was young, had touched and shaped something in me that had not been affected in the same way before or since, and had therefore taken on a singular, and possibly outsized, importance as the years had passed. Something about my experiences here had established an unbreakable hold upon my memories, I said, and I felt its presence all the time, every day, night and day; sometimes strongly, sometimes weakly, but always present. And all kinds of small, random events could fire these memories into motion, I told him: the smell of rain approaching on a warm breeze, the sight of waves crashing violently against tall, sharp rocks, or striking a golf ball late in the day into a fine mist. And I had never wanted to leave, had despaired when leaving became necessary – and had most likely come to idealize and festoon ridiculously my recollections of the place.

Oddly enough, I felt no hesitation at relating these kinds of intimate thoughts to this person to whom I had only just been introduced. Wanton personal disclosure was not at all my normal mode. However, something about him – or the setting, or the entire experience of return - prompted revelation and candor. Soon we came to the crest of a small rise. I realized we had circled around to the back of the depression in which the caretaker's shuttered home sat so alone. We halted and looked at the rear of the dwelling and, beyond it, the blue-green sea, dotted with squadrons of birds curving and soaring against fantastic sheets of clouds.

"What exactly do you do here?" I asked him.

"A bit of everything, actually," he said with a shrug and, now, a bantering tone. "A caretaker cares for his kingdom."

I smiled. "But seriously," I persisted. "What do you do up here?"

The litany of his multifarious duties then came forth. He took readings and surveys for calculating the populations of the many species of seabirds that nested upon the island. He tended to injured members of the flocks, arranged treatment for those with minor injuries and dispatch for those that could not be saved. He gave lectures and tours and acted as an educator. He tracked and rescued visitors who wandered off the trails and lost themselves in the bleak heather, or ventured too far upon the cliffs and found themselves stranded, unable to find their way back to safe ground. In the short summer-time he grew a garden. He catalogued the state of the flora, alert for signs of natural or man-made damage, and logged reproductive and health trends among Skomer's furred and feathered denizens, always on the lookout for evidence of disease. He repaired the footpaths. He took meteorological readings. He unloaded the weekly deliveries of groceries and supplies. He filled out applications for grants and funding proposals, submissions to assorted foundations and government departments. For the safety and edification of visitors, he kept up the various informational signs and placards that dotted the island – pointing the way back to the dock, describing the unique purplish vegetation in the hollows and bogs, sketching the original outlines of now-obscured Norse cooking sites or forges, reduced today to undistinguished piles of rubble on the ground. There was really no end to his labor, he declared, no limit to his responsibilities, large and small. And all of them, I reflected, discharged upon this stark, lonely rock, emplaced long ago in the thrashing seas off the mouth of the Haven, as if Skomer Island itself was meant, in some mystical way, to guard the Haven's unspoiled Arcadia and fend off the wildness beyond.

"I don't want to leave either," the caretaker concluded – echoing what Sam had told me earlier. "Most people can't understand it – but this is where I think I ought to stay and do my work."

By this time, we had made our way down into the depression and around to the front of the house. It looked old and weather-beaten, but sturdy. Sam and Terry moved aside to discuss some matter concerning the tour boats' summer schedule, and I tried to peer into a window while their attention lay elsewhere. I was curious about how he lived all alone in this spartan setting, and thought I might spy some clue inside the house. The windows were dark and opaque, however, and I discerned nothing. I returned to his conversation with Sam just as it was ending – something about a recent heavy rain having washed out several of the footpaths, causing more visitors than usual to wander off and lose their way. Then Terry shook my hand with a serene and simple expression and, I thought, a trace of bemusement in his face, saying he hoped I had found in my return what it was I had hoped to find. Then he turned and entered the door of his solitary home.

Sam and I lingered a few moments longer, watching white-caps rise and fall in the churn of the ocean. Seabirds raced and shrieked in the wondrous canopy above. The wind blustered unsparingly and huge clouds formed in towering masses, then fell apart and sped past overhead in torn threads, like insubstantial spirits fleeing ashore to shelter. On the far western edge of the horizon, a bank of thunderheads began to shape. Later, it would storm. Or maybe it would dissipate, I reflected, so fickle was the weather. Rabbits scampered across our path, the gray pallor of the sky darkened, the sea rolled and roiled in the distance, and I began to feel the languid fatigue that had trailed in my wake the entire day.

I turned to look at Sam. His gaze remained over the water, his face impassive. "It's a good life here, isn't it," he remarked after a moment, as if the idea had just come to him. *Yes*, I thought, *without a doubt. Just not mine.*

We had tarried longer than expected on our little island outing, and it was late in the afternoon when we caught *The Minerva* on her last run of the day, recrossing Jack Sound to the mainland in the thinning light. We berthed at the flimsy wooden dock and the day-trippers clambered out. I thanked Sam for the tour. We made our way uphill to his truck, then headed back to Dale, where Caron had arranged a small group for dinner. I was leaving in the morning and, after the late hours of the reunion, looked forward to a quiet final evening.

At Sam's house in Dale, which sat back from the crescent of the beach, we rendezvoused with Jenkins and Hugh and Caron, Aiden Lloyd, Martin Owen, Gwen Thomas, and Erin Jaworski – daughter of another Pole who had found his way to Milford after the war. They had only just arrived and gathered in his yard, which enjoyed an expansive, open view across the harbor.

The waters of the cove lapped smoothly. Divers and windsurfers in bright wetsuits were coming ashore at the end of the day. Blue and red sailboats bobbed in the water – just as they had years ago, when Caron and I had ridden the bus to Dale and strolled along the seawall bordering the shoreline. The sun was falling in the west, and streams of fiery light spilled through cracks in the clouds that had filled the sky all day, glinting sharply on the tranquil channel. We stood chatting and watching the sunset; watching as the colors shimmered upon the placid face of Dale's protected bay, as the orange deepened to red, then purple, till the bay grew black and the air cooled and the clouds parted to reveal the first evening stars glittering above. Only then, as if on some silent signal, did we move on.

We had dinner at The Trafalgar, an old stone-walled pub set on a point where the breakwater juts out into the bay. It was a subdued and muted meal – Erin kept repeating that she didn't want the evening to end – and then it came time to say goodbye. We walked outside, where the water swashed quietly and the voices of people putting away their boats or their diving gear came to us faintly out of the darkness, as if from a faraway place. There were farewells all around, and as we broke up Caron and I walked briefly beneath the full, yellow moon, along the embankment overlooking the inlet, where the sailboats were now just shadows jouncing in the dark, like old memories dimly seen.

"We walked here a long time ago," I said.

"I remember," she said, and took my hand. "I told you I hadn't forgotten."

Then we said goodbye as well.

Hugh drove me back to The Crescent. Early the next morning, in a gray and drizzly mist, I caught the train to London.

# THE FOLLOWER

I watched the speckled sea from the window of the airplane as it climbed above the Atlantic, heading back to America, and it suddenly seemed to me that our lives resemble the waves that cross the ocean. They emerge from a dark and distant, formless depth, far away and far from sight. They take shape, gather, build, and move relentlessly forward, toward landfall on some waiting shore, insensible of their end and the countless multitude that have come before. On and on they race, through day and night, night and day, toward final annihilation on the approaching brink – where they crest and then collapse, their waters spilling into the sand and returning to the sea, where other waves are forming, building, and racing anew toward that same demise. And thus each wave is new, yet made of the leavings of the old, and its end ordained.

Some waves tower high, and foam and froth like the swells that pound the craggy cliffs at St. Anne's Head. Like some men's lives, they roar and howl as they approach and pass and shatter on the rocks, spectacular and grand. Yet others roll in regular rhythm, steady, constant. And still other waves are but a ripple, barely a wrinkle on the indifferent countenance of the vast and unknowable sea. While the great waves crash and thunder, and the steady waves speak forever in their even, constant voice, these little ripples murmur softly in a quiet key. And in the tumult of the world we fail to catch their rippling sigh. We gaze awestruck at the extravaganza of the huge and howling waves. Or we become hypnotized and sedated by the steady, rolling, drone of the steady, rolling waves – and the modest whisper of the small and humble wavelets is lost and forgotten, or never heard at all.

When I was young I saw the massive breakers crash against Stack Rocks' broken limestone cliffs, and the rolling waves barrel lazily across Newgale's supine, spreading sands – but the call I heard most clearly was the murmur of the ripples in the sheltered waters of the Haven. I heard it first upon a sparkling morning stepping sleepily from a train, blinking in the bright sunlight, to behold flocks of brilliant white gannets circling in the crystalline sky. I heard it beneath my feet crossing the bridge into Hakin at dusk, after the myriad sounds of the day had fled and left the water to speak alone. I heard it standing forlorn on the platform at Milford Station one cool summer twilight, a train's engine hissing like an angry spirit and my father calling me to board. I heard the soothing murmur when I returned to Milford in my dreams, and its singsong chant lingered in my mind when I awoke. Some people thrill to the giant waves, but I was captured by the gentle murmur and the gentle ripples – captured forever, for I never forgot them, never escaped them, never renounced them, and always sought them.

The great waves and tiny riplets alike meet their appointed ends upon the shore, and thus it matters not to which you are devoted. But I became a follower of the murmur of the gentle ripples in Milford Haven when I was young, and kept faith for many years, then returned when I was called, where it sounded in me once again and made me glad.